THE
LAST RIDE OF
CALEB O'TOOLE

ERIC PIERPOINT

sourcebooks
jabberwocky

Published by Sourcebooks Jabberwocky, an imprint of Sourcebooks, Inc.
P.O. Box 4410, Naperville, Illinois 60567-4410
(630) 961-3900
Fax: (630) 961-2168
www.jabberwockykids.com

Library of Congress Cataloging-in-Publication Data is on file with the publisher.

Source of Production: Versa Press, East Peoria, Illinois, USA
Date of Production: July 2013
Run Number: 20656

Printed and bound in the United States of America.
VP 10 9 8 7 6 5 4 3 2 1

This book is dedicated to children everywhere. For within them lies great courage and inspiration.

And to the memory of my father, Robert Pierpoint, who was also my best tennis and fishing buddy.

1

THE BURNING OF GREAT BEND, KANSAS, 1877

★ ★

Caleb O'Toole ran through the blazing streets until he thought his heart would burst through his chest. The night air was filled with the choking smoke and ash of fires that had been started by a mob of terrified townsfolk. They were burning down the houses of the dead, of those who had perished in the cholera epidemic that had spread throughout the population of this cattle town in the middle of Kansas. It wasn't just the fires and the cholera that had the citizens in a panic. Murderers and thieves were about.

"Tilly!" Caleb shouted as he desperately searched the streets for his little sister. He ducked down the alley past the Last Chance Saloon. "Til…" he gasped, choking from the smoke. Tears streaked his face, tears that came from the grief of having lost his loving father to the deadly grip of cholera just two days before. Caleb had buried him with his own two hands. And now his beautiful mother was gravely ill with the disease.

Caleb stopped, his hands on his knees, trying to catch his wind. *CRACK!* A shower of sparks warned him as the sign from Mrs. Greeley's Finery crashed down from above. Caleb dove out of the way just in time. He yanked off his hat and slapped away the sparks that burned through his shirt. "Tumble!" he called. During the confusion of the night, scared by the screams and the gunshots, their crazy dog, Tumble, had run off and little Tilly went looking for him.

Caleb raced past the train depot, but there was no one around. Trains hadn't stopped there in weeks because of the cholera. He dashed over to the schoolhouse where his father had taught, thinking that perhaps Tilly went there. He ached knowing that his father would never again be that wise, sturdy figure who stood out front and kept the boys in line as they filed into the little school. Caleb darted around to the back. There was still no sign of his sister. He vaulted over the schoolyard fence, then leaped onto the wooden walkway that connected all the stores along Main Street, peering into the windows along the way. Fine brick buildings stocked with brightly colored wares were mixed in with the old wooden shacks that were relics of the past before the cattle boom hit some seven years ago. No Tilly anywhere!

The loud crack of a gunshot stopped Caleb in his tracks. Just ahead, a huge man with a smoking revolver, wearing a hat and a long black duster, backed out of Jim Jackson's Mercantile. The flash of a shotgun blast lit things up from inside the store. The man in the duster whirled around and fired back as he tossed a bag over his shoulder. Mr. Jackson, mortally wounded, crashed through the glass storefront, the shotgun dangling from his helpless fingers. Suddenly, the big man looked at Caleb and raised his pistol. Caleb dove behind a rain barrel.

"I see you there, boy," said the mountain of a man as he advanced on Caleb. "Come on out now."

Caleb held his breath, his heart pounding in his chest. *Run*, his mind screamed, but his legs felt like lead. The sweat of his fear trickled down his back. Carefully, Caleb peered around the barrel. In the firelight, he caught a glimpse of the man's fat cheeks under his hat, his mouth set in a gleeful grin. The big man's gun roared. A chunk of the rain barrel blew up near Caleb's head and he felt the sting of wooden splinters in his face. He could hear the man chuckle to himself.

"There he is!" a voice cried.

"Over at Jackson's!" another shout rose. "Get him!"

Caleb's attention was suddenly drawn to a commotion coming from the street over by Town Hall.

The huge killer turned to face the advancing men and snapped off three shots. He quickly ducked away, using the cover of smoke to escape. The men raised their rifles and fired back, shattering a window just feet from Caleb. He bolted like a deer from his hiding place, fearful that he might get gunned down in the crossfire.

Caleb raced for his life. As he turned down the alley, he saw three men in masks toss lit torches into the Andersons' home. There was no one alive in the sad old house. All had perished in the epidemic. One of the men lost his mask as he threw his torch. It was Henry Kalbe, a nasty, skinny do-gooder. Kalbe cheered and shook his fist as the curtains in the house caught fire.

"Out evil!" shouted Kalbe, nearly frothing at the mouth. He suddenly saw Caleb and his crazed eyes lit up in the blazing fire as if he was possessed. "We'll be a comin' for yours, Caleb O'Toole! The devil is in your house too!"

Caleb sprinted down the street to the Sheriff's office. As he burst through the door, the black mustachioed Sheriff W. W. Winstead and Deputy Daniel Foley tossed a drunken man roughly into an already crowded jail cell. They quickly swung their rifles toward Caleb. Caleb hit the deck and the lawmen jerked their guns up at the last second. Foley's knees were knocking, but the Sheriff was a tough and steady western man, as much cactus as Ponderosa pine. It took nerves of steel to stand up to the gunfighters and thieves that passed through Great Bend. One look into the deadly calm of Sheriff W. W. Winstead's piercing eyes would usually send the outlaws packing.

"Lord, Caleb!" growled the Sheriff. "I nearly blew your head off! What are you doing out? You best get home to your family."

"Tilly's gone! I can't find her anywhere," said Caleb as he picked himself up off the floor. "And someone just shot Jim Jackson. Killed him cold."

"Son of a skunk! You get a look at the shooter?" The Sheriff continued to reload. Deputy Foley, shaking from the violence of the night, checked his Colt pistol.

4

"He was big, real big. Wearing a long black duster."

"Black duster, you say?" Sheriff Winstead jammed more shells into his Winchester rifle. "Third time I've heard about him today. Lord help him when I find that thieving snake."

"And Henry Kalbe and some men just started burning up the Andersons' house. They were wearing masks."

"Kalbe! I'll have his hide, that crazy fool. Daniel! Get some men and sweep the other end of town. Some cowboys are fixin' to run a herd of cattle out the south end. I'll see if any'll help out and head over to the Andersons'. Anybody robbin' or settin' fires, shoot 'em down!" The Sheriff shoved a Colt revolver into his holster.

"Right, Sheriff," said Foley. His hands shook as he racked a shell into his Winchester. "Heaven help me." He closed his eyes, drew a deep breath, and took off out the door.

"But, what about Tilly?" pleaded Caleb. "We can't find her and I've been looking all over." Caleb felt his throat catch at the thought of his little sister somewhere in the midst of all the mayhem.

"Lord knows what you've been through, boy, but you best get home and look after your family." said Sheriff Winstead as he grabbed Caleb and headed for the door. "We'll look out for Tilly. Go on now."

"Yes, sir." Caleb stood for a second to gather himself as the Sheriff hustled down the street. *There is no way I'm going home without Tilly*, he thought as he sprinted down the road.

Caleb dodged and ducked his way through the alleys

between the stores, desperately avoiding anyone. He knew he could get his head blown off by friend or foe. When it seemed that he had exhausted his search, the thought struck him like a thunderbolt. The Thatchers! Why didn't he think of them sooner? The old couple who owned the bakery on the edge of town always gave Tumble his share of muffins and treats. Tumble might head there!

Caleb raced down Main Street toward the Thatcher house. He was running out of time, and he had no use for caution. As he ran, he was blind to the glass smashing on his left. A scream was heard coming from somewhere in the smoke, but Caleb kept his legs pumping. Ahead of him, a shot rang out, and Caleb's heart jumped. It came from the edge of town. It came from the Thatcher house!

So desperate was Caleb's purpose that he didn't see the dark-clad stranger astride the black stallion in the road. He ran headlong into the beast and crashed to the ground. With his head ringing from the impact, Caleb looked up, half expecting to stare into the gun of the man who shot Jackson. But instead of the high-pitched cackle of the murdering thief, the voice Caleb heard was so low and dangerous it shook Caleb to his boots.

"Watch yourself, boy," said the stranger as he stared hard at Caleb.

Atop the fierce stallion rode a tall, lean man in a long dark coat, with a square jaw and eyes under a black hat that were so piercing they could cut glass. His right hand gripped the handle of the Colt pistol at his side; his left held the reins of the coal-black horse. A Spencer rifle rested in a scabbard; the initials "N.V." were carved into the gun's stock and burned into the leather saddle. The firelight played shadows on the stranger's face. He seemed to exude calm and a kind of dangerous power at the same time. Like an unlit stick of dynamite. He sat deadly still upon the huge horse and took in the chaotic rage around him like he was born to it.

"My...sss...sister!" was all Caleb could muster as he shook his senses together and picked himself up off the ground. A muffled boom and flash of light tore his attention away from the mysterious stranger. Several shots rang out. The flicker of fire danced from a building in the distance. The Thatcher house was burning. Then he heard the scream. Tilly's scream.

"Tilly!" called Caleb as he took off down Main Street. He could hear Tumble now too. The little dog was in a barking frenzy. At fifty yards away, Caleb saw his little blond sister standing in the middle of the street in front of the Thatcher house. Tumble was at her side. A rider in a long black duster was circling Tilly, and laughing at her.

"Let's go, boys!" called the rider. "We ain't got all night!"

Two more riders in black dusters emerged from the dark, carrying bags of what was probably loot. Caleb's heart stopped. The biggest of the two held the reins of a riderless horse. It was the man who shot Mr. Jackson! The three men circled his sister, taunting her and laughing. Tumble snapped at the hooves of the horses, determined to protect his best friend. One of the horses kicked Tumble full in his ribs, but the faithful dog would not relent. If Tumble managed to attach his jaws to that horse's leg, there would be no letting go.

Caleb ran with all his might to his sister, choking back his fear. He had no weapon, but that didn't stop him. He dodged through the stomping legs of the horses and covered his sister with his body as the men circled them. A wiry man in a black duster emerged from the burning Thatcher house to the porch. He threw a sack over his shoulder, drew his pistol, and fired back inside. Old Mr. Thatcher, holding onto his wounded wife, staggered to the doorway. He raised his revolver and fired wildly, causing the thieves to scatter for an instant and yank their horses away from the burning house. Quick as a snake, the wiry thief shot the old man in the shoulder and spun him to the floor, his poor wife falling beside him. As the outlaws advanced on the house, Caleb used the distraction and grabbed Tilly, then ran and took shelter behind a big oak tree. Tumble raced around the hooves of the stomping, kicking horses that tried to rid themselves of the four-legged cyclone.

"Tumble!" cried Tilly as she attempted to run back into the street for her dog.

"Shhhh! Tilly, be quiet," pleaded Caleb.

"Let's go, Nathan!" shouted the leader of the murderous gang. "Get it done!"

"No…no…please!" cried Mr. Thatcher. He reached painfully over and held his wife who was bleeding from the heart. He tried to raise his hand to surrender. But the wiry killer would have none of it. He seemed to take his time to enjoy the moment, relishing the power of the kill. The Colt shot its flame. The Thatchers lay dead.

Caleb held Tilly to him and clamped his hand over her mouth. They were witnesses to this murder, and Caleb knew the gang could well turn on them. As he peered carefully from behind the tree, he saw one of the riders draw his pistol and fire at Tumble, who was dashing around the horses' legs. He missed as Tumble ran underneath his horse.

"Dang dog," muttered the rider and aimed for a second shot, the others laughing at him.

Tilly squealed and twisted and finally broke from Caleb's grasp. "Tumble!" she screamed. Caleb dove for her and hauled her back behind the oak tree. His heart pounded as he sneaked a look to see if they'd been discovered. The four black riders shifted around on their horses and stared toward the tree. Slowly, they advanced on Caleb's hiding place. He knew he should make a run for it, but his legs felt frozen. He watched death come to call as if he were a terrified rabbit waiting for a pack of wolves.

Suddenly, the crash of gunfire somewhere up the street stopped the outlaws in their tracks. They urged their horses together, pistols pulled, straining to see the source of it. Thundering hooves pounded ever closer. Three more rifle shots scattered the thieves. They fired back blindly as two of their horses began to rear and buck. Out of the smoky darkness, the mysterious stranger came, his dark coat swirling behind him. He galloped toward them on the black stallion like he was sent from Hades. Crouching low, the reins in his teeth, he fired his rifle as he charged down Main Street, a deadly knight on a warhorse.

The murderous thieves returned fire, but then quickly regrouped and spurred their horses out of town, choosing to make off with their loot instead of risking it with this ferocious unknown enemy. The night swallowed them up as if they were never there. Brave little Tumble, determined to finish the job, took off in a barking fit after the horses.

Caleb held fast to Tilly as the stranger galloped to the Thatcher house. The rider sheathed his rifle and swung his leg over the stallion's neck all in one motion and hit the ground running. He leaped onto the porch, then into the house, which was now engulfed in a blazing fire. The man tried to beat back the flames and drag the Thatchers from the burning house, but it was useless. The flames grew all around him as he cradled Mr. Thatcher and put his ear to the old man's heart.

"There he is! He's over here!"

"He's robbin' the Thatchers!"

"That's him! Shot Jackson too!"

Caleb turned to see a half dozen angry men rushing down the street toward them, Deputy Foley in the lead. They drew their pistols and fired on the tall figure in the doorway. The stranger dove from the burning house to the porch and drew his Colt. He raked his hand over his gun, fan-firing as he leaped from the porch to the big black stallion. Foley hit the ground hard as his men scattered for cover behind the bushes and trees in the side yard of the house. As the mysterious rider spurred his horse, he then holstered his empty Colt and drew a smaller pistol, a Remington, from his boot. Like lightning he fired on the men, pinning them down. Caleb watched in amazement as the lone gunman held six men at bay. Foley and his men were no match for this man of war. They were forced to lie in cover.

Sheriff W. W. Winstead, Winchester in hand, suddenly emerged with two men from the alley on the other side of the house. No sooner did he raise his rifle to fire than the dark rider drew his Spencer rifle, spun in the saddle, and blasted the railing of the porch near the lawman's head. Sheriff Winstead's shot went wild as splinters from the shattered wood raked his face. Two more quick shots drove the Sheriff's men under the porch of the burning house. The huge black stallion, controlled only by the grip of the rider's knees, crashed into the bleeding, cursing Sheriff and sent him sprawling to the ground.

Caleb, his arms around a trembling Tilly, watched in awe as the dark rider twisted backward in his saddle and fired his Spencer rifle, spurring his horse out of town while laying down a barrage of cover fire.

Suddenly, all was quiet. The man had vanished. The Sheriff picked himself up, staggering from the collision with the stallion. Deputy Foley emerged along with the men from their hiding places. Caleb took Tilly from the cover of the big oak tree. Tumble was nowhere to be seen.

"You men!" barked the shaken Sheriff as he yanked a splinter from his bleeding face. "Get a bucket brigade ready."

"No way we're saving Thatcher's house, Sheriff," offered Deputy Foley.

"I ain't thinking about saving Thatcher's, it's the one next to it I'm worried about. Daniel, get William Torrey over at the telegraph office. Put out the word we got a murderer headin' north."

"Sheriff!" Caleb called as he went to the Sheriff, Tilly in hand. "He didn't do it!"

"Lord, Caleb, what in tarnation are you doing? Going to get yourself killed out here!" growled Sheriff Winstead.

"But, he's not the one, Sheriff. There were these other…"

"No buts. You take Tilly on home now. Stay off the street. I mean it." Sheriff Winstead bellowed as he grabbed one of the men. "You boys get those buckets goin'!"

Caleb was about to protest once more, but he gathered Tilly to him. A tremendous sadness suddenly entered his body, a feeling that washed over him like a dark nightmare.

Mother.

2

A MOTHER'S WISH

★ ★ ★ ★ ★ ★ ★ ★ ★ ★ ★ ★ ★ ★ ★ ★ ★ ★

Caleb's fifteen-year-old sister, Julie, ran out of the house as he neared home. He had carried little Tilly halfway across town and his arms ached from the effort. Caleb could see the pain in Julie's pretty face, the control she tried to muster as she reached out for Tilly. Her big blue eyes, caught in the firelight of a burning house, betrayed her.

"She's calling for us, Caleb," Julie said, trying to put up a good front. "There isn't much time. She was hanging on 'til she saw you. Come, Tilly."

Caleb let Julie take Tilly. He felt numb as they hurried toward their little house. The home used to hold so much happiness, but now his heart was breaking with the fear of what may be waiting for them inside.

★ ★ ★

Caleb stood by the bed as Julie dutifully and lovingly stroked their mother's hair and mopped her brow. She and Tilly had the same flowing golden hair his mother used to have. Once beautiful, his mother was a shell of her former self, exhausted from nursing their father while fighting the dreaded cholera herself. Day by day, she faded alongside her husband. Julie cared for her at her bedside while Caleb saw to the chores and the care and feeding of his horse, Dusty. He fought tears as he saw his mother's eyes flicker open. Where they used to be sparkling blue, now they were yellowish with fever. The lovely face that lit up the house with laughter and song was now shriveled with sickness.

"Children," Mrs. O'Toole said in a whisper. "Come closer."

"Yes, Mother," Caleb said as he and Tilly went to her side.

"There isn't much time. They'll come and set fire to this house."

"I won't let them. I'll get the rifle," Caleb said defiantly.

"Listen to me carefully, children." Mrs. O'Toole reached out weakly for her son. "Caleb, I need you to be strong. Like a big oak tree. You must be brave and never waver from the task I will ask you to do. Promise me."

"Yes, Mother," said Caleb as he choked back his tears.

"Hitch Dusty to the wagon. And Julie…"

"Yes, Mother?" said Julie as she mopped her mother's fevered face.

"You are a most special young woman now. Take care of your sister as I know you will. Gather all you can. You must leave Great Bend. No one in this town will take you with all the sickness." Mrs. O'Toole burst into a coughing fit.

"A gang of thieves just killed the Thatchers," said Caleb. "Jim Jackson too."

"I saw!" cried Tilly as she snuggled into her mother's arms. "He was a dragon. His teeth were all black and he was breathing fire. He said he would find me and eat me."

"She's scared," said Caleb. "Those men nearly trampled her in the street."

"Oh, come here, princess." Mrs. O'Toole held Tilly close to her. Then she unfastened a dainty necklace from her neck. On the silver chain was a locket. "You wear this around your neck and I will always be with you. Right by your heart. See?" Mrs. O'Toole popped the locket. "You will always be safe. There's your father and me on this side. And who's that?"

"Me," cried Tilly softly. "Julie and Caleb."

"That's right. Julie, Caleb, this is what you must do." She leveled her eyes at them, drawing on her last ounce of strength. "Go north to the Oregon Trail. Get on the Western train."

"But, Mother," exclaimed Julie. "We can't leave you."

"You must. Folks here have lost their senses. Caleb," she said as she pressed her son to her one last time, "over there...on the dresser. A letter from your Aunt Sarah in Montana Territory."

Caleb went to the dresser and picked up the letter, his heart pounding.

"We've sent her a wire and a thousand dollars," Mrs. O'Toole said weakly, gasping for air. "You must find Aunt Sarah. She has always agreed to take you in, should anything happen to your father and me. It's all in the letter. There's a little extra money in the jar in the kitchen to help along the way." Caleb's mother suddenly shook with pain. After a few moments, she seemed to relax, as if she was resigned to dying.

"Mother, no!" cried Julie as she held her mother.

"Mommy! Mommy!" sobbed Tilly.

CRASH! The sound of breaking glass rang out. Caleb went to the window. Through the smoke and the night, he saw several men brandishing torches a few houses down the street. He could hear Henry Kalbe's shrieking voice above the din. Shots rang out as the victims of Kalbe's insane mob tried to defend their house.

"Go, children. Hurry," said Mrs. O'Toole weakly.

Caleb could no longer fight the sting of his tears as he held the letter in his hands. Julie looked over at Caleb, the depth of her sorrow pouring from her watering eyes. Tilly sobbed at her mother's breast.

"Where?" was all Julie could say. Caleb couldn't speak.

"Montana…the Bitterroot," whispered Mrs. O'Toole. Then Caleb's mother closed her eyes and breathed her last.

★ ★ ★

Caleb raced to the barn to hitch up his faithful gray horse. Gunshots came from just a few houses away. Dusty nervously stomped and started as Caleb led him over to the buckboard. Kalbe and his mob were closing in. Caleb gave the leather strap a mighty tug as he cinched up Dusty's harness. His father's single-shot, fifty-caliber Sharps rifle leaned up against the barn. It was a breechloader and a good hunting rifle. Next to it was a Colt revolver and a few boxes of ammunition. He quickly carried them to the wagon. In the lantern's light, he caught his reflection in the window of the barn. He picked up the Sharps. Time seemed to stop. The heft of the big gun and the weight of his mother's dying wish filled him with fear and uncertainty. He knew little of his Aunt Sarah. It was a treacherous journey of over a thousand miles to her ranch in the rugged Bitterroot Mountains of Montana Territory. There were countless perils between Great Bend and the gold fields of Montana. Caleb took a deep breath. At least they might be safe once they reached the train in Kearney Junction. He thought if they could just make it there, they could ride the rails past the Indians, murderers, thieves, and other dangers that lay in wait along the Oregon Trail.

Julie came running from the house with an armload of supplies. "We've got enough food for a few days, a bit more if we stretch it. Some blankets, extra clothes," she said bravely as she piled them into the buckboard. "And here are Father's maps from school. But there is so much; all the photographs and the books. Caleb, just to leave it all behind is…"

CRASH! Kalbe and his men had arrived, shouting to the heavens as they threw their fiery torches into the front window of the O'Toole house.

"Out devil! Out evil!" Kalbe's reedy voice rang out.

"Satan be gone!" shouted another.

"Get Tilly!" urged Caleb as he tossed a hatchet and some rope onto the pile in the wagon.

"Tilly is still with Mother!" cried Julie as she ran back into the house. "Tilly!"

Caleb pulled back the hammer, slammed a shell into the breech of the Sharps, and crept around to the side of the house. His hands shook as he raised the big rifle to his shoulder. Henry Kalbe and his insane little mob had grown in size. Caleb counted a dozen hooded men, all armed with guns and torches. He knew that if he fired the Sharps, they would surely turn on him and he would perish in a hail of bullets. He carefully eased the hammer back as he lowered the rifle, then he ran back into the house after Tilly and Julie.

Caleb tore through the growing blaze to his mother's room. Julie was trying to pry the terrified little Tilly away from their poor departed mother.

"Tilly. Tilly, come!" Julie exclaimed.

"No!" cried Tilly as they managed to break her free. "I'm not leaving Mommy!" She kicked and screamed as Julie carried her down the smoke-filled hallway. Quickly, they bolted through the kitchen and out the back door. Caleb ran to untie Dusty from the fence. He climbed aboard the wagon and grabbed the reins. Julie carried little Tilly to the other side, pulled herself up, and sat by Caleb. Tilly buried her head in Julie's arms and sobbed.

Caleb glanced back at their once happy little home, the dream home that was now burning to the ground with their poor mother still inside. He looked at Julie's grief-stricken face.

"She's with Father, Caleb," said Julie. Caleb saw something more than tears in his sister's eyes. She was tough. They both knew that even though they had lost nearly everything, they still had each other.

"Ya, Dusty!" yelled Caleb, giving the reins a shake. As they pulled away from the burning house and dashed down Main Street, Caleb heard the roar of gunfire and the shouts of the Sheriff and his men over the din. They raced along the bloodied streets of Great Bend, where killers and thieves had destroyed the lives of innocent and decent people. He turned Dusty hard to the road north. Caleb prayed the three of them would survive this flight into the hidden dangers of the unknown.

"Woof!" Make that four. Tumble ran furiously through the smoke, struggling to gain on Dusty and the wagon.

"Tumble!" Tilly shouted and clapped her hands for the little dog.

"Come on, boy!" yelled Julie as she climbed into the back of the buckboard.

Tumble, his four feet flying, emerged from the smoke and raced to keep up with them, determined not to be left behind.

"Tumble, up!" cried Julie. And up he went. He gave a great leap and landed with his front paws in the back as Julie helped pull him in, his little legs scrambling to hold on. Tilly climbed into the back and threw her arms around the feisty little dog. Tumble rewarded her with a fierce licking.

"Dusty! Go boy!" said Caleb as he gave the reins a mighty shake.

Dusty bolted forward. The buckboard shot Caleb and his sisters out of Great Bend for good.

THE DASH TO THE NORTHERN TRAIN

★ ★ ★ ★ ★ ★ ★ ★ ★ ★ ★ ★ ★ ★ ★ ★ ★ ★ ★ ★

Caleb clutched his Sharps rifle and slammed it against his shoulder. The hairs on his neck pricked up as he strained to look out the window. Thunder and lightning blew up the night as the rain lashed against the little dugout hunter's cabin that sat by the Smokey Hill River. Something was moving among the trees outside the cabin. Julie quickly blew the candle out. After several days of rough travel on the road north out of Great Bend, a fierce storm broke out. Try as they may, they could no longer push through the deep mud of the rugged road. They decided to wait out the weather in the stinking, musty hole in the earth with a slapped-together roof and wooden floor. For four days, they sat huddled among several old buffalo hides that lay stacked in the corner, leftovers from a time when the beasts still roamed the Kansas prairies. Things smelled pretty bad inside, but at least the broken-down dugout kept most of the rain off them.

Caleb caught a flash of movement near the wagon. His

heart hammered against his chest as he heard Dusty whinny in alarm. He tried to get a better look at whatever was outside, but in the lightning flashes, he could only catch glimpses of Dusty nervously shifting around.

"See anything out there?" Julie said as she grabbed hold of Tilly and held her tight. Tumble growled a warning that said that there was something he didn't like lurking outside.

"No, but Dusty is acting like something's up," said Caleb as he peered through the window.

"Maybe it's the dragon!" cried Tilly as she buried her head against Julie's shoulder. She was tormented by visions of the black-cloaked men who murdered the Thatchers in Great Bend, terrified that the black-toothed one would find her and eat her.

"I see something!" Caleb yelled.

"Indians?" whispered Julie.

"No. It jumped on the wagon." Just then Dusty let out a loud, screaming whinny. Caleb gave the door a mighty shove, aiming the rifle at the moving shapes in the dark. The lightning flashed again. Wolves! They were all over the wagon, tearing into their supplies. One huge wolf leaped onto Dusty's back, but the powerful horse bucked and kicked out his hind legs, shaking off the wolf. Caleb aimed and fired, just missing the snarling beast. The wolf rolled along the ground, then gathered himself to attack Dusty once again as the other wolves scattered. Caleb reached into his pocket for a bullet, trying with all his might to remain calm. He fumbled it and it fell to the ground as precious seconds ticked away. Finally, he locked in another one and pulled back the hammer. Dusty reared and stomped with his front hooves, keeping the wolf at bay. Caleb fired again, but this time the rifle wasn't snug against his shoulder, and the hard kick from the gun sent him reeling against the dugout. The wolf leaped onto Dusty's back as Caleb scrambled desperately to his feet and reloaded. In a split second, Julie was at his side. Julie let loose on the wolf as fast as she could, the Colt revolver spitting flame. Caleb fired again, and the wolf jumped off Dusty and dashed away into the cover of the trees. Tumble raced from the cabin like the devil's wind and charged through the trees after the huge wolf.

"Get 'em, Tumble!" shouted Tilly as she came running out the door.

"Tilly! Get back in there!" Julie snagged little Tilly and pushed her back into the cabin. She then lit a candle, and holding a bucket upside down over it to keep it dry, walked outside, kicking the door shut behind her. Caleb held his rifle at the ready as they went over to check on Dusty and the wagon.

"Is he OK?" asked Julie as she held the candle up for Caleb to see.

Caleb stroked his horse to try to calm him. "Easy, boy." Caleb felt around Dusty's neck and shoulders. "It doesn't look like it got its teeth into him. There are a few deep claw scratches, but nothing serious. I'll take care of it in the morning."

"Oh, no! They got most of our food. Look." They could see

that the wolves had torn off the wooden top of their supply chest. Their teeth marks were visible, even on the metal hinges. Soaked to the bone, Caleb took another look around, thinking that any animal that could do this to wood and metal could make short work of them. A snap of a branch in the tree line startled him and he raised the Sharps quickly. It was Tumble, jogging proudly back. The wolves had fled.

"Good boy, Tumble," Caleb gave the little mutt a scratch on the head.

"Saved the day," Julie added with a smirk.

★ ★ ★

"Kearney Junction is still pretty far off. Maybe we should head to Red Cloud." Julie sat in the cabin, studying a map in the candlelight.

"No!" exclaimed Tilly. "We'll get attacked!"

"No, Tilly, not the Indian, Red Cloud. I mean the town. Folks named it after him." Julie managed a laugh as Tilly snuggled fearfully into her arms. "Besides, Chief Red Cloud doesn't fight anymore. He went to Washington to try to make peace for his people."

Caleb smiled sadly as he listened to Julie talk about the once fierce Sioux Chief. It reminded him of happier times of being gathered around the family supper table, listening to his father rail against politicians in Washington for breaking many of the Indian treaties. He would often peer from around his newspaper and snap off a question about the Indian Wars or politics. If you didn't know the answer, he would hand out paper and pen and with a stern look say, "Write it down, son!" Then he would grin and ruffle Caleb's hair. He did a lot of writing during supper. Julie, it seemed, always knew the answers.

"I don't think the railroad goes through there yet," said Caleb. "Maybe we should head east to Kansas City, pick up the train there."

"Too far. Our food won't last." Julie chewed her lip as she ran her finger along the map.

"What if we head west?" offered Caleb.

"There's nothing. You'd have to go all the way to Colorado. No, Red Cloud is our best bet. Looks like it could be about a hundred miles." Julie studied the map and stroked Tilly's hair. "We could stock up on food and then head north for Kearney Junction. Closest train is there. According to the map, we can take it all the way to Utah. Then we head up to Montana Territory."

Caleb kicked himself for not thinking of bringing their food in at night. That was one mistake. The other was not reloading the Sharps fast enough. He vowed to practice. "How much money do we have?"

"About fifty dollars. But that should get us to Virginia City. The letter says the thousand dollars is in the bank there. We'll pick it up and then find Aunt Sarah's ranch. We could always sell Dusty for more money in Kearney Junction before we get on the train." Julie looked at Caleb's crestfallen expression.

"I'll never sell him," said Caleb, shaking his head at

the thought. He couldn't imagine his world without his faithful horse.

"Sorry, bad idea. We'll find a way to take him on the train," said Julie as she wrapped Tilly in her blanket. "We better head out as soon as the rain lets up." She rolled up the map and snuggled beside Tilly. Then she brought out the Colt pistol and rested it at her side. "Can you take the first watch?"

Caleb nodded his head, then reached for the Sharps and brought a stool over to the window. No way was he going to let anything else happen that night. This time he stuck a spare bullet in his teeth.

★ ★ ★

Seven days later, exhausted from the insufferable Kansas heat and nearly starving, they made it to Red Cloud. Caleb, his hands raw from handling the reins, drove the buckboard through the little town. The hammering and sawing of people building new shops echoed through the dusty street. Smaller than Great Bend, Red Cloud was booming in anticipation of the coming railroad. It seemed everyone was out making preparations for the Fourth of July. Banners were being strung, flags raised, and a brass band played in the town square. They rode past a mercantile, the undertaker, a bakery, and the drugstore. There was an outfitter store, dress shop, barber, church, hardware store, and a loan office. Cattle were driven through the street by dusty cowhands. A number of peaceful Pawnee Indians sat trading their wares. Compared to the troubles in Great Bend, Red Cloud was heaven. It all seemed so civilized. How strange it felt compared to what they had been through. Suddenly, Julie reached over and squeezed his arm.

"Caleb, pull over into the alley." Julie smiled at the Sheriff, who was watching them out of the corner of his eye as he talked with a well-dressed woman holding a brightly colored parasol. The woman pointed toward the wagon. "Real easy so we don't attract attention." She gave the Sheriff a polite nod as Caleb guided Dusty behind the Smith Brothers' store.

Caleb caught on immediately and gave the reins a shake. Dusty yanked the buckboard quickly down the alley and out of sight. Then they doubled back, bypassing Red Cloud, and came to a stop in a grove of trees near a wide river about a mile away. Julie began stripping off her filthy dress down to her undergarments.

"Should have thought of this before." She then grabbed Tilly's clothes and nodded toward the river. "Let's clean up before we head back to town. Folks seeing us come in from the south, frightful as we look, they may get suspicious. Chances are some will know of the cholera in Great Bend and they might be on the alert. That would scare the entire town of Red Cloud."

"Should dry in no time in this heat," said Caleb as he jumped in the river, clothes and all. The cold water felt good. He squeezed his blistered hands, trying to get some life back into them. "I'll head to that outfitter store later and see what I can get. You and Tilly should probably stay here."

"Go in from the north and if anyone asks…"

"I'll tell them I'm from Kansas City."

★ ★ ★

Caleb managed to lay in a few supplies for the trip north. They stayed hidden outside Red Cloud to rest for two days, bathing discreetly in the water from Republican River, sleeping at night under their wagon. Then they rode north without any trouble for four more days until they finally reached Kearney Junction.

Caleb drove Dusty over the bridge that spanned the Platte River. In the distance, he saw railroad tracks and steered Dusty over toward the train depot. They had traveled nearly two hundred miles in a few weeks. They should be proud of themselves.

"Looks kind of dead," said Julie, looking around for signs of life. For a town that was a hub of the Northern Railroad, it seemed strangely deserted. A few people could be seen farther up the street, but it was eerily quiet. Two pack mules hitched to a railing brushed at flies with their tails in the summer heat. A lone dog sauntered slowly to the middle of the road and lay down, stretching without a care in the world. Caleb eased the wagon over to the train platform. He jumped off the buckboard and tied Dusty to a post. Julie climbed down and held her arms out for Tilly and helped her down. "Let's look around."

★ ★ ★

The depot office had a "CLOSED" sign on the door. Caleb peered inside the windows as Julie and Tilly searched along the track. Finally Caleb spotted the depot master who was napping inside, hat over his face. Caleb banged on the window until the man got up and shuffled to the door.

"Can't you read?" said the grouchy little man. "We're closed!"

"When is the next train due in?" asked Caleb.

"Ain't one." sniffed the man. "They ain't runnin'." Tumble decided he didn't like him and gave a low growl. "You hold on to that dog of yours."

"Tumble, here!" called Tilly, and the dog reluctantly obeyed.

"What do you mean, there's no train?" said Julie. "They were running in Great Bend, at least they were until the cholera came."

"There's a railroad strike a comin', haven't you heard? Word is it's gonna happen next week. Whole country's a mess for it." The depot master folded his arms and snorted.

"A strike? But we have to get to the Bitterroot," said Caleb.

"The Bitterroot? On the train?" laughed the depot master.

"Yes. We're to take the train west toward Utah and head north to Virginia City," offered Julie as she studied the letter.

"Well, you wouldn't get far, even if there weren't no strike," said the depot master as he shook his head. "They only got part of the Montana route built. They're still workin' on it. No tellin' when it'll be ready to travel. You best head back where you came from."

"So, how do we get there?" Caleb asked the man, glancing at Julie's crestfallen face.

"Only way is to wait for the wagon train to build up near Dobytown like they did in the old days. Head out on the Oregon Trail, then up the Bozeman Trail to Montana Territory. Take you at least a couple of months or more. Daggone dangerous on the Trail. Between the killers and the thieves, I'd say your chances ain't worth a bucket of mud. Worse, the Sioux are pretty riled up between here and there."

Caleb shivered at this news, for the Oregon Trail was a massive and dangerous undertaking. Pioneers began the journey from the Missouri River in eastern Kansas and traveled some two thousand rocky miles through Nebraska and the rugged territories of Wyoming and Idaho. It was the only direct route and it was a treacherous one. Some made it safely in huge ox-driven wagon trains all the way to California and Oregon, looking for gold or a better life. But here they were, just three children and a little buckboard. Besides the thieves, murderers, and hostile Indians, there were also bears, mountain lions, tornadoes—all sorts of unknown dangers. Caleb knew that their chances were slim because so many pioneers perished. They were buried in shallow graves alongside the Trail.

"Did you say wait until the wagon train builds up?" Caleb tried to shake off his fears as he looked into the setting western sun.

"For protection. Troops'll be riding in pretty soon for escort. No one goes through these days until they got better numbers on account of the Indians and all. Folks going it alone are dead meat. They need to wait for maybe thirty more wagons before the next one heads out. Until then, nobody in their right mind goes it alone."

"How long?" asked Caleb.

"Best guess is a week or two."

"Where's Dobytown?" Julie pulled Tilly to her, wrapping her in her arms.

"South of the Platte River a few miles outside old Fort Kearny. Can't miss it. Watch your hat, though. That is one mean town. Now, you three move along, I've got work to do." The fussy little man shuffled off to some imaginary task, leaving Caleb, Julie, and Tilly standing forlornly by the empty railroad tracks. Caleb took a deep breath, grabbed Dusty's reins, and eased the wagon away from the tracks. Silently, Julie helped Tilly up with Tumble, and then she climbed aboard.

★ ★ ★

"What are we going to do, Caleb?" worried Julie as they rode alongside the tracks.

"I don't know. I guess we'll head to Dobytown and wait for the wagon train and go with them."

"But, we'll need to stay for a week or so, and then pay them to take us on. We'd never make it alone," said Julie. "Our money will never last. Maybe we should go back to Great Bend."

Caleb looked long at Julie as they rode south in the late afternoon sun over the bridge that spanned the Platte River. The idea of going back to the violence and sadness of Great Bend was out of the question after weeks of travel. Their only real option was to head to Aunt Sarah's ranch. It was a hard choice to make, but at least they would have a home, and some money.

★ ★ ★

A few miles later, they trotted past the tall wooden fence that surrounded the dismantled Fort Kearny. Old barrels and boxes lay strewn about from the days it served as an outfitting depot for pioneers headed for the Oregon Trail. A burned-out service wagon stood next to a broken-down cannon, reminders of years past when Fort Kearny provided protection for settlers against Indian attack. Parts of the fence had been taken apart or sagged in neglect. Even an old Pony Express sign dangled from a chain, clattering in the hot breeze. Caleb had often dreamed about being a Pony Express rider, but the company was shut down when the railroads came, way before he was even born.

A half-hour later, they entered the run-down, ramshackle place called Dobytown. There were a few dusty, broken-down buildings; some looked like they were made out of mud. Suddenly, several drunken cowboys galloped past at breakneck speed, firing their pistols into the air. Caleb jerked Dusty to the side, leaped into the back of the wagon, and reached for his Sharps rifle. Julie grabbed Tilly and held her head down, then drew her Colt.

"Yeehawwwww!" A cowpoke let out a whoop as he lit a string of firecrackers and hurled them from his horse. Cowboys piled out of the saloon doors next to the livery. A red, white, and blue Fourth of July banner flapped in the breeze in front of the saloon. Caleb stuck his head up and watched as one of the cowhands leaped on his horse and raced along the dusty street. The other men cheered as the galloping cowboy pulled his pistol and fired at the telegraph poles as he tore past them. Then he stopped and reloaded, turned around, and fired six more shots.

"Twelve in a row and I hit every skunkin' one of 'em!" he boasted as he jumped off the horse. He collected some money from the others, who slapped him on the back as they went back inside the Dobytown Saloon. Caleb saw an old stableman struggling with some horses. Curious, he watched the old man limp into the barn, dragging the horses in after him.

"I have an idea," Caleb said as he turned Dusty around and headed toward the livery.

★ ★ ★

"You say you'll do the muckin' and the groomin' for the chance to bunk down? No pay?" said the old stableman.

"That's right." Caleb said. "Just until they get the wagon train together, then we'll go."

The stableman scratched his head at the prospect of being

able to take it easy on his aching back, eyes brightening at the thought of taking naps when it suited him. After all, it was nearly sundown, and there were about a dozen horses to tend to. "Tell you what, lad. You can have that big double stall in the back. Just put yourself down some fresh hay, and after you get settled in, you can start by brushing down that big black over there. Can you shoe?"

"Yes, sir!"

The stableman's eyes lit up at that piece of good news. "That seals the deal. Now, the way I work it, whatever horse gets tied up out front, bring 'em inside for feed and water. But this big black here needs a shoe on the hind left. When you're done with that, brush him down and tie him to the rail outside. His owner's headin' out tonight."

★ ★ ★

Caleb brushed the big black stallion with long gentle strokes. The huge horse's flanks rippled as the bristles tickled his hide. The saddle was an Army issue. A leather scabbard held a gleaming Spencer rifle. He was tempted to hold it, but common sense got the better of him. Suddenly, he got goose bumps. He pulled off the saddle and scabbard and set them on the top rail of a stall. *It couldn't be*, he thought, as he ran his fingers over the initials that were carved into the stock. "N.V." His mind flashed on the mysterious stranger and the big stallion that last terrible night in Great Bend, his mad charge into the ranks of the black-coated murderers. He turned back to the black and continued to brush it, studying the scars along its flank. This was a true warhorse.

Caleb heard Tilly crying and looked over at Julie as she raked fresh hay into the horse stall they were to bunk in later.

"Here." Julie took the locket from Tilly's neck. "See how pretty she is? Just like you. And Father is so handsome." Together they studied the tiny photo of their parents.

Caleb shut his eyes. He could picture them clear as day. "Want to hear a story?" Julie asked Tilly. Hearing Julie tell a story like their father brought an ache to Caleb's heart as he brushed the black horse.

"Once upon a time?" sniffled Tilly, brightening a little at the thought of inventing a new story. She snuggled close to Julie in their bed of hay, grabbing onto Tumble.

"Well, once upon a time, there was…"

"A beautiful princess!" Tilly always wanted her stories started in this fashion.

"A beautiful princess, and she…"

"Was locked in a dragon's cave!" exclaimed Tilly as she snuggled in tighter next to Julie.

"It's always about the dragon now," said Caleb. Exhausted as he was, his night was not near over.

"Yes, since that night." said Julie sadly.

"I'm going over to the saloon. Maybe they'll let me wash some dishes or something and give us some food."

"Thank you, Caleb," said Julie, her eyes shining in gratitude for her brother. "But be careful. This town seems kind of wild." She turned back to Tilly and continued her story.

"I will." Caleb gave Dusty a pat as he took him outside and tied him up next to their wagon. Then he went back for the black. He hoisted the saddle onto the horse and cinched it tight. Carefully, he secured the Spencer rifle and scabbard, once again noting the "N.V." carved into the stock. He wondered if the hands that carried it into battle were the hands of the dark rider of Great Bend. He led the stallion outside and tied him carefully to the rail. Satisfied that the horse wasn't going anywhere, he headed to the Dobytown Saloon.

4

THE DOBYTOWN SALOON

★ ★

You want to what?" said Red at the back door of the saloon.

"Work for food?" said Caleb to the saloon lady with the flaming red hair. "My sisters and I are sleeping in the livery until the wagon train heads out."

"Land sakes, boy, Dobytown is no place for children. This mud hole is nothin' but a snake pit. It's full of killers and thieves. They'll take your life as quick as they'll take your money. Heck, soldiers won't even come around here. You best take your sisters and ride on out."

"We've got nowhere to go," pleaded Caleb.

"Red!" barked a voice from inside. "What in tarnation are you doing talkin' with that boy? I got a business to run!"

"Please?"

"Sit tight. I'll see what I can do." Red softened as she looked hard at Caleb. Then she disappeared into the saloon. Caleb could hear her talking with the man inside over the sound of the piano. After a minute, she came back outside.

"All right. Tom says to put you to work. But just for tonight," said Red as she motioned Caleb inside.

The Dobytown Saloon was hopping. Some cowboys were whooping it up, drinking away the trail dust and playing poker. Tough-looking men, six-shooters on the bar in front of them, silently stared into their whiskey. The piano player kept it lively, his long, skinny fingers dancing over the keys and filling the saloon with favorite tunes. Caleb washed and dried glasses and set them on the long wooden bar. Saloon girls dressed in brightly colored dresses sashayed past and ruffled his hair. Smoke from cigars cast a blue haze across the room. Suddenly, two drunken cowhands broke out into a fight. One of them reared back and punched the other and knocked him out cold. Immediately, the burly cowpoke picked him up and threw him right past Caleb, straight through the saloon doors and into the street. The other cowhands barely noticed. *No wonder Father never let me go with him inside the Last Chance Saloon in Great Bend*, Caleb thought.

"Hang in a little longer and we'll fix you up some supper. You've earned it," said Red as she shoved some dirty glasses into Caleb's tired hands.

"Thanks, Red. I'll work all night if I have to." Caleb said, for he and his sisters needed every dime he made.

"Hey, Tom!" yelled Red to the bartender. "What do you say we keep this kid? Cute, ain't he?"

Tom looked up from the bar and slid a bottle of whiskey over to some dusty cowboys. "It's gettin' late. Give him his grub and give him the boot."

Red laughed and gave Caleb a wink. "I'll give you a boot," she said to Tom. "Right up your…" Red stopped in her tracks. She went white as a ghost. The creak of the saloon doors silenced the din of the room. Things seemed to stall in time for a few seconds. Caleb turned to see what she was looking at and felt his knees almost buckle. It was the stranger from Great Bend. The dark rider who tried to save the Thatchers. He stood tall and dangerous, about six foot three. The hands that gripped the swinging doors looked to be made of iron. A black hat covered his hair but couldn't hide the piercing eyes and whiskered jaw. A Colt revolver strapped to his hip stood ready under the long dark coat. Some of the cowboys looked up from their whiskey to take in the stranger. Others could not meet the intense gaze of the man.

"Lord, no…" said Red, her breath catching in her throat. She took Caleb by the elbow and led him around to the side of the bar. "Just my luck. Of all men to show up in this godforsaken town."

"Why…who is he?" Caleb's mind raced.

"It's William Henderson! The Killer of Quick Creek! They must have let him out of prison." Red took a deep breath to compose herself. "Whatever you do, Caleb, steer clear of him." Too late. William Henderson caught Caleb's eye, the man's steely stare turning his legs to water. Caleb felt a shock to his boots. He had heard about the former war hero who went crazy and killed three Union soldiers, a cold-blooded killer who was locked up in Fort Leavenworth prison. Cowboys shifted clear as the tall, dark figure passed through the swinging saloon doors and made his way along the bar. Caleb felt the grip of Red's hands on his shoulders as Henderson walked over to them, the eerie quiet giving way to the heavy sound of his boots.

"Boy," said William Henderson, as he stood towering above them, his voice a rumble. "Why don't you make yourself useful and bring a bottle of whiskey to that table over there." He pointed to a lone table against the wall. He then nodded to Red and touched his hat. "Red. Been a long time."

"William…yes…uh…long time," Red managed to choke.

"Give him this," said Red as Henderson sat down at his table. Shaking, she grabbed a bottle and a glass and shoved them into Caleb's hands. "Then stay out of his way. I've worked every saloon this side of the Missouri River. Believe me, I know the man. He's nothing but a coldhearted killer."

The man may be a killer, but he was also something else. Caleb had seen it himself in Great Bend when Henderson drove off four murderers and tried to save Mr. Thatcher. In his heart, he felt something wasn't right. Caleb drew a breath and made his way over to Henderson's table. He put the bottle and glass in front of Henderson, who then poured himself a shot. Caleb stood before the man and tried to control the shaking in his knees.

"That night in Great Bend. It was you, wasn't it?" asked Caleb nervously. Henderson drank his whiskey and surveyed the saloon.

"Must be somebody else you're thinking of," he replied in a low growl.

"You tried to save Mr. Thatcher. I saw you," Caleb said.

Suddenly, Henderson reached up and took hold of Caleb's shirt, drawing him close. "I tell you, boy, you must be talkin' about another man. You don't know me and I don't know you," Henderson said in a low whisper as he poured himself another shot of whiskey. "Do we understand each other?"

"Yes, sir," Caleb gulped.

"Good. Now go on about your business." Henderson released Caleb, then pulled his hat down over his eyes and leaned back into his chair.

Caleb moved away from the table. He vowed to keep his mouth shut, leave this Henderson alone, and get back to making money off the cowhands. Suddenly, the saloon doors burst open. Four men in grimy black dusters and black hats shook the trail dust off as they bellied up to the bar. Caleb nearly bumped into the biggest one. As he looked up into the huge man's eyes, his mind reeled. These were the thieves who shot Mr. Jackson and the Thatchers! The man stared hard at Caleb, then burst into a big grin. Caleb fully expected the worst, but the man did not appear to recognize him. Caleb breathed a sigh of relief and edged over to the other end of the bar, thankful that it had been dark and smoky that night back in Great Bend. He vowed to keep his head down, his mouth shut, and try to stay out of their way.

"Red!" shouted the oldest one who must have been the leader. He was big and mean-looking with greasy black hair. His face had the look of perpetual rage. "It's gonna be a long night. Line 'em up and keep 'em comin'." He had black teeth!

Quickly, Caleb turned away, remembering Tilly's vision of the black-toothed dragon.

"Well, well. If it ain't the Blackstone boys!" shouted Red, one eye on Henderson. "Eli Blackstone, you have made my night. Girls, get over here and leave those other worn-out doggies. We've got some real company!" Caleb was nearly trampled by the money-hungry saloon girls as they shrieked with delight and sashayed over to the Blackstones.

As Caleb hustled through the night, he felt a little safer. He found that working hard and minding his own business was the best course of things. He made money too, and as he did, he learned the names of the murderous Blackstone brothers. There was Eli, or Blacktooth, who was the oldest. Then Davey, or Mountain Man, who killed Mr. Jackson. The youngest was named Earl and he had a face like a rat, skimpy whiskers streaking out from under a pointy nose, eyes darting in a beady stare. Rat Face picked at an angry sore on his neck as he threw down a shot of whiskey. Then there was Nathan, the one who shot the Thatchers. He was an ugly, vicious-looking man with deep scars on his face and the black eyes of the dead. Caleb shuddered to look at him, for it was like being stared at by a rattlesnake.

Just then, the swinging doors opened and a burly man walked toward the bar, a Sheriff's badge pinned to his chest. The man shot the hairs up on Caleb's neck as he gruffly shouldered his way past him. There was something shifty and cruel in his nature. Immediately, the bartender set down a shot of whiskey.

"Sheriff Wayne!" bellowed Blacktooth.

"Eli," grinned the Sheriff as he tossed down the whiskey. Caleb saw Henderson pull his hat down farther over his eyes.

"Thought we'd have us a little fun," Blacktooth said with a chuckle, leveling his gaze at Sheriff Wayne. Caleb shot a look to the Sheriff and noticed a sly wink. "Want to join us?"

"No," said the Sheriff with a snicker as he set his glass on the bar and walked toward the door. "You boys have your fun. Be good now."

"OK, Sheriff Wayne, we'll be sure and do that," sneered Snake, who suddenly appeared behind Caleb with a saloon girl in tow. He took hold of a whiskey bottle and started to drain it, then laughed and poured the last of it on Caleb's head, slamming the bottle on the bar. "What are you lookin' at, boy?" Caleb sputtered and wiped the burning whiskey from his eyes. "More whiskey!"

Caleb, his eyes stinging, went behind the bar, his mind racing. He figured he should make his exit, but since they didn't seem to recognize him, money and food were his main concern. If he did a good job, maybe he could talk Tom into letting him come back and work at the saloon until the wagon train was ready. Then he and his sisters would be all right. Caleb pulled a bottle of whiskey from the shelf and headed back.

"What we need is a little poker game!" whooped Mountain Man as he stalked over to the card table. "Bring that whiskey over here, Bottle Boy!"

Caleb hustled over with the bottle. Mountain Man,

Snake, and Rat Face surrounded several cowboys who were in the middle of their poker game. Mountain Man picked up an old cowpoke and tossed him from his chair like a rag doll. Then he took a seat and reached for a deck of cards. The three remaining cowboys exchanged dubious looks. Caleb dubbed them Eye Patch, Long Beard, and Irishman, and all seemed pretty reluctant to play. Eye Patch got up to leave, but Snake slammed him back into his chair.

"Fill us up, Bottle Boy!" said Rat Face, his sinister rodent grin and beady eyes challenging Caleb. Snake and Blacktooth held their glasses out to Caleb, and he filled their whiskey glasses while Mountain Man dealt the cards.

"Now this little game is called Davey's Draw," Mountain Man giggled.

"Forget it, I'm out." The Irishman rose from his chair. Snake slammed him back down as Rat Face drew his Colt. Eye Patch and Long Beard sat frozen, figuring they had better go along with the game.

Caleb felt Blacktooth's hand on his shoulder. "Fill theirs up too, boy," said Blacktooth, indicating the empty glasses on the poker table. "Can't forget our manners!" said the killer with a chuckle. Caleb glanced over to Henderson's table at the other end of the saloon. Henderson sat quietly, hat down over his eyes. Like the ticking clock on the wall, Caleb could almost hear the beating of his own heart as he filled up the poker players' glasses.

★ ★ ★

Deeper into the evening, Caleb felt the fatigue hit him like a steam engine when he heard the words that could change a night of fun on the town into a deadly rampage.

"That's cheating!" shouted Irishman. Everything stopped. The piano player ducked down, the girls stopped laughing, and all conversation came to a halt. The air took on a menacing stillness, like the gunpowder smell of a shot fired. Quickly, Mountain Man grabbed Irishman in his huge fist. The other cowboys edged carefully away from the poker table. Caleb looked over to see Henderson slowly pull his Colt revolver and hold it at the ready under his table.

"What did you say?" Mountain Man held Irishman in his grip.

"I had three nines!" said Irishman in protest.

Blacktooth dropped Red like a sack of potatoes and walked slowly to the table and checked out the cards. "Well now, Mr. Englishman, my brother Davey here's got a full house. In these United States of America that beats three of a kind."

"News to you, I'm Irish. He had two fives, everybody saw!" squealed Irishman. "He cheated and drew twice!"

"Everybody?" Blacktooth asked in a deadly voice. "Who here seen that?" Rat Face and Snake grabbed the handles of their Colts and stared down the room, itching for a fight. No one spoke. Mountain Man hung onto the sputtering Irishman like a bear playing with a fish.

Blacktooth snatched Caleb's bottle away and drank, smacking his lips from the bite of the whiskey. Then he shoved it back into Caleb's shaking hands and roughly brushed him aside, sending Caleb crashing into the wall just feet away from Henderson's table. Wiping the burning whiskey from his lips with the back of his hand, Blacktooth took a murderous stroll around the saloon, looking for a victim. None dared meet his gaze. Cowboys shifted on their feet nervously. No one wanted any part of him. Finally, his eyes rested on Henderson and he leveled his deadly stare at him. Caleb's breath caught, knowing at any second things could explode like a violent storm.

"You seen that?" hissed Blacktooth to Henderson. Henderson, hat over his eyes, sat calmly with his hidden Colt pointed under the table at Blacktooth. Furious that Henderson ignored him, Blacktooth demanded again. "I'm talkin' to you, mister!"

"I heard you," replied Henderson quietly.

"I asked you if you seen that." Blacktooth moved his hand to his Colt. Caleb's eyes widened as Henderson tilted his hat up and stared back at Blacktooth. The other cowboys in the saloon cleared the area around Henderson's table. Caleb held his breath as the two men faced each other down. The saloon was as quiet as a church, yet crackled like a lit fuse.

"Well, I can't see much of anything from here, now can I?" Henderson was dangerously calm. "But if you ask me if three nines beats two fives, I'd have to say it does. I heard a man say he had three nines, so I guess he wins."

"Hear that? I win, he says!" choked Irishman, struggling in Mountain Man's grasp.

"You callin' my brother a cheat?" challenged Blacktooth, his mouth breaking into an ugly black snarl. "Get up!"

Caleb could almost sense Henderson pulling back the hammer of his Colt. His mind raced, his heart pounded, for there he stood against the wall, clutching the whiskey bottle, standing between a murdering thief and the Killer of Quick Creek. At any moment, the bullets would fly and his own blood could splatter the walls of the Dobytown Saloon. Thinking fast, he slowly crossed over to Henderson's table. The old clock quietly ticked as the two gunfighters continued to stare each other down. Carefully, he poured whiskey into Henderson's empty glass, trying to keep the bottle from clinking against it. He brought his other hand up to keep it steady.

"Can't forget our manners," said Caleb in a shaky voice as he filled Henderson's glass. Blacktooth, his hand on his Colt, stood poised to unleash a barrage of lead. But then, a flicker of amusement appeared across Blacktooth's face.

"Manners!" Blacktooth roared. "Bottle Boy says we can't forget our manners!"

Caleb looked at Henderson. "A full house beats three of a kind, right, mister?" Caleb quietly pleaded. "That's right, isn't it?"

Henderson eyed Caleb for what seemed like an eternity. Then slowly he reached for the whiskey glass, his right hand still under the table on his pistol. Caleb held his breath as Henderson brought the whiskey to his lips and drank. Satisfied, he then set the glass back down on the table.

"That's right," said Henderson as he gave Caleb a sly wink.

"He says a full house wins!" said Caleb to Blacktooth.

"Here that, Davey?" said Blacktooth, his mouth set in an ugly grin. "The boy says you win!"

"That's it. I'm out! I'm not losing what I have to a cheater!" said Irishman as he broke free from Mountain Man's grip.

Snake lashed out suddenly and pistol-whipped Irishman to the floor. "Can't quit now, Irish. New hand!"

Blacktooth sneered victoriously at Henderson and headed over to the poker table. Henderson pulled his hat down over his eyes, easing his hand off his Colt. Caleb breathed a sigh of relief as Red hustled over with a plate loaded with food.

"The Lord did give you some smarts, Caleb. You best get yourself out of here for tonight." Red ruffled Caleb's hair. "We'll see about tomorrow."

"Thanks, Red." Caleb took the food gratefully and headed through the swinging doors. The cowboys were drinking again, the girls laughing, and the piano player playing. The Dobytown Saloon was hopping once more.

5

THE GUNS ROAR

★ ★

Caleb picked up his Sharps rifle and sat against the wooden stall in the lantern light. More horses had been left out front while he was in the saloon and he'd dutifully brought them in for feed and water. Now, he could finally rest. Tumble was curled up nearby, snoring softly. Tilly lay snuggled against Julie like a raggedy angel, still clutching a favorite little doll that they'd managed to bring along for her. Julie slept with her arms around Tilly in motherly protection, her golden hair fanned out in the hay. Caleb took a rag from his back pocket and cleaned the rifle's barrel and stock. He pulled the hammer back and peered into the chamber, then blew away some specks of dirt. He took out a bullet and slid it in, mindful of the click it made when it was snug in the chamber. Next, he squeezed the trigger and eased the hammer down. He leaned back in the hay and closed his eyes as exhaustion washed over his body. Images of his burning home, his dying mother, the wolves, and the Blackstones flickered across his mind. He heard Dusty give a quiet snort outside the barn door. Then Caleb fell into the deepest sleep of his life, the Sharps slipping from his grasp into the hay beside him.

★ ★ ★

"That's it. The dapple-gray horse there. She's all I've got," a strange voice said. Caleb could not move himself to wake. He could feel someone suddenly shaking him, but he could not open his eyes, so deep was his sleep.

"Well, she's ours now!" answered a dark and sinister voice.

"Caleb, wake up!" he heard Julie say, feeling her trying to shake him from his slumber.

The CRACK of a fist against flesh jolted Caleb awake in time to see Irishman fly through the open barn door and land in a heap. The four murderous Blackstones, drunk and dangerous, barreled in behind him. As Blacktooth reached down and yanked up Irishman, his evil eyes rested upon Tilly, who snuggled deep into Julie's arms.

"Well now. What do we have here?" leered Blacktooth as he dropped Irishman into a pile of manure.

"It's the dragon!" exclaimed Tilly. "It's him!"

Blacktooth stared hard at Tilly. Then his mouth broke into an ugly black grin. "What do you know? You're a long way from Great Bend now, aren't you?"

"Bottle Boy, too, if my memory serves," cackled Mountain Man.

"Told you he was that same kid," said Rat Face.

Caleb searched the hay all around him. The Sharps that had fallen from his grip was buried beside him. Suddenly, he felt the heavy rifle and struggled to bring it to bear. In a flash, Snake was on him, jerked the Sharps from his hand, and tossed it aside. Then he shoved Caleb over toward Mountain Man. Caleb lashed out and caught the huge man with a solid kick in the shins, but Mountain Man held him in his fist and just laughed. Suddenly, he backhanded Caleb across the face. Caleb's head exploded with light and he went flying, landing in a heap, his ears ringing from the blow. He tried to get back on his feet, but Mountain Man clamped a ham-sized fist around his throat. Caleb struggled to breathe, the blood roaring in his ears.

"Tumble! Get 'em!" Tilly managed to gasp as she struggled in Julie's arms.

Tumble charged from the stall and set upon the Blackstones in a barking rage, snapping his mighty little jaws at Mountain Man's feet. Mountain Man kicked at Tumble and nearly dropped Caleb when Rat Face picked up a shovel and silenced the loyal mutt with a blow to his head. Tumble yelped once, then lay still.

"And I sure remember that dang dog," laughed Rat Face as he tossed the shovel aside.

Caleb could feel the life squeezing out of him. Try as he might, he could not break from the big man's grip. He punched at Mountain Man with both his hands, kicking out with his feet, fighting for his life. Finally, Mountain Man released him and he crashed to the ground, gasping for breath.

"Stop!" Julie ran to her brother. Blacktooth reached out and snagged Julie by the hair. "No…please…" cried Julie as she struggled in the big man's grip.

"Well now, looks like we got a whole family of brats here." Blacktooth stared at Julie like a fox at a hen.

"What do you think we should do with 'em, Eli?" said Snake, moving in for a closer look.

"Ask me, it throws a kink in things," said Rat Face. "I say we get rid of 'em."

"Look, I want none of this," exclaimed Irishman suddenly. "You have my horse. Let me go."

"Shut up!" Mountain Man lashed out and smacked Irishman across the head. "We better take care of 'em. Bottle Boy and the little princess here, they be witnesses, Eli."

"Got a point there, Davey," growled Blacktooth.

Caleb lay dazed, his ears ringing and his vision blurred by Mountain Man's blow to his face. Through the haze, he saw Julie struggling in Blacktooth's grip. Little Tilly sobbed as she lay in the straw of their stall. Tumble was crumpled up just a few feet away, blood pouring from a gash in his head. He could hear Dusty, tied up outside, screaming a high-pitched whinny.

"Please. We won't say anything," pleaded Julie as Blacktooth yanked her close.

"You leave my sister alone!" cried Tilly as she ran from the stall to Julie. Blacktooth grabbed Tilly and tossed her to Rat Face like a little rag doll.

"Ha! Look out for this one!" joked Blacktooth. "Hold on

to her, Earl!" Rat Face grabbed Tilly and held her tight as she kicked and screamed.

"No!" cried Julie as she raked her fingernails across Blacktooth's cheek, drawing blood.

"Feisty little puma, you are." Blacktooth laughed and wiped some blood from his face. "Looks like we've got a little business to take care of, my brothers. Let's saddle up and take 'em out of town. Gag 'em first. Davey, get some rope."

"Right good idea, Eli." Mountain Man grabbed some rope from one of the stalls.

As Caleb felt his strength return, he saw the Sharps lying ten feet away, half hidden in some hay. The tip of the long barrel gleamed in the lantern light. He edged slowly toward it on his belly, thinking if he could just get to it, they might stand a chance. As Julie put up a mighty fight against Blacktooth, Caleb chose his moment. Mustering all his courage, he dove toward the rifle. In an instant, he brought it to his shoulder, pulling back the hammer with a resounding *CLICK*.

"Stop!" Caleb leveled the Sharps at Blacktooth's chest. Terrified, he knew they could easily gun him down, and in fact seemed to be amused by his show of bravery. The four Blackstones stood silent, shoulder to shoulder, daring Caleb to pull the trigger. Caleb held his ground.

"Well, Bottle Boy, what are we going to do about you?" Blacktooth snarled as he held Julie tight against him.

"I say shoot him. Gonna have to deal with them anyway," said Snake as he rested his hand on his Colt. "He's only got one bullet in that Sharps of his." Rat Face tossed Tilly away.

Mountain Man dropped the rope and slid his enormous hand to his pistol.

"Good idea, Nathan," said Rat Face. "I say on the count of three! One…"

"Two…" chuckled Blacktooth, his black eyes boring into Caleb. Julie lashed out with a kick to his shin. Blacktooth grabbed Julie's hair and held her in front of him.

"Caleb!" cried Julie as she fought against Blacktooth.

"Let her go!" Caleb knew this may be the final moment of his life. The Blackstones would kill as soon as breathe. The blood roared in his ears and his heart thundered in his chest. Suddenly, the sound of the cocking of a pistol rang out behind him.

"You heard the boy," said the deep voice. William Henderson, Colt pistol in his hand, stalked with deadly purpose through the barn door. He stood beside Caleb and boldly stared into the evil eyes of Blacktooth, leveling the Colt at his head. "Let her go."

No one moved. Blacktooth held Julie in his grip, then finally let her go. "You best back out of here. This ain't your business."

"I'm making it my business." Henderson trained his gun on the murderous brothers. "You men drop your guns, real easy."

"We should get the Sheriff," said Julie.

"Good! Why don't you go on and do that?" chuckled Blacktooth.

"No! He's in with them!" exclaimed Caleb, remembering the curious exchange in the bar.

"Noticed that, did you, boy?" said Henderson. "I said lose the guns."

The Blackstones held their ground, pure rage pouring from their eyes. So tempted they were to draw on Henderson, their hands itched for the handles of their revolvers. Surely they could kill him if they all fired at once. And just as certain, each knew Henderson would kill two of them, or maybe three, before they got the chance. The Killer of Quick Creek stood rock-steady, almost daring them to make a move. Slowly they unbuckled their gun belts and let them fall to the ground. Julie grabbed Tilly and backed out of the way.

"You," Henderson said to Julie. "Gather your things and take the little girl out of here. That your wagon outside?"

"Yes, sir." Julie jumped into action.

"Can you hitch it up?" Henderson kicked the Blackstones' guns away.

"I can," Julie said as she grabbed Tilly and their things and hustled out of the barn.

"Boy, aim that rifle of yours at that ugly fellow on the end." Henderson motioned toward Snake. "If he moves, shoot him."

Caleb nodded and shifted his rifle to Snake and pointed it straight at his head. Snake glared at him with dead viper eyes as Caleb fought to hold the big gun steady.

"Those your horses?" Henderson pointed his Colt at Blacktooth, indicating the horses behind him.

Blacktooth silently stared back, aching to get his hands on his gun.

"I take it that's a yes." His gun covering the Blackstones, Henderson picked up the rope Mountain Man dropped and slapped at the flanks of the horses, driving them toward the barn door. "Ya! Git!"

"You're a dead man," hissed Blacktooth as the horses raced out of the barn.

Henderson faced Blacktooth and the two men locked in a deadly stare of destiny. Then Henderson reared back and backhanded Blacktooth across the mouth, splitting his lip. Blacktooth hit the ground hard.

"Guess I'll be going now," said Henderson. "Son, get in that wagon."

Caleb's heart pounded so hard he swore he could hear it. When he backed out the barn door, he turned to see Julie hitching up Dusty. Tilly suddenly jumped from the wagon and raced past Caleb into the barn. "Tumble!" cried Tilly.

"Tilly, no!" shouted Caleb.

"Get her out of here!" exclaimed Henderson.

Tilly darted past the Blackstones to try to save her dog. Rat Face lunged at her as she ran near him and took her to the ground. He clamped an arm around her and held her in front of him, using her as a shield. Caleb ran toward his sister, blocking Henderson's aim. "Get down, boy!"

The Blackstones suddenly dove for their guns. Blacktooth shot first as Henderson jerked his Colt up to avoid Caleb. It was a lightning bolt that wounded Henderson in his side. Henderson fired back as Blacktooth ducked behind a mound of hay. Mountain Man raised his gun to fire, but Henderson, with the calm of a man who had seen many battles, whirled around and fired first, killing Mountain Man instantly with a shot to the heart. Rat Face grabbed his gun and scurried away with Tilly, taking cover in a stall. In the panic and confusion of the moment, Irishman bolted toward the barn door, but fell dead to the ground, shot in the back by Blacktooth.

Snake rose from behind an old service wagon and drew a bead on Henderson's back. Caleb swung his Sharps and fired. The report of the big rifle filled the barn and Snake grabbed for his ear. Caleb had shot it half off, adding yet another scar to Snake's ugly face! Quickly, he reached for another bullet to jack into the Sharps, precious seconds passing as he struggled to reload. Tumble sprang to life and launched himself at Rat Face, burying his teeth in his leg. Rat Face, yowling in pain, let go of Tilly and tried to beat Tumble away with the butt of his Colt. Kicking off Tumble, he drew on Henderson. Caleb swung the Sharps toward Rat Face. He fired, but missed as the rodent man dove for cover.

"Get her out of here, boy! Go!" yelled Henderson, reaching for the spare Remington revolver in his boot. Caleb grabbed Tilly and dragged her toward the barn door. Blacktooth vaulted a stall and hid behind some bales of hay. Henderson shot the lantern above and flames cascaded over the hay and Blacktooth. Blacktooth beat at his flaming duster, firing wildly at Henderson. With both his guns blazing, Henderson managed to keep the three Blackstones pinned down. Henderson backed toward the barn door to cover Caleb as he struggled to get Tilly and Tumble to safety.

"Come on, Caleb!" shouted Julie as she held Dusty and the wagon steady.

Caleb scrambled into the back of the wagon with Tilly. Henderson fan-fired his Remington and backed out of the barn as flames began to devour the inside. When Henderson had fired his last shot, he reached for a loose bridle that was draped over the rail and lashed the door shut. There was a crash of gunfire from the inside and the door splintered from a hail of Blackstone bullets. Caleb reached down and pulled up Tumble, then covered Tilly with his body. "Go, Julie!"

"Ya, Dusty!" yelled Julie, giving the reins a mighty shake. Dusty shot down the street. As they raced away, Caleb looked back and saw the wounded Henderson trying to mount his black stallion. Henderson, hit in the leg, went down under the thunder of the Blackstone guns. In a split second, Caleb made his decision.

"Turn back!" exclaimed Caleb as he scrambled in front with Julie.

"No, Caleb!"

"They'll kill him, Julie! He saved our lives!"

Julie yanked Dusty around and sped back the other way. Lights were already appearing in the night as the townsfolk raised the cry for fire. As they pulled up to the barn, Caleb leaped off the wagon and ran to Henderson. Blood was pouring down the gunfighter's forehead. Henderson struggled to get up, but fell into Caleb's arms. The Blackstones fired from within the burning barn, trying to escape the flames. Hands broke through the splintered door and yanked at the bridle that held it shut. Caleb tried with all his might to drag Henderson to the wagon. In moments, the Blackstones would break free.

"Julie, help me!" cried Caleb. Julie reached down under the driver's seat and came up with the Colt. She fired the pistol at the barn door as she ran to help Caleb. Together they heaved Henderson into the wagon. Caleb vaulted in front and grabbed the reins.

"Hang on!" yelled Caleb as he shook Dusty's reins, driving the buckboard out the west end of town. Henderson, bloodied and unconscious, but alive, lay facedown next to Tumble. Julie clutched Tilly hard to her chest in the back of the buckboard. Shouts of "Fire!" echoed in the street and drunken cowboys staggered out of the saloon. Caleb urged Dusty on as fast as the horse could go. He dared not look back. He could imagine the Blackstones' rage. Mountain Man was dead. Caleb had wounded Snake. But right now, his main concern was to get them out of Dobytown!

★ ★ ★

On they galloped through the night as Dusty pulled the little wagon along the Oregon Trail. They stopped for nothing as mile after mile disappeared under the mighty gait of Caleb's faithful horse. Caleb's heart pounded out a beat to Dusty's flying hooves, fearing the Blackstones were not far behind. Finally, miles away from the rat hole called Dobytown, in the light of the moon and heading west, Caleb looked back.

As he slowed Dusty, he thought he could hear the soft thunder of a horse's hooves. His breath caught as a dark shape galloped easily toward them. Caleb grabbed his Sharps. He brought the heavy rifle to his shoulder and sighted on the shape as it came alongside the wagon. Then he relaxed.

It was Henderson's horse. The black.

6

THE KINDNESS
OF STRANGERS

★ ★

Two days later, Caleb urged Dusty through a small cluster of trees in the early light of dawn. Henderson's horse was tied to the wagon. They had pushed hard along the Oregon Trail and had covered thirty or forty miles. Dusty was breathing hard and needed a rest. There had been no sign of the Blackstones. Once, they spotted a small band of Indians against the distant sun. Fearing for their lives, Caleb and Julie grabbed their guns and watched breathlessly as the Indians rode to within a few hundred feet of the wagon. One of them raised his hand. Caleb raised his hand in return. The Indians walked their horses slowly toward the wagon across the flat, endless plain. Fortunately, they turned out to be friendly Pawnee, not the fierce Sioux. They were just curious and looking to trade. There had been no sign of other travelers, no wagon trains in sight. A lonely graveyard of trash and broken-down wagons dotted the road. Folks often lightened their loads as the miles went by on the Oregon Trail. The strewn items were ghosts of pioneers past. There was even a rocking chair sitting forlornly alongside the road.

It was nearly sunrise when Caleb carefully surveyed a little farmhouse they had come upon. Beyond exhaustion, he weighed his options. They needed food and sleep. Henderson had to have a doctor or he would surely die. It was a wonder how a man could lose so much blood and still be alive.

"I think we should see if they can help," whispered Julie as she held little Tilly beside her next to Caleb. "Besides, Tilly needs to stop for a while and rest. She's not feeling too well."

"All right, I'll go down there and see." Caleb picked up his Sharps.

"Better let me do it. They see you with that gun, they might get nervous. Keep watch here." Then Julie pocketed the Colt and jumped off the buckboard.

Caleb nodded and settled in with his rifle and put his arm around Tilly. He felt her forehead. It did feel hot. He glanced at Henderson. He was unconscious, but still breathing. Try as they might, they couldn't stop the flow of blood from his wounds.

Julie was at the door in mid-knock when it suddenly opened, a light flaring up from the inside. An old, skinny farmer appeared, gripping a single-shot Enfield musket that was probably left over from the Civil War. Julie turned and pointed toward Caleb. The farmer nodded and went inside. Julie signaled Caleb to head down.

★ ★ ★

"It was Indians, you say?" said the farmer's wife, Mrs. Whitticker. She was a very stout older woman with a pleasant face. The farmer's son, Billy, stood in the corner. He looked to be about seventeen. His ears stuck out and his face was covered with pockmarks. Farmer Whitticker was busy tending to Henderson, who was lying in a bed. The gunfighter's shirt was torn open and the gaping bullet wound in his side bled heavily. Henderson's pants were ripped up the side. That last bullet had smashed the bone in his leg. The farmer had wrapped a cloth around the wound to stop the bleeding. The crease of Henderson's head wound revealed the white of his scalp, but at least it didn't bleed much anymore.

"Yes, ma'am," said Julie.

"Mrs. Whitticker," the farmer said as he picked out a piece of the bullet from Henderson's side and placed it into a china bowl with a clack. "Why don't you take these girls into the kitchen for some of that stew you made last night? I'm sure they could use a bite. Look pretty hungry. And that young'un don't look too good."

"No, she don't, Daniel." Mrs. Whitticker felt Tilly's head. "She's fevered. Come along, Julie, is it? We'll fix up something."

"Yes, ma'am, thank you for your kindness." Julie took Tilly's hand and followed Mrs. Whitticker out the door.

"What's your name, boy?" said Mr. Whitticker as he cut away Henderson's shirt.

"Caleb O'Toole, sir."

"You say you're out of Great Bend? Where you headed?"

"Montana. Up in the Bitterroot." Caleb grabbed a cloth and swished it around in a bucket of clean water and handed it to the farmer, who continued to clean Henderson's chest and arms.

"Long way, the Bitterroot. Long way. So you say some Indians ambushed you on the trail?" The farmer tied off a stitch in Henderson's side. He then ran a cloth down Henderson's arm, searching for farther damage.

"Yes, sir. Over by Little Blue River." Caleb watched the man's expression change as he examined Henderson's hands. Brutal scars around Henderson's wrists revealed years in prison. *Fort Leavenworth prison*, Caleb thought as he remembered the story of Henderson's past. Caleb watched the farmer as he studied Henderson's scars.

"Well, this man needs a doctor. I've done all I can for him." Whitticker checked the bandage on Henderson's side and then washed his hands in the bucket. "Billy."

"Yeah, Pa?" said the big-eared son.

"Head over to the depot and telegraph over to Kearney. Then see if there's a doctor handy at Fort McPherson. Might get one over here in a day or so." Whitticker looked hard at Henderson. "Boy, it would be a good idea if you stay in here and keep an eye on your father."

"Yes, sir," said Caleb as the farmer and his son left the room. A warning bell went off in Caleb's head. Something in the farmer's eyes left him wondering if the Whittickers believed their story. He tried to sort out what to do when Henderson's hand shot up and grabbed Caleb.

"Get us out of here, boy," Henderson whispered weakly as he bent Caleb's ear close to him.

"We can't move you," replied Caleb quietly. "You could bleed to death."

"Listen to me," Henderson gasped as he pulled Caleb closer. "We've been lucky so far, but that farmer's kid is going to stir up Sheriff Wayne and the Blackstone gang once he starts banging away on a telegraph, not to mention that Sheriff Winstead from Great Bend, who's probably on my tail. Blabbing your name and all. That happens and we're all sunk. Word gets out, there won't be a town or Sheriff around that won't be on the lookout for me. Or you."

"But you didn't do it," insisted Caleb. "It was the Blackstones that killed the Thatchers. I saw it."

"And you and that little one are witnesses. You got it, boy?" Henderson coughed and grabbed his side. Blood oozed from the bandage. "There's no telling how close the Blackstones are right now, and they'll be scouring the country for you. They'll check every telegraph office there is. They'll see all of us dead before they die themselves. You can count on it. I know the kind."

Suddenly, Billy galloped past the window on his horse. Henderson was right. They had to get out of there. Mountain Man was dead, they were witnesses to two murders in Great Bend, and he himself had shot the ear off Snake. Caleb decided he'd better get Julie, gather everything, and get back on the trail fast. He hustled to the kitchen. Julie was sitting on the floor against the opposite wall next to the kitchen table, Tilly curled beside her. Julie tried to signal him with her eyes when the cock of a rifle was heard.

"Now move over there by the wall with your sisters and we'll just wait." Farmer Whitticker emerged from the little mud room to the right of the kitchen, his wife following close behind. He held the Enfield musket steady as a rock as he motioned Caleb over to the wall. Caleb moved slowly toward his sister, then stopped midway when he caught her eye. He had to think fast.

"I don't know what you're up to, but I bet no good," said Mr. Whitticker. "Man nearly shot to death by Indians? Over at the Blue River? Mostly just Pawnee around these parts and we ain't had trouble with them for some time. We'll just see what Sheriff Wayne has to say over in Kearney. Troops from Fort McPherson will likely get here by tomorrow. Lots of bad folks on the trail stealing and robbing and we don't cotton to any. Who's to say you ain't some of them?"

"It's all right, we're not thieves," said Caleb as he took two steps to his left toward the pantry. "Could you see yourself to just let us go? We won't be any trouble."

"No. You just sit over there, now," sniffed Whitticker as he motioned Caleb with his gun. "Don't care how long it takes. We'll get to the bottom of this."

"Yes, we will," said Mrs. Whitticker with a huff, nodding in the direction of Henderson and the bedroom. "We don't stand for his kind. Man's been in prison, I know it."

"That's a nice rifle. Bet you fought in the war with it, Mr. Whitticker? A single-shot Enfield, right?" said Caleb as he gave Julie a look. He carefully backed away another step toward the pantry, opening the space between him and Julie.

"That's right. And I'm a dead shot with it too." Whitticker moved toward Caleb.

Caleb took a breath, hoping that his sister would take his clue. He need not have worried. The *CLICK* of Julie's Colt cocking might as well have been a thunderclap in the little kitchen.

"Mr. Whitticker," said Julie calmly. "I have a Colt pistol aimed right at the back of your head. Six shots. Please don't make me nervous. Put your rifle down."

"She does, Daniel," said Mrs. Whitticker in a shaky voice. "Better do as she says."

The knuckles of the farmer's fingers were white with fury as he gripped his Enfield musket. He was trapped. Six shots to one were not good odds at all. Slowly he leaned his rifle against the stove.

"Go on then. Get yourselves out of here," said Whitticker as he went over to his wife.

"Now, the two of you get in the pantry. You'll be fine in there until your son gets back." Julie motioned the old couple with her Colt. Defeated, Farmer Whitticker led his wife into the pantry.

"I'll get Dusty and the black ready." Caleb shot into action. "Then I'll come back in and we can get Henderson in the wagon."

"Hurry, Caleb," said Julie as she shut the pantry door and gave the latch a twist.

Caleb picked up the Enfield and ran outside. He tossed the rifle to the side of the barn. Then he hitched up Dusty. The black knew something was up and stomped in anticipation. Tumble vaulted into the wagon and began to bark up a storm. Caleb bolted back inside to get Henderson. Julie had him sitting up. He groaned in pain as he tried to stand. He sagged suddenly, and the two of them moved to either side of him, catching the big man before he fell. With his leg shattered but bound and his side roughly sewn by Farmer Whitticker, Henderson was in pretty bad shape. Finally, they half dragged the gunfighter outside and helped him into the back of the wagon. Julie grabbed Tilly and lay her beside Henderson, covering her in a blanket. Then she hopped aboard and took her place beside Caleb.

"That was quick thinking back there, Caleb," said Julie as she checked her Colt. "Where should we head now?"

"West." Caleb gave the reins a shake. "Dusty, ya!"

7

THE TERRORS
OF THE TRAIL

★ ★ ★ ★ ★ ★ ★ ★ ★ ★ ★ ★ ★ ★ ★ ★ ★ ★ ★ ★

Push harder!" yelled Caleb as he rammed his shoulder
into the right rear wheel of the buckboard. Julie leaned
into the other wheel, but try as they could, they were stuck
smack in the middle of a flash flood. The rain had beaten
them steadily for two days since they left the Whitticker farm
some thirty miles behind. Trying to cross the river earlier that
morning to the small grove of trees just north of them had
proved a mistake. Now they were at the mercy of a terrible
summer storm. To the south, a massive tornado was bearing
down on them. Caleb had to scream above the great roar
of the giant black funnel. Several other smaller ones that
never touched down brought torrents of rain. There seemed
nowhere to hide, the landscape was so flat. Water, mud,
and rocky debris from the flood cascaded all around them.
Most of their supplies had washed down the river, and Caleb
and Julie fought desperately to save what remained. Tumble
had nearly drowned, fighting against the sudden rise of the

Platte River. Now he sat shivering in the buckboard, howling, exhausted as the screaming black tornado carved up the prairie. "It's no use, Caleb!" Julie slumped against the wheel. Perhaps a hundred yards away, there was a rise of earth that led to a rocky outcropping. It was their only hope. The giant funnel cloud tore a path directly toward them.

"Dusty! Ya!" Dusty pulled mightily but the wagon wouldn't budge. "I'll get the black!" Caleb stood in the wagon and grabbed the rope that held the stallion. Desperately, he pulled the big horse closer. Caleb silently punished himself. He should have seen this coming, but flash floods happened so fast on the prairie. He still had his Sharps and the large heavy box that held tools and a few remaining trinkets of their past. They also had their father's maps and Aunt Sarah's letter, but their blankets had washed away along with their food and their clothes.

Carefully, Caleb mounted the huge black horse. *Lord, he is big*, thought Caleb. Dusty was big too, and Caleb could ride him for all his worth. But this one fit the likes of Henderson. The horse seemed to know he was being given a task, for he let Caleb guide him to the side of the wagon. Together, he and Julie helped the wounded Henderson onto the black. Barely able to hold himself up, Henderson slumped forward in the saddle, arms around his horse. Then Caleb got on as Julie handed him the reins. Slowly, the powerful horse fought against the current until they were safely on the bank of the rocky rise. He tried to ease the big man off the stallion, but the gunfighter was too heavy for him and they both crashed to the ground. Henderson painfully rolled to his side and began to drag himself to the shelter of the rocks. Caleb grabbed the reins of the powerful horse and pulled himself up. He then scrambled back up onto the saddle and went back for Tilly. He brought the black to the rear of the wagon and jumped aboard, gathering his terrified little sister in his arms. Tilly held tightly to Caleb's neck as he placed her on the saddle of the stallion. He swung his leg up and settled in behind her, grabbing her tight with his free hand and reaching for the reins with his other. Slowly, they made their way to the riverbank. He jumped off the horse and carefully pulled Tilly to him. Then he took her to the shelter of the rocks and laid her down by Henderson. Caleb then rode back to the wagon and fished out the long rope he had packed in the big tool chest. He tied it to Dusty's harness, mounted the black, and tied the other end of the rope to the saddle horn.

"Ya, boy! Go!" The huge horse dug into the river rock, the muscles on his wet flank bulging. The tornado, just a half-mile away, advanced in a deafening roar, its black and silver funnel bent and twisted as it tore up the Nebraska plain. Sheets of rain pelted them mercilessly.

"Dusty! Come on!" yelled Julie as she took hold of the reins and gave Dusty his command. "Ya!"

Finally the wagon lurched forward. Caleb and Julie, working as a team, managed to pull the wagon back around. Then as quickly as the tornado came, it vanished. Not two hundred yards away, the funnel cloud began to draw back into the black sky. They were spared. As they pulled out of the muddy overflow of the river, water cascaded from the wagon. Then lo and behold, two fish flipped and flopped from the buckboard and landed next to Julie. She dove quickly for the fish.

"Well," said Julie as she scrambled for the fish. "We've got supper!"

★ ★ ★

The campfire lit up the rocks around them as they roasted the two trout on sticks. Their shelter had proven to be a real find. The craggy stones above them kept the wind and rain away and there was enough room so they could all lay down on the hard-packed dirt. They were dry. Pieces of charred wood lay scattered about, evidence of pioneers or Indians past, who must have sought refuge in the cavelike structure. Still, there was enough good wood to build a fire. It was fortunate they still had matches in a tightly sealed jar in the tool chest. The rain continued to fall. Lightning flashed in the distance. Caleb shook his head silently at the new state they found themselves in. It was a pretty hopeless one. He knew it was probably not a good idea to keep the fire going too long. He didn't want to attract attention. But tired and wet as they were, and powerfully hungry, he figured it was better to risk it. They had to shed most of the clothes on their backs to dry them by the fire. Tilly lay next to Tumble for warmth. Julie took one of the trout and offered it to her, but she refused it.

"She won't eat, Caleb." Julie drew Tilly to her. It wasn't like Tilly to not eat. Something had to be wrong. Tilly cried softly in Julie's arms. "Want to hear a story, Tilly? Once upon a time?"

"No," Tilly whimpered as she reached for the chain still around her neck. She opened the locket and looked at the only remaining picture of their parents.

"I'll check on Dusty and the black," said Caleb sadly as he took a last bite of fish. "Save some of the trout for Henderson in case he wakes up." He leaned over to Tilly and kissed her cheek. "She's still got a fever."

"I know. I'm worried, Caleb." Tears glistened in Julie's eyes.

★ ★ ★

Caleb stood in the rain outside the rock shelter a short distance from the campfire. He felt like crying himself, but vowed to stay strong. Strong like a tree, his mother said. After all, what good would crying do?

The flood seemed to be slowing. Dusty and the black seemed no worse for wear with their thick hides. He figured they were about sixty or seventy miles west of Dobytown. Already, they had been through more dangers than they ever could have imagined. What else would lie ahead? With no money, no supplies, and Henderson close to death, they were hamstrung. It was hard to know what to do. He couldn't just leave him to die. If they came upon a town and handed him over to a doctor, it would only be a matter of time before the law or the Blackstones caught up with him. And then there was their own trouble with the Blackstones.

They would keep coming for them, he knew. Caleb hoped that if they could somehow shake them off their trail and make it to Montana, they would be safe. He took the saddle and blanket off the black. Then he slung the black leather saddlebags over his shoulder and hoisted Henderson's heavy Spencer rifle.

Caleb headed back to the fire and sat down. He checked the rifle and placed it and the saddlebags next to the boulder beside him. Julie's eyes were closed from exhaustion. Tilly was curled up in her sister's arms, staring at her locket. Something about her breathing worried Caleb. He shivered and threw another half-burned log on the fire to help stave off the chill of summer rain. Caleb eyed Henderson's saddlebags. Curious, he reached over and loosened the leather strap. He fished around inside the bag and pulled out a metal object. He held the piece of metal toward the fire to see.

"Man could get himself killed for that." Henderson stirred weakly. He reached his hand out. "You want to give me some of that fish?"

Caleb tore off a piece of trout and handed it to him. "I wasn't going to take it. I mean, I was just looking to see if there was anything we could use. I took the saddle off the black and I brought your rifle and the bags in to dry."

"Name's Pride."

"Pride?" asked Caleb, not sure what the man was talking about.

"My horse." Henderson gnawed on the fish weakly and gazed out at the night rain. "Been with me for years. Fought in the war together. Nebraska Volunteers. I was a scout all along the Platte River Road. Been stuck in these same rocks fighting the Sioux years ago. Thought I was dreaming. And that thing you're holding I should have thrown away, as much good as it does."

"What is it?" Caleb turned the piece of metal over in his hand.

"Medal of Honor. Awarded by President Abraham Lincoln himself." Henderson managed a bitter laugh. "They took everything I had after the war. Sent me to Fort Leavenworth prison. Got out a few weeks ago. At least I got my Pride back," Henderson said with a painful chuckle. "And my medal."

"You killed some Union soldiers," said Caleb warily. "I read about it."

"They were Redlegs. Red-booted soldiers who stood against slavery but then turned into murderers and thieves. They went around the countryside, robbing and killing folks in the name of the war." The firelight revealed a deep hate in Henderson's eyes.

"Jayhawkers," said Caleb. "Weren't they called that too?"

"That's right," said Henderson in a deadly whisper. "They killed my wife and baby. Burned our house to the ground. Seven of 'em. After the war, I caught up with three." He reached into the pocket of his tattered shirt and pulled out a beautiful necklace. A gold locket sparkled in the firelight. With excruciating sadness, he held it to his chest. "This is all I have left."

75

"Quick Creek. I remember the story. They say you were a hero during the war but then you went crazy."

"Well, they got the crazy part. I don't figure to get my mind right until I get the other four. They're out there somewhere. If I make it out of this mess, I'll find 'em," Henderson said as he coughed up some blood.

"I want to see," Tilly said weakly. She held out her hand to Henderson. The gunman painfully reached for her and gave her the necklace. Tilly took it and popped open the tiny locket. "They're in heaven with Mommy and Daddy." Tilly handed her own necklace to Henderson. "See?"

Henderson looked long at the pictures of the O'Tooles. Tilly crawled weakly next to the big man and nestled into him. Caleb watched the war hero turned gunfighter grow tense at the first touch of his sister. Then he seemed to slowly soften as he let little Tilly snuggle in. Together they looked at the pictures in the firelight.

"You have to wear it over your heart," said Tilly as she tried to put Henderson's necklace over his head.

"Don't fit. That's why I keep it here in my pocket. Still over my heart. See?" Henderson noticed the sadness written on Caleb's face. "What happened to your kin?"

"It was cholera," explained Caleb.

"How long?"

"Three weeks ago…I think," said Julie, her voice catching with the memory. "Come, Tilly. Caleb, if you can take the first watch, I'll wake you. She needs to sleep." Julie gathered her sister in her arms as Tilly held her hand out to Henderson.

Carefully, he placed the locket in her hand, and then pocketed his own necklace and closed his eyes.

"What was it like?" Caleb asked the gunfighter warily. "Prison, I mean."

Henderson lay staring out at the night as the fire crackled beside them. For the longest time, he said nothing. "You don't ever want to know, kid." He reached for a stick that lay nearby and tossed it on the fire. "Leavenworth wasn't so bad after what they did to me at Fort Scott. At Scott, I took the whip on my back too many times. Kept me chained to an iron ball. Then they transferred me to Fort Leavenworth about five years back and some laws stopped that kind of thing. Instead, they put me in a hole. Solitary confinement, they called it. No windows. Didn't see the sun for years."

"How did you get out?" asked Caleb

"An old friend found one of the Redlegs that was around that night in Quick Creek. Made him confess. The Army didn't want to, but they had to let me go." Henderson closed his eyes and let out a big sigh.

Caleb figured he had gotten about all he could out of Henderson. He reached for his Sharps and shoved a bullet into his teeth. His senses were alive as he surveyed the prairie. The rain had let up and a piece of the moon was peeking out from the clouds. As quickly as the flood had appeared, it had vanished to a trickle.

"Boy? Give me your rifle." Caleb handed Henderson the Sharps warily. "Cartridges," commanded Henderson as he took the rifle. Caleb handed him the bullets and watched as the bloodied man painfully held the rifle in his left hand. "Take that one out of your mouth and watch." Henderson inserted a bullet in the webbing between each finger of his right hand. He pulled back the hammer of the big Sharps and slammed a shell into the breech. Then he pretended to do the action again and again, pulling back the hammer and cramming another shell from the webbing of his fingers.

"The shell ejects, then you reload quick, see. You can kill four men that way," said Henderson as he handed Caleb the Sharps. "When you can do that at a gallop, then you might just survive out here." Then Henderson rolled over with a groan.

"How did you do that?" Caleb said as he picked up the bullets. Carefully he arranged them in the webbing of his fingers. He pulled back the hammer and tried to jam a shell into the chamber, but it tumbled to the dirt.

"Practice," said a low rumbling voice. "Keep a sharp eye out, now."

★ ★ ★

"Caleb!" cried Julie as she shook her brother awake in the morning sun. "Caleb, wake up!"

Caleb shot awake and reached for his rifle. His sister knelt before him, tears streaming down her pretty face. "What's wrong?"

"Tilly! It's cholera! She's got the shakes!"

Caleb crawled on his hands and knees over to his little

sister. She was convulsing terribly. He gently felt her fore-head. It was hot. He knew the signs. Both their parents had died this way. A terrifying feeling washed over him. They had to get help and fast or Tilly could die in a matter of hours.

"Get her in the wagon!" cried Caleb as he ran to hitch up Dusty.

8

COTTONWOOD SPRINGS

★ ★ ★ ★ ★ ★ ★ ★ ★ ★ ★ ★ ★ ★ ★ ★ ★ ★ ★

Caleb rode Pride like a man possessed alongside the Platte River in the blazing Nebraska heat. It took him all morning to become accustomed to the big horse, but more and more he felt a part of him. At a full run, he smoothed out like glass. The huge warhorse glistened with sweat and pounded the ground in a thunderous beat. Desperately, Caleb searched the horizon for signs of anyone who could help them. Tilly was fading fast. If he didn't find some kind of help, she would surely perish. He turned in the saddle at a full gallop and looked over his shoulder for Julie. He could still see her in the distance, driving Dusty and the buckboard as fast as his loyal horse could pull them. The little wagon flew after him across the scorching prairie, kicking up the drying mud from the storm.

Caleb tore up a small rise to the top for a look. The plains were mostly flat, and looking out from the hill, he could see miles in any direction. The green and gold prairie grass grew tall over the clay-colored landscape. Ahead the river carved through shallow rocky ravines. It felt vast and lonely. Caleb stood in the saddle and his heart fell. Nothing. No one. All morning, Tilly shivered and shook, cried out in her agony. Along the way, he had stopped several times for anything useful lying on the Oregon Trail. Julie spotted several yards of cloth in a thicket and she had draped it over her sister to shelter her from the noon sun. Dehydration was Tilly's worst enemy, and Julie filled some bottles she had spotted along the trail with river water and forced Tilly to drink.

Lord, Caleb cursed to himself, there must be someone around. He was just about to head back toward Julie and the wagon when something caught his eye. Just the slightest glimmer in the sun. A reflection! "Pride! Go! Ya!" Caleb squeezed the big black stallion with his knees, and the horse shot forward with a surge of power. He raced down the hill and back to the trail, urging Pride straight west. He squeezed Pride again and the horse responded mightily, his head straining forward and his tail flying straight back in the wind. Caleb's heart pounded, for as fast as Dusty was, he was no match for Henderson's horse. On he raced until Caleb could see what was causing the reflection. Wagons!

★ ★ ★

"Hold it right there!" shouted the wagon master as Caleb rode toward the front wagon. It was hardly a big train, more like a few families who stuck together and decided to go it alone on the trail. There were just six horse-drawn ordinary farm wagons traveling in single file. These were not the big Calistoga type, or the Prairie Schooners that were pulled by oxen and could carry thousands of pounds. He eased Pride to a stop and raised his hands as rifle barrels suddenly appeared from the cloth covers, or bonnets, of the wagons. Caleb could hear the *CLACK CLICK* of the cocking weapons from the travelers hidden inside. Julie brought the buckboard to a halt some yards away, skillfully reining in an exhausted Dusty.

"We need help!"

"You ought to know better than to ride up on someone like that, boy!" said the wagon master as he lowered his Winchester. "Liable to get yourselves shot."

"We've got a sick child!" pleaded Julie.

The wagon master thought for a second as if weighing the pros and cons of slowing their trip to help out. "Bess! Says they got a sick child!"

Instantly, a frowning woman stuck her head out from the second wagon. She had on a white head cover and bib. She studied Caleb for an instant, then looked over to Julie. Julie leaped off the wagon, gathered Tilly in her arms, then carried her toward the wagon train.

"What's wrong with her?" asked Bess as she climbed down from the wagon.

"She's burning up with fever. We think she's got cholera." Julie brought Tilly over to Bess, whose face changed in an instant. Fear crossed her face as she recoiled from Julie like she'd seen the devil.

"Cholera!" shouted Bess.

The wagon master grabbed Julie roughly and marched her back to the buckboard. "You can just turn right around and ride away from here. We got enough of our own troubles!"

"Please!" Caleb exclaimed. "She needs help. She won't last."

"Says she's got the cholera!" Bess scrambled back into her wagon and shouted to the others inside. Caleb could hear alarmed voices responding to the news. Several more rifles appeared from the wagons. Caleb backed Pride away a few steps. "Keep her away from here! Get away!"

"Please. Please help us!" cried Julie.

"Move on, hear?" The wagon master raised his Winchester and leveled it at Caleb. "Cottonwood Springs is a few hours west, then south. Take the left fork. Get a doctor there! Go on now!"

★ ★ ★

Three hours later, they made Cottonwood Springs, a few miles south of the Platte River. Along the road, they passed some Indians heading toward town, some walking and some on horses. Caleb recognized them as Arapaho. *Most likely the Indians are looking to trade*, thought Caleb. He pulled Pride to a stop about a half-mile outside town, Julie and the wagon right behind him. He figured he should hide Henderson, for riding in with the gunfighter was attention they could ill afford.

Caleb led Pride to a cluster of trees about a hundred yards

off the road that looked like it would serve as good cover. If Henderson was right in his thinking, towns up and down the Platte River would have heard the news about the shoot-out in Dobytown, the murders in Great Bend, and their run-in with the Whittickers. Caleb had seen a telegraph office when they rode toward Cottonwood Springs. The Blackstones and Sheriff Wayne would be casting their net. He had to keep Henderson out of sight.

"Go on, kid," whispered Henderson as if he read Caleb's mind. "Leave me be. Just help me over there, then go take care of your sister." Henderson nodded to a big oak tree.

Caleb and Julie carefully laid the gunfighter down on the other side of the big tree. Henderson's wounds were oozing blood and fluid. It was hard to figure how the man was still alive. Caleb tied off Pride a short distance away so he could drink from a little brook. He left the saddle on the horse, then he filled Henderson's canteen and placed it next to him. "Better go, kid." Henderson reached for his Colt and placed it by his side.

★ ★ ★

Caleb drove the wagon through Cottonwood Springs. It was the sort of outfitter town that sprang up along the Platte River and the Oregon Trail. In its heyday, it was most likely prosperous as the pioneers replenished their supplies for their journey. When the Northern Railroad came, the wagon trains dwindled and these old towns had fallen on hard times. Caleb passed a few shops, the livery, church, and a saloon, searching for a doctor. He made a mental note of them as he drove Dusty hard. Several folks crossing the main road had to jump from their path. Then he found what they were looking for. A sign hanging just the other side of the street from the Sheriff's office.

DOCTOR LEE M. JEFFERSON MEDICINE AND SURGERY

Caleb brought Dusty to a halt. He cast a wary eye at the Sheriff's office and vaulted from the wagon. He stared through the window of the doctor's office. Julie jumped down and grabbed Tilly in her arms and rushed to Caleb. "Is there anyone in there?" she said breathlessly.

"I think I see someone. Come on," said Caleb as he ran to the door.

★ ★ ★

"It's cholera all right," said Doctor Lee M. Jefferson as he examined Tilly, who was stretched out on a table. She could barely open her eyes. He then wheeled a squeaky old instrument stand over to the table and began some preparations. He picked up a cloth and poured some alcohol over it. Instantly the room smelled of medicine. "How long has she been like this?"

"Several days," said Caleb as he held Tilly's tiny hand.

"Our parents had it weeks ago," said Julie despondently.

"Dead, I take it?" asked Jefferson matter-of-factly. Caleb nodded to the doctor. "It can happen this way. Sometimes it can take ten days or so for someone to catch it. She's lucky to make it this far, little thing. Some are dead in a day. Sorry to say I don't hold much hope for her." Jefferson shook his head sadly. Then he began to swab Tilly's wrist with the alcohol.

"What are her chances?" said Julie, fighting tears as she gently stroked her little sister's face.

"Fifty-fifty at best. Fifty-fifty." Then Jefferson picked up a razor. Carefully, he sliced a vein in Tilly's wrist. Then he placed her hand in a bowl next to her. The blood began to drip slowly into the bowl. "Best thing is to bleed her."

"Bleed her?" Caleb was horrified at seeing his sister's little hand resting in the bowl.

"Get that infected blood out. Then we'll see if she'll come around." Jefferson looked over at Caleb and motioned him toward the door. "Might take some time before we know anything. You both don't need to be here."

"Caleb, I'll stay with her," said Julie.

Caleb headed toward the door. "I'll be back after I pick up some supplies from that feed store we passed."

★ ★ ★

Caleb eased Dusty down Main Street, Tumble at his side. He remembered there was a general store at the other end of town. As much as he wanted to stay at Doc Jefferson's office and be with Tilly, he knew they had to lay in supplies quickly if they were to continue on the Oregon Trail. There was one main problem. They had no money. Caleb pulled up to the store and climbed down, tying Tumble to the wagon. He brushed past several Arapaho Indians. Known as traders, they milled around the various goods and supplies stacked near the door, looking to exchange their skins and furs for anything they could use.

Caleb peered through the window. A man behind a counter was talking with a woman customer. He stepped inside the store to the sound of a bell signaling his entrance and casually checked out the shelves that were stocked with everything a pioneer could use: sacks of feed, canned goods, and sugar. There were tools, clothing, and blankets. Caleb knew he needed too much to even ask for a handout and he had nothing but his horse and his Sharps to deal in trade.

"That will be five dollars and sixty cents, Mrs. Tuttle," said the skinny-necked owner of the store. Caleb gave the man a quick glance as he tended to the lady who was finishing up her shopping.

"Thank you, Mr. Dodder. My, things are getting so expensive. Business must be picking up with the wagon trains coming around again," said Mrs. Tuttle as she gathered up her things.

"Yep. Had a big one come through last week. Don't expect things to last once the railroad starts runnin' again. Sign of the times. I hear your boys had a tussle with some of the Pawnee up on the ridge," said Dodder, his Adam's apple bobbing up and down. "Gall-darn Injuns."

"The Pawnee claim it was these Arapaho. My guess, it was some Sioux. Either way, it's getting so you can't hang on to your stock these days." The woman sniffed her disgust.

"Too many comin' around here beggin'," said Mr. Dodder, nodding in agreement.

Caleb held a can of beans in his hands like it was gold. He could pocket it, he thought. Who would know? After all, no one would blame him if they knew of their hopeless plight. He started secretly shoving food into his pockets when the thought struck him. Stealing! He just couldn't do it, even if they were in such dire straits. He could hear the voice of his father scolding him. One thing about the O'Tooles, they were honest. He began to put the cans back on the shelf when the barrel of a rifle pushed into his chest.

"What do you think you're doing, you little thief?" said Dodder as he grabbed Caleb's collar.

"I was putting them back, sir, I swear." Caleb struggled briefly in Dodder's grasp, and then stopped, worried the rifle might go off accidently.

"What's that in your pocket, then, boy?" asked Dodder.

Caleb reached in his pocket and started to put one last can back on the shelf. Dodder stopped him.

"No, you don't!" exclaimed Dodder. "That's evidence!"

"Boy needs to be taught a lesson, Mr. Dodder," offered the snooty Mrs. Tuttle.

"That's my thinkin'. A visit to Sheriff Ed ought to do it!"

With righteous fury, Mr. Dodder marched Caleb at gunpoint outside and started toward Sheriff Ed's office.

Tumble bounded from the wagon in a barking fit, snapping the rope tight as he nipped at the feet of Dodder. Startled, Dodder kicked hard at Tumble, who answered by snatching Dodder's pant leg in his mighty jaws and giving it a good rip. Fortunately for Dodder, the rope held fast.

"Keep that dog away, boy, or I'll shoot him!" Dodder tried to jerk his pants from Tumble's jaws.

"Tumble, no!" shouted Caleb. "Back in the wagon, boy." Tumble gave Dodder one more growl and did as he was told, leaping back aboard the buckboard.

Dodder marched Caleb down Main Street toward the Sheriff's office. Several townsfolk cast disapproving looks his way as the skinny store-owner prodded him in the back with his rifle. He felt both humiliated and angry with himself and kept his head down as Dodder hustled him along. Julie appeared from Doc Jefferson's office. Tears streaked her face as she ran toward them. "Caleb!" she cried. "Oh, Caleb, it's real bad. We can't wake her up!" As she caught up with them, she noticed Dodder's hand on Caleb's collar and the gun barrel pointed at his back. "Caleb, what happened?"

"Don't worry, I'll clear things up," answered Caleb.

"Move on out of the way, missy," Dodder said with a sneer. "Boy was caught stealing!" Then he forced Caleb into Sheriff Ed's office. Julie went white as a ghost, struggling with this horrible turn of events. Then quickly she turned on her heel and ran down the street toward the wagon.

★ ★ ★

Caleb stood before Sheriff Ed, his head hanging in shame. He was devastated that he had now caused more of a problem. He shifted nervously, trying to figure a way out of the mess he was in.

"So this is it?" asked Sheriff Ed as he held up the can of beans. He shook his head and stroked his gray beard at the trivial nature of the so-called crime. "This is your evidence?" One deputy, lounging on a cot in the jail and eating his lunch, began to snicker. The other deputy leaned against the wall cleaning his pistol. He eyed Caleb with amusement as he raked his hand across the cylinder of the six-shooter.

"That's it!" answered Mr. Dodder. "Caught him red-handed. Do your duty, Sheriff!"

"Who is this boy, anyway?" Sheriff Ed shuffled through some papers on his desk.

"Never seen him before," answered Dodder.

"What's your name, son?" Caleb hesitated until the Sheriff poked a finger in his chest and looked him square in the eye. "Boy, give me a name."

Caleb stood still and silent, unwilling to tell his name.

"Young girl over at Jefferson's called him Caleb. Sheriff, I could tell he was up to no good the minute he came into my store," sniffed Dodder, his Adam's apple bobbing up and down.

"Shut up, Horace," snapped the Sheriff. "I am sick and tired of you bustin' in here over every little thing that goes on in your dad-burn store. This ain't nothing, hear me? Now here's your gall-darn can of beans. I'm just gonna let him go."

"I remind you of your duty, Sheriff!" squawked Dodder. "I'm on the election committee, and if you want to stay Sheriff, you arrest this young criminal!"

"Dad gummit, Horace! I got bigger fish to fry. I got Indians stealing from ranchers and burning down telegraph poles, ranchers shooting Indians, thieves, drifters, and drunks!" Sheriff Ed snatched up some papers and started peeling them off, shaking them at Dodder. "On top of it, I just got a wire telling me to be on the lookout for a murderer on the loose in these parts who happens to be none other than William Henderson. Sheriff Blackstone says he shot one of his brothers in Dobytown. And that's after he killed some folks in Great Bend, according to a Sheriff W. W. Winstead. Looks like he's headin' this way with three kids and a dog packed into a wagon, and if you think young Caleb here is so all-fired important, you can have this job!" Suddenly, Sheriff Ed stopped and stared at one of the papers. Then he leveled his gaze at Caleb. "Caleb, huh? Last name wouldn't be O'Toole would it? The same Caleb O'Toole out of Dobytown?"

Caleb's heart sank while his mind raced. Sheriff Wayne was also a Blackstone brother! And now they all knew their names and where they were headed! Old Farmer Whitticker, not to mention Red from the Dobytown Saloon, must have been talking. Sheriff Ed rose from his desk and peered into Caleb's eyes.

"Well, now, Caleb," said the Sheriff. "I don't suppose you have an ugly dog with a big mouth with you, do you?"

"He sure does!" squealed Dodder. "Darn near bit my leg off."

"Would that be Henderson over at Jefferson's? Says here he was shot up pretty bad. He over there getting himself patched up, boy?" Sheriff Ed leaned hard on Caleb. "You tell me now, make it easy on yourself."

"It's my sister," replied Caleb. "She's got cholera."

"We'll see." Sheriff Ed took Caleb roughly by the shoulders and marched across the room to the jail cell. He shoved Caleb inside and slammed the steel bars closed. "You can stay in there 'til we straighten things out. Men, I think we got ourselves a murderer here in town."

Instantly the two deputies began to check their guns as the Sheriff reached for his Winchester. "Horace, you head over to the Hickory Saloon and get some of the boys. Tell them we're lookin' for a killer that might be shot up some. Start at the south end of town and work your way north. I'll check the doc's. One way or the other, we'll find this Henderson son of a snake!"

"Don't bother. You've already found him," said a deep voice coming from the doorway.

Three shots blasted the Sheriff's office and the deputies scrambled for cover. Sheriff Ed, Winchester in his hand, spun around and faced the smoking barrel of Henderson's Colt pointed straight at his head. The smell of gunpowder filled the room. Caleb dove under the cot he was sitting on. After a few seconds, he peered out to see Henderson, white as a sheet, blood seeping from his side and his leg, limp toward the Sheriff.

"You men drop your guns if you want this man to live."

Henderson kept his pistol pointed right at the Sheriff. Instantly, the deputies dropped their guns. Sheriff Ed laid down his rifle. Mr. Dodder, his Adam's apple working overtime, held on shakily to his Winchester. "You too." Henderson lashed out with his Colt and knocked the skinny man on his head. Dodder dropped his rifle and crashed into a heap.

"You'll hang for this, Henderson," said Sheriff Ed.

"Then you'll be hanging an innocent man, not that it matters," growled Henderson. "Open up that cell and let the boy out."

"Julie's over with the doctor. He's bleeding Tilly," said Caleb as he picked himself up off the jail floor. Sheriff Ed opened the steel bars and let him out.

"Not anymore, he's not," muttered Henderson. "Darn fool near killed her. Julie's got her in the wagon." Henderson nodded toward the Sheriff. "Caleb, take his keys. Lock 'em all up."

Caleb took the Sheriff's keys. Henderson gestured toward the jail cell, and the four men crowded inside. Then Caleb locked the steel bars and stepped away. Henderson swayed on his feet as he backed away to the door.

"Come on, boy," said Henderson. Caleb hustled to the gunfighter just as he sank toward the floor in pain.

Caleb helped Henderson over to Pride. Several townspeople ducked for cover as Henderson blasted two more shots in the air. Julie pulled up in a rush with the wagon. Tilly was laid out in the back. Henderson whistled and Pride went down to his knees, bending low so Henderson could climb onto him. Then Henderson lashed his left hand to the saddle horn. Satisfied he was secure on Pride, he whispered to Caleb. "No matter what, follow Pride and don't stop for nothing. Tilly's got one chance." Pride rose to his feet proudly as Henderson circled him to the north.

"What?" cried Caleb as he jumped aboard the wagon and grabbed the reins from Julie. Julie leaped in back and held Tilly. "Where are we going?"

"An old friend." Lashed to Pride, Henderson shot down the main road north.

★ ★ ★

Caleb pulled Dusty to a sudden stop a mile outside Cottonwood Springs. There was one thing he had to do. Caleb reached for the Sharps rifle and crammed a shell into the breech. He pushed the sight up and searched high on a telegraph pole about a hundred feet away.

"Caleb! We'll lose Henderson!" cried Julie, seeing Pride gallop away on the northern road.

"One last thing." Caleb spotted the telegraph wire connected to the pole some fifty feet up. He aimed and fired the big rifle. The first shot nailed the connector, but the wire was still hanging. Quickly he slammed another bullet into the Sharps. He took a deep breath and squeezed the trigger. The telegraph wire split and flew off the pole. "That'll slow them down," he said, stashing his rifle. Then he grabbed the reins and gave them a great shake. "Dusty, ya!"

THE GREAT BLUE HAWK

★ ★

I see him!" Caleb shouted from the rocky cliff above. Julie waved from the wagon below. She held Tilly and bathed her forehead gently, trying to keep her cool. Caleb said a silent prayer as he hurried back down the steep, rocky slope toward his sisters, grateful that he had finally caught up to Henderson. They hadn't seen Pride for over an hour. The big warhorse had disappeared down a ravine. Finally they picked up its signs. Tracking had been difficult. The barren landscape had afforded them little cover in their flight along a little-used road miles south of the Oregon Trail. They had lost Henderson several times during the past day and a half, but Caleb was able to make the right decisions tracking Henderson. Sometimes it was a blood trail left on a bush, or a hoofprint in the mud. He had noticed Pride had part of his right front hoof missing. More and more, Caleb's senses came to life on the trail. He knew they had turned west and his guess was they were headed toward the craggy rock peaks far off in the distant sun, so he kept driving the wagon to where he figured Pride was taking them. The guess paid off.

A half hour later, Caleb pulled Dusty through the sagebrush and into a circle of scrub pine trees that guarded what looked like a pass between the low hills. He guided Dusty through the pass, following Pride's hoofprints in the sand. There stood Pride, in the middle of a clearing. Henderson lay unconscious across the saddle, still lashed to his huge black horse.

"Caleb," asked Julie breathlessly. "I don't like it." She pulled Tilly to her and cradled her in her left arm. Then she took out the Colt.

"I don't like it either." Caleb grabbed his Sharps. Suddenly the *CLACK CLICK* of many guns cocking filled the air. Caleb whirled around and aimed his rifle at the sounds.

All at once, they were surrounded by Indians on horseback who emerged silently from the scrub trees and rocks. Several ponies were loaded with game from a hunt. They slowly circled around the wagon, rifles and bows pointed at the O'Tooles. Caleb decided to drop his gun and raise his hands. He nodded to Julie and she dropped her Colt. They were no match for a dozen or so rifles, and offering themselves peacefully was perhaps their only chance of staying alive.

A barrel-chested Indian Chief, dressed in an old U.S. Army coat and wearing a single hawk feather in his long black hair, rode slowly from the boulders. He got off his horse and held his hand out to Pride. Pride pawed the earth and, to Caleb's amazement, walked slowly to the man and sniffed his hand.

Carefully, the Indian checked out Henderson, talking low to the gunfighter and gently shaking his shoulder. Henderson finally managed to turn his head to the Chief. Caleb could hear him mumble something. Then he said something to the rest of the Indians. The Chief gave a signal and one of the hunters leaped off his horse and walked to the wagon. He held out his arms to Julie.

"Give us the child," said the Chief. "Have no fear. We will help you. This Henderson and I are old friends."

Julie looked to Caleb, her desperate eyes searching her brother's. "It's our last chance, Caleb. They're Pawnee, so it should be all right." Caleb nodded and she handed little Tilly to the hunter, who quickly mounted his horse. The others grabbed Pride's reins and they disappeared through the winding pass with Henderson. Then the Chief leaped onto his horse and advanced to the wagon.

"I am Blue Hawk," said the Indian. "Come."

★ ★ ★

Caleb and Julie followed Blue Hawk through a series of cuts in the ravine. They rode along a river for a few miles until they came to a modest cluster of scrub pine trees. As they entered the grove of trees, the chattering of voices could be heard. Gradually the sound grew until they came to a clearing overlooking a peaceful Indian village. All around were earth huts built near the side of the rocky river. The mud homes blended into the sparse clumps of trees and bushes of the prairie. Caleb was surprised to see so many Pawnee people, as most had been moved to a reservation in Oklahoma after a big battle with the Sioux at Massacre Canyon. Many of the women and children were tending to the crops that grew in the mud banks. They ceased their labor and watched curiously as the hunting party drew near. Some drew their children closer as they saw Henderson atop Pride, wary of any danger the new visitors might bring into their midst. The hunters dropped off their kill and immediately the Pawnee women took the game away to be processed.

Blue Hawk dismounted and began to speak in Pawnee to several of the women. One of the women pointed and ran upriver, while the others took Tilly from the hunter on horseback and disappeared into a hut. Henderson was carefully gathered from his horse and taken inside.

"Don't worry, they will be safe. We have sent for Talking Crow." Then Blue Hawk shouted to the others. The Indians took Pride, Dusty, and the wagon away and led Caleb and Julie to another hut. "First, you must bathe. Then you will eat and rest."

★ ★ ★

Caleb lay in the animal furs, drinking from a gourd. He was getting used to the earthy blend of nourishing herbs. He had bathed in the cool river, his first bath in many days, and he began to feel better. Several of the women had taken Julie to another part of the river where she bathed unseen by the men. They had slept for twenty-four hours straight. Julie lay quietly next to him. Their clothes had been washed, scrubbed, and returned to them clean. Tumble was given food, and he snored with contentment in the corner on his own patch of fur. Suddenly, the cloth curtain over the entrance was drawn aside and a beautiful woman with raven-colored hair and dark eyes came in, dressed in rugged pants, boots, and a bloodstained man's shirt. She was tall, slim, and maybe thirty years old or so. A little younger than Caleb's mother, he thought.

"They call me Talking Crow," she said in perfect English. "My real name is Anna Maria Consuela Kathleen Sullivan. You can call me Doctor Sullivan if you must. Or Kathleen. What is the little girl's name?"

"Tilly," answered Julie, rubbing the sleep from her eyes. "I'm Julie, and this is Caleb."

"Well, Julie and Caleb, I am doing what I can for Tilly. She is lucky to be alive at this point. She needs rest and fluids. I think I can help her. Cholera can kill in a few hours or it can take time, but my hunch is she'll be all right in a few days."

"Oh, thank the Lord. I mean, thank *you*," Julie cried happily.

Caleb felt a great relief wash through his body. "The doctor in Cottonwood Springs wanted to bleed Tilly," he said.

"Doctor Jefferson, I know him. He's an old fool. He could have killed her. No, a mixture of herbs with water, rice, bitter gourd, citrus, and onion should do it. My father read up on the experiments curing cholera using hydration and herbs.

He figured out how to fight it from the latest news from Europe and told him, but Jefferson wouldn't listen. That old crackpot will bleed anything. It's his stubborn way." She held her hand out and Tumble ambled over to give her a sniff.

"Your father was a doctor?" asked Julie.

"An Irish doctor married to a Mexican woman, my mother. He was a legend. Killed by a Sioux arrow a few years after my mother died. The Pawnee loved him when he pretty much cured the cholera around here. He had heard about Louis Pasteur of France and his new theory about heating water to kill off germs. He figured out it was probably contaminated water that spread cholera, though many disagreed with him. But my father felt he was right. You should stay away from drinking river water or water near where there are people."

"We were all drinking water from the Platte," said Caleb.

"Well, you're lucky then," said Dr. Sullivan. "Around here, Blue Hawk has them boil it. Smart."

"And now you're a doctor too?" asked Julie.

"You find that hard to believe?" sniffed Dr. Sullivan, raising her eyebrow. "Most do. Pretty rare they say."

"I've never heard of a real woman doctor," offered Julie curiously.

"Learned by my father's side, but it was my beloved mother who put it into my head to do it. She was quite a lady. Got my degree in Cincinnati, Ohio, at the University. It's one of the few places there are for women to do that sort of thing."

"I didn't know you could do that. Most girls I know would never have dreamed of it."

"Well, get used to it. It's coming. Who knows, you might have the gift of it." She winked at Julie. "I was raised to think I could do anything I want if I put my mind to it." Dr. Sullivan laughed. "Part of being the daughter of two very opinionated people. Irish and Mexican and they fought all the time. And loved. With them, it was the same."

"What about Henderson?" asked Caleb.

"Henderson's another story. I stopped the bleeding but the infection is everywhere, and he's been shot so many times, it's a miracle he's still among us. Just pulled out two slugs and I'm working on the third one. The bullet nearly shattered the bone clear through. Most doctors would amputate the leg right away, but I'm thinking I might not have to. They're cleaning him up right now. He's pretty weak, but he's putting up a fight. How did you end up in the company of a man like that?"

"It's a long story," said Julie.

"Good! I like conversation." Dr. Sullivan reached out her hand to Julie. "Come, I could use your help. If you can handle it, you might learn something."

"My help?" asked Julie as Dr. Sullivan pulled her toward the door.

"It's a long shot, but I'm going to try to save Henderson's leg, set it, and stitch him up. Fought me over the chloroform, but he should be about ready with all the whiskey I gave him. It's going to hurt. Caleb, you come too," ordered Dr. Sullivan. "I might need you to hold him down."

★ ★ ★

"Son of a skunk!" roared a staggering Henderson as he broke away from Caleb and two of the Pawnee women. "Get your daggone hands off me!" he cursed as he hobbled around the hut like a wounded buffalo in a drunken rage. Part of his leg bone poked out through his skin. Henderson crashed to the earthen floor, writhing in pain. Immediately, Caleb grabbed Henderson by his good leg and the two Indian women jumped on his arms. Dr. Sullivan took hold of the broken leg by the thigh.

"Listen to me, Henderson!" ordered Dr. Sullivan. "Your choice is lose the leg or let me get the bullet out and try to set it. If you don't calm down, we will have to just knock you out, and I will have to amputate. You will hobble around the rest of your life, if you manage to live through it. And that is a big if. The infection may kill you. Do you understand?"

"I'm not gonna let some woman doctor butcher me!" growled Henderson.

"I ought to let you just die on your own for that rather ignorant remark," answered Dr. Sullivan as she folded her hands across her chest and stared hard at the gunfighter. "Maybe the sawbones you were used to during the war would do a better job? All right then, so be it. You're on your own."

"Fine!" Henderson stuck an arrow in his teeth and bit down hard. "Set it then."

"Good, let's get to work. Caleb, take hold of his broken

leg at the ankle. When I say, pull hard as you can and twist to the left," said the doctor. "Can you do that?"

"Yes," answered Caleb as he gripped Henderson's ankle. He watched in fearful fascination as the doctor grabbed a sharp knife that a Pawnee woman had taken from a pot of boiling water. She carefully sliced the skin around the broken bone. She then poured some of the boiled water into a small pot and set it near Henderson's leg, instructing Julie to clean the wound with a cloth. Julie's face colored for an instant and she hesitated.

"There'll be a lot of blood. If you can't take that, you're not for this business," snapped Dr. Sullivan.

Julie nodded and began to clean Henderson's wound, her squeamishness gradually giving way to brave determination. Dr. Sullivan pointed out some bone fragments and Julie plucked them out carefully. Together they sterilized the wound with alcohol. "See there?" Dr. Sullivan poked into the leg deeper.

"The bullet!" exclaimed Julie. Dr. Sullivan dug into Henderson's leg with a pair of long tweezers and pulled out a large piece of lead. "All right now, Julie, you hold on to Mr. Henderson's good arm, and Caleb? Are you ready?"

"Yes, ma'am! Pull hard and twist left!" Caleb tightened his grip on Henderson's ankle as Julie took hold of Henderson's arm.

"Lord," said Henderson weakly. "Hurry up, dang it!"

"Now, Caleb!" ordered Dr. Sullivan as she held on to the upper part of Henderson's leg. With a mighty pull and a twist, Caleb popped Henderson's leg back into place with a *SNAP*. Henderson let out a groan and went limp, passing out from the pain. "Good job," said the doctor as she inspected the leg. "Caleb, thank you. You can go now and check on Tilly if you want. Make sure she drinks more of this." She handed Caleb a jug of the earthy-tasting herb water. "Julie, pass me the needle and the stitching thread. This you'll want to learn. When we're done with that, we'll make a splint."

Caleb watched for a minute as his sister eagerly went about the task of learning how to stitch a wound. He had an instant respect for this doctor and a new understanding of how capable his sister was becoming. "Come, Tumble." Caleb headed out the door. Tumble jumped up eagerly. "Let's go see Tilly."

★ ★ ★

It was a week later, and Tilly was almost as good as new. It was nearing time to leave the Pawnee village. Caleb was afraid if they didn't go soon, it would be winter by the time they made the Bitterroot Mountains. Waiting for Henderson would be impossible. He survived, but his leg was of no use. He would have to remain in camp. For a while, it was safe. The Pawnee had set up observation points and were keeping a lookout. The Blackstones were nowhere to be found.

Caleb smiled to himself as Tilly snuggled beside Julie on some furs in the main hut near Blue Hawk. She loved to hear his stories. Other Pawnee men sat on their mats among the different-colored lodge poles in a circle and smoked. They watched as Blue Hawk, who was a medicine man as well as Chief, took the pipe and made his offering to Tirawa, the force in the sky the Pawnee believed created their star gods.

"The gods created the humans and all things." He passed the pipe to Caleb and began to tell the story of the ancient Morning Star ritual, describing the capture of young girls that the Pawnee believed would ensure them a good year ahead. Caleb admired the hawk feathers that adorned the long wooden pipe. Observing from the others, he clamped his palm over the hole at the end of the pipe and drew the smoke into his lungs. When Blue Hawk got to the part of the story about human sacrifice, Tilly let out a loud shriek. Caleb choked on the smoke. His lungs practically exploded, throwing him into a fit of coughing.

"These things are no longer done," offered Blue Hawk, giving Caleb a hard pat on the back. He chuckled as he noticed a wide-eyed Tilly squirming under her sister's arms. "There is much that has changed. We used to roam the land and hunt the buffalo. But the railroads came. We even helped build the tracks. We are mainly farmers now. Between the Sioux and the white man, we try to live in peace."

Caleb, somewhat embarrassed and a little dizzy from the smoke, passed the pipe back to Blue Hawk. Wanting to redeem himself, he reached into his pocket and stuck three bullets into the webbing of the fingers on his right hand. Then he reached for his Sharps rifle with his left. Blue Hawk watched as Caleb pulled the hammer back and quickly crammed a shell into the breech. Blue Hawk broke into a toothy grin.

"Henderson showed me that. I've been practicing," said Caleb.

"That was good." Blue Hawk nodded in approval as he smoked his pipe. "Henderson was the best at it. First time I saw him do that we were at a full gallop riding with the Second Nebraska Cavalry. We came down on some Sioux warriors in the Dakotas at Whitestone Hill."

"That was General Sully!" Caleb whispered to himself, remembering his father's condemnation of the attack. "He massacred the Sioux for killing settlers in Minnesota."

"Once we saw what was happening, Henderson and I stopped fighting," Blue Hawk said sadly. "I have no love for the Sioux. But these were peaceful people and had nothing to do with what happened in Minnesota. General Sully did not care. He was out to kill Indians. It was not right these things happened."

Caleb took the pipe and puffed thoughtfully for a moment as Blue Hawk recalled his years of riding with Henderson along the Platte River against the Sioux Indians. "Later we fought together for the North during the war. We were scouts. I never saw a fighter the likes of Henderson. Course we were younger. Lots of winters have passed."

"Were you there at Quick Creek?" asked Caleb. "When Henderson killed those Redlegs?"

"No. But I was with him when he found his wife and

child dead and his house burned down after the war," Blue
Hawk said sadly. "Henderson was never the same after those
men butchered his family. We went our separate ways. His
heart turned very dark. After the war, he tracked and killed
three of those men. Troops caught him and locked him up
for many years. Some of my people found one of the Redlegs.
We convinced him to confess. Roughed him up pretty good.
They finally had to let Henderson go."

"That was you?" Caleb asked excitedly.

"Took you long enough! I'm lucky I didn't rot in that
prison!" Henderson, held upright by two Pawnee men, bellowed at Blue Hawk as they carried him into the hut. Dr.
Sullivan entered right behind him. "Lucky I didn't keel
over in the hands of Talking Crow here. It's witchcraft these
women doctors perform. Not real medicine like a man!"
Henderson gave Caleb a wink. He enjoyed getting a rise out
of Dr. Sullivan as he began to feel better.

"You mean just cut your leg off and let it go at that, I
suppose. Then beat you over the head with it. Would you
have preferred that?" Dr. Sullivan answered in a huff, getting
a smile out of Julie.

"Wouldn't do much good," joked Julie. "He's pretty
hardheaded."

This got a big laugh out of Blue Hawk, who chattered
along with the other Indians, translating. They seemed to
find the exchange pretty funny.

"Tell me a story. Once upon a time!" Tilly said suddenly.
Caleb smiled. *She must be feeling better*, he thought. Caleb

felt warm in the company of the Pawnee people. It reminded him sadly of his mother and father.

Blue Hawk laughed. He liked little Tilly. He said something in Pawnee to the rest of the men and they all laughed. "Henderson, tell about the time we held off ten rebels in that saloon back in sixty-four."

"Ten?" Henderson winced as the two Pawnee men leaned him against the side of the hut. "It was four! You must be getting old, Blue Hawk. Though I don't see how you saw anything, since you hid under the piano!" Tilly then crawled over to Henderson and tucked herself in his arms.

"My gun jammed!"

"Convenient. Never would have gotten into that mess if it weren't for me trying to save your hide," growled Henderson.

"You got us into that one!" exclaimed Blue Hawk. Then he signed and talked with the other Indians, who all chuckled at the story. "What was the name of that woman who shot at you?"

"Pearl, I think," said Henderson thinking back on the event. "And she was shootin' at everything."

"Men and their stories," muttered Dr. Sullivan. "I'm sure accuracy is not an issue here."

"Tell it once upon a time! In a magic castle!" cried Tilly.

This stopped Henderson and Blue Hawk. The hut fell silent, and all the Pawnee looked around in anticipation. Finally, Blue Hawk signed, trying to explain what Tilly meant. This caused even more confusion.

"You have to tell it her way," offered Caleb.

"Well," said Henderson. "Once upon a time in this saloon, I mean magic castle, Blue Hawk and I got into this gunfight and we…"

"It was a knight!" said Tilly, causing Henderson to stumble. "And a servant!"

"She likes stories about King Arthur and castles," said Julie.

"Anyway," Henderson continued reluctantly. "We were surrounded by these rebs in the, uh, castle who started in on Blue Hawk, the, uh, servant, I mean…"

"Servant!" Blue Hawk replied indignantly. "I was never the servant. Why don't you be the servant?"

"It's just a story, dang it," protested Henderson to Blue Hawk.

Blue Hawk chattered away with the other Pawnee Indians. One warrior, Running Horse, made what seemed to Caleb like a snide comment and Blue Hawk rebuffed him, causing the others to laugh at Blue Hawk.

"Anyway, the local saloon lady…" Henderson continued.

"The beautiful princess!" exclaimed Tilly delightedly.

"Yeah, uh, the beautiful princess started going crazy…" said Henderson.

"The dragons with black teeth were looking for the princess!" exclaimed Tilly.

"Actually, the dragons were trying to run off without paying for the princess's frog." Henderson scratched his head, trying to figure out how to continue. "So she took out a gun…"

"No! The princess knew the dragons killed the muffin

people, so they were going to eat her! Then she took out a magic fire wand!" cried Tilly.

"Magic fire wand, and started shooting up the saloon, I mean castle," said Henderson.

"And turned the dragons into fish!" said Tilly.

Blue Hawk translated, trying to keep the other Pawnees up to date with the story. With this last piece of news, the Indians broke out in great discussion. Blue Hawk threw his hands up in the air and halted all conversation.

"We are confused," said Blue Hawk. "We understand that the rebel white men are the dragons and a dragon is an ugly spirit that breathes fire. But a wand that can change a dragon into a fish? How does this happen? We also want to know who the muffin people are and why the dragons are interested in the frogs."

"This is ridiculous!" said Dr. Sullivan as she and Julie laughed and held on to each other. The Pawnee thought it all deadly serious and leaned forward to hear the explanation.

"Look, daggone it!" roared Henderson in frustration. "I took out my magic fire wand and started changing the rebs, uh, dragons into fish. Blue Hawk, the servant…"

"I'm not the servant!" shouted Blue Hawk indignantly.

"Blue Hawk," continued Henderson, "couldn't change any dragons because his wand jammed!"

"And the knight was the fastest with his wand in the whole magic castle and he saved the princess!" cried Tilly. "The end!"

"Well, it was something like that," muttered Henderson.

Blue Hawk rapidly translated as the Indians gasped and

nodded, delighted with Tilly's version of the story. When they were satisfied, Running Horse got up and started talking, pointing to Henderson. Blue Hawk nodded in agreement.

"They want to see how fast you are with your wand," said Blue Hawk to Henderson. "They have heard of you for so many years, how Henderson was the fastest draw on the Oregon Trail. I told them it was a long time ago and maybe those years are past." Blue Hawk winked at Caleb.

"Oh yeah, we'll see. Give me a gun!" Henderson struggled in his splint, and the two Pawnee Indians stood him up in the center of the hut. One of them handed Henderson a Colt. He tried to hold it with his left hand, but the pain from bullet wounds in his side and shoulder were too much. Then he used his right hand and jammed the gun into his trousers. Blue Hawk readied his pistol and faced him in the hut, the two warriors staring each other down. Caleb took Tilly and stood to the side.

"What?" cried Dr. Sullivan. "No, he can't. This is absurd. I just took three bullets out of the man."

"Quiet there, Talking Crow," said Henderson. "I know what I'm doing."

"Julie, men are some of the stupidest beings on the planet. Whatever you do, don't fall in love with one," warned Dr. Sullivan.

"Oh, so you like him?" giggled Julie as she shared the joke with Caleb. Caleb had heard Henderson and Dr. Sullivan banter back and forth enough to think something was up between them.

"What!" protested Dr. Sullivan. "Certainly not, he's a complete idiot. Watch and learn."

"On the count of three," said Blue Hawk.

"Go ahead!" growled Henderson. "Soon as Talking Crow shuts up."

"One…two…three!" Blue Hawk drew quickly, but Henderson fumbled with his Colt and it fell to the ground. Blue Hawk won, to his great surprise. All the Indians began to clap him on the back as he proudly raised his hands.

"It's not my gun hand!" protested Henderson. "Tell them, Blue Hawk. You remember!"

"No. You've slowed down," laughed Blue Hawk. "Maybe you need a new wand."

"You got turned into a fish!" cried Tilly.

The crack of three gunshots in the distance delivered the news that shook Caleb to his feet. Instantly he looked for his Sharps as a Pawnee warrior ran into the hut. He spoke rapidly to Blue Hawk, and suddenly all the men grabbed guns and bows and ran outside. Blue Hawk faced Caleb and Henderson, deep concern etched in his proud face.

"They are here!" said Blue Hawk. "These Blackstones. You must go now."

10

TAKING PRIDE

★ ★ ★ ★ ★ ★ ★ ★ ★ ★ ★ ★ ★ ★ ★ ★ ★ ★ ★

Caleb pulled Dusty around, and he and Julie rushed to load their wagon. Tilly held Tumble and crouched in the back. Some of the Pawnee men leaped onto their mounts and headed down one side of the river. Several more men took off down the other way as Blue Hawk stormed from his hut with his Winchester. Near the pass that led to the Pawnee camp, the gunfire continued in what sounded like a fierce fight. Pawnee women ran up carrying food, a couple of pots, and a few blankets and set them in the wagon. The women, children, and dogs began to head west for safety while four men rode up to either side of the wagon.

"Go now," said Blue Hawk to Caleb. "We can try to throw them off, but we can't get into much of a fight with them or we'll have the government troops riding down on us like the old days. Jumping Dog and some of my men will ride north with you to the Oregon Trail, then west for a ways and see if you can hook up with a wagon train." Blue Hawk gave

Tilly a bear hug. "There are four of these Blackstones. They think we are Sioux here." Blue Hawk explained. "We have some of their arrows and we shoot near these men. They see these Sioux arrows and they get frightened. Nothing scares folks like the Sioux. My warriors will try to drive them south down the river. It will give you time, but not more than a day or two."

"Thank you, Blue Hawk." Caleb shook the big Indian Chief's hand. "We will repay you some day." Blue Hawk nodded, then he and Running Horse took off down the river.

Several Pawnee men on horseback rode up with Pride. One of the horses was pulling Henderson, who had been lashed to a wooden sled. Caleb, Julie, and Tilly ran to meet him.

"Listen, boy." Henderson drew Caleb near to him, the old ferocity having returned to his eyes. "Be smart out there, trust no one. I'd take you to Bitterroot myself if I could, but right now I'm not much use to anyone. And having a man like me around will only get you into more trouble."

"Where will you go?" asked Julie.

"Somewhere where he can heal, if he's ever going to use that leg again," said Dr. Sullivan as she hurried over to them. In her hands she carried an old leather bag, which she handed to Julie. "Julie, this is for you."

"What is it?" asked Julie.

"My father's medical bag. It's all I have left of him, but I have a hunch you'll need it on the trail. Hurry now." She gave Julie a hug and kissed Tilly.

"I'll take good care of it," said Julie, her eyes glistening with gratitude. "Thank you for everything, Dr. Sullivan." She took Tilly's hand and climbed aboard the wagon.

"Boy," said Henderson, "I need you to do something for me." Henderson whistled and Pride trotted over. "Take Pride."

"What?" said Caleb, confused.

"Treat him right, and he'll treat you right. He just might save your young hide." Henderson's eyes told Caleb that this was a sacrifice of the greatest degree. "It took a brave man to head back into fire and do what you did for me back in Dobytown." Henderson held out his hand and Caleb shook it. "Go on, now."

"Yes, sir," said Caleb. "I'll take good care of him."

Caleb picked up his Sharps rifle and stuck it into the scabbard that used to hold Henderson's Spencer rifle. Then he adjusted the stirrups and mounted the great warhorse. Instantly, Pride snorted and pranced as Caleb led him over to the wagon. Julie tucked her Colt pistol next to her and grabbed the reins and guided Dusty away from the Pawnee camp. The four Pawnee men led them through the rocky pass to the trail. Once they neared the clearing, Caleb spotted the horses of the Blackstones. He could see dark figures in the hills far away, smoke coming from the guns. He prayed Blue Hawk would be true to his word and somehow throw the killers off track. And Caleb knew in his gut they would come after him if it took the rest of their days.

For several days, the four Pawnee Indians led Caleb and his sisters along the Platte River. A merciless mid-July sun beat down on them, but thankfully, they had been safe. They hadn't seen a wagon train, but they had some luck, for travelers before them had thrown away some items to lighten their load. Caleb loaded a large cask of bacon onto the wagon. At least they could eat that after the food that the Pawnee had given them was consumed. There was also a large tarp that had been discarded, and they figured a way to rig it for shade on the wagon. There was even a piano sitting by the trail. But no sign of the Blackstones. Blue Hawk had succeeded in pushing the killers farther south. Caleb knew at some point they would have to cross the river and head north to Montana Territory on the Bozeman Trail. At times he tried, but the river ran deep. As the days passed, Pride felt more like a part of him. The big horse responded to his new rider, and Caleb took great care of him, for he understood the importance of Henderson's gift. Pride could outrun any of the Pawnee horses, and he figured that would come in handy. Along the way, his Indian companions would often display their skills, riding and shooting. Caleb would try to match them, often nearly losing his balance and falling off Pride, only to grip the saddle horn to keep himself upright. The Pawnee would laugh at his awkwardness in a good-natured way.

Toward the end of the day as the prairie cooled, the leader, Jumping Dog, suddenly galloped past Caleb, letting out a war whoop. As he passed, he let go of his horse's reins and grabbed his rifle. Jumping Dog then stopped his horse and turned him around, racing back to the group, aiming his rifle as if to shoot. Then he suddenly brought his horse to a stop with just his legs, pretended to fire his old rifle, and then swiftly sheathed it. He grinned at Caleb in challenge.

All right, Caleb thought, *we'll just see what I can do.* "Ya, Pride!" cried Caleb as he gave the big horse a squeeze with his legs. Pride shot forward, Caleb holding on tight. After about a hundred yards, he turned Pride back to the group. As they picked up speed, Caleb dropped the reins and, thinking on what Jumping Dog did, reached toward his Sharps and brought it to his shoulder. This was easy, he thought, for Pride was smooth as glass. Caleb spurred Pride at breakneck speed toward the Pawnee Indians. Julie and Tilly stood in the wagon to watch, clapping their hands for Caleb. Caleb, full of new-found confidence, raised his rifle and let out a whoop, shifted his weight back, and pushed his legs forward, thrusting his feet deeper into the stirrups. Pride took the signal and slammed to a halt. Caleb flew out of the saddle and over Pride's head. *BLAM!* The Sharps fired as it hit the ground and Caleb crashed into a heap. The Indians ducked for cover, then, seeing Caleb and everyone were all right, began to laugh. Embarrassed and bruised, Caleb brushed himself off and picked up his Sharps. Even Pride, standing stock-still, seemed to be laughing at him.

"I know what I did." Caleb walked over to Pride. Gingerly, he reloaded his rifle and climbed back into the saddle.

"Caleb," said Julie with a snicker. "Now I'm beginning to understand what Dr. Sullivan means about men being stubborn."

"I can do it," answered Caleb. "I just need to…"

"Practice," said Jumping Dog with a toothy grin.

Caleb set his jaw and guided Pride to the trail. He took a deep breath, picked up the reins, and gave Pride a squeeze with his knees. "Ya!" Caleb cried, and again the black horse took off. On Caleb went, getting a feel for Pride as he let go of the reins. For a while, he just concentrated on the rhythm of the horse and the feel of him pounding underneath. As they bolted over the sandy trail, Caleb could feel every muscle twitching beneath him. With the slightest pressure, he could push Pride faster, while a gentle lean back would slow him down. Tremendous joy filled Caleb's heart as the warhorse seemed to obey his every command. Joy was something that was slow to return to him after the tragedy of Great Bend. Caleb discovered a strength in himself he never knew he had.

After what seemed like several miles, Caleb reached for his Sharps. Carefully, he raised the big rifle to his shoulder. He sped along the Platte River until he spotted an old broken wagon wheel resting in the trail ahead. He took aim. He could sense pulling the trigger. Carefully, he balanced himself as he pretended to fire his Sharps, then he leaned back and stuck his feet forward, giving Pride the signal to stop. Caleb stopped perfectly! Elated, he pressed forward to give the wonderful horse a pat.

Suddenly, the sound of screaming women and children filled the air. Up ahead was a band of Indians, their horses loaded with their tepees and belongings. Some were bathing in the river. The Indian women yelled and grabbed their children, pointing toward Caleb. Caleb jerked Pride to the side. His head was nearly blown off.

Caleb felt the whistle of a bullet fly by his head. Another shot was fired some hundred yards away, and Caleb whirled around in the saddle. Fear gripped him, and he froze as six Indians rode down on him with one purpose. To kill him. Pride twisted underneath Caleb, awaiting a signal from him. Was he to rush forward and meet the battle or would his new master turn him and run? Panic filled Caleb for a moment. Then he made up his mind. Run!

Caleb squeezed Pride with his knees and the huge horse reared and then leaped forward as if he were shot out of a cannon. In a blast of power, Caleb rode Pride on a race for his life. He could see the Indians try to surround him, but they couldn't quite head off Pride. On Caleb drove Pride at breakneck speed, and the more Caleb relaxed, the faster they went. Now he had a plan. Outrun them, yes, but he had to keep them away from Julie and Tilly. Caleb led the Indians on a chase through the scrub brush, over the rocks, crashing through streams. They fired on Caleb as he raced on. A bullet buzzed past Caleb's ear and took part of his hat off. The Indians were expert riders and shot with deadly accuracy. Now he needed to act or die. Caleb let go of the reins and reached for his Sharps. As he did, he stuck three bullets into the webbing of his right hand. He calmed himself as he turned in the saddle to face the Indians who trailed Pride by perhaps a hundred yards. Caleb shifted his weight and, with his knees, suddenly guided the warhorse to his left. Carefully, he sighted down on the lead Indian and let loose. The blast of the big Sharps nearly threw Caleb off his horse, but he quickly recovered. The lead Indian, surprised, veered off. Caleb quickly slammed another bullet into the breech and fired. The shell ejected and he immediately reloaded just the way Henderson taught him. In rapid fire, Caleb held the Indians off. None of them struck, but it was enough to give him the distance he needed to escape their fire. Caleb reached into his pocket at a full gallop and grabbed a handful of bullets. Quickly, he loaded the Sharps. He raced Pride around in a long circle. On they ran, but the Indians lost ground. They had met their match in Pride. Eventually, they slowed to a stop. Miraculously, they seemed to give up. Caleb thought about firing again, but there was no need. Then he saw why. His four Pawnee friends were lined up ahead, rifles in their hands and sighting in on the pursuers.

Jumping Dog shot his rifle into the air. Then he urged his horse forward to meet the attackers. In peace.

★ ★ ★

"They are Arapaho," said Jumping Dog as he returned to Caleb. All the Indians had lowered their rifles and followed a ways closer. They seemed fascinated by Pride. Julie held the wagon back a short distance and hung on to Tumble in case he had any ideas of stirring things up. "They think you attack their women and children as they bathe in river. They have lost many of their people to white men. I tell them you don't mean harm."

"It was my fault. I surprised them up the river. They shot at me and I tried to outrun them." Caleb tried to keep himself from shaking from the ordeal. Jumping Dog signed with the Arapaho and they gestured back.

"They want to know the young white warrior who rides like an Indian. They say they have never seen such a horse. I tell them I teach you," Jumping Dog said proudly.

"Yes. Tell them I say you are a good teacher," smiled Caleb. "And you teach me to shoot too."

As Jumping Dog spoke with the Arapaho, their leader began to gesture all around him. He looked confused as he explained something to Jumping Dog and finally all the Indians put up their hands, shrugging their shoulders.

"He says I am not such a good teacher for shooting. You miss and they knew not what you shot. They say you need to practice," said Jumping Dog with a grin. "But they think you ride good."

Again they spoke at length. Then the Arapaho turned their horses and galloped away, the trail dust kicking up behind their horses as they rode back toward their camp. They were a people who traveled fast and light, who could pack up their belongings and tepees within an hour. Battle had taught them to fight or flee quickly. Caleb had nearly been shot off his horse when he galloped into their midst, but he and his sisters were safe. He breathed a sigh of relief, for he had been lucky. He made a silent vow to be more careful.

"They say there is big wagon train some miles up ahead. We rest for tonight. Tomorrow we ride hard to Ash Hollow," said Jumping Dog as he trotted past Caleb to the wagon.

Ash Hollow! Caleb knew of it. That was where the pioneers gathered on the Oregon Trail and lowered their wagons with ropes by hand down a treacherous hill to the road below. It seemed a monumental task, but you could then cross to the North Platte River from the south. A wagon train had been spotted! Perhaps their luck had changed. Caleb's hands finally stopped shaking.

★ ★ ★

Wagons! For miles! Caleb reined Pride to a stop at the edge of the impossibly steep trail. Below, perhaps a mile away, was the wide Platte River. In the distance beyond, wagons were disappearing into a growing cloud of dust. As Pride danced along the edge of the near vertical hill, Caleb looked around to figure a way down. There seemed no way to get their buckboard safely to the bottom without riding some distance away and making their way back. Time was everything and it would be hard to catch up. If they were to travel in the safety of this wagon train, they had to join up with them now. As the wagons drew farther away, Caleb saw his solution. Just ahead at the edge of the clifflike trail were several long ropes! This was where the wagons were lowered over the side.

"Ready?" cried Caleb as he and Julie stood holding the reins of Dusty and Pride. After they had emptied the wagon of their supplies, Caleb hitched the two horses to the wagon with the long ropes left by the pioneers. Their Pawnee friends held the wagon steady at the edge of the steep trail some two hundred feet away.

"Yes!" Jumping Dog and the three other Indians began to push the wagon over the side. Once the rear wheels went over, they grabbed hold of the ropes and braced themselves. Keeping tension on the ropes, Caleb and Julie carefully backed Dusty and Pride a few feet toward the lip of the hill as the wagon disappeared over the side. The rope snapped taut and held! Then they began to back Dusty and Pride toward the edge as the wagon slowly inched toward the bottom below.

"It's working!" exclaimed Julie as she coaxed Dusty slowly backward. Jumping Dog and another Pawnee man held their knives, ready to cut the ropes in case of any problem. "Back, Dusty!"

"Easy, Pride," said Caleb as the big warhorse strained against the weight. "How much farther?"

"Almost there!" shouted Tilly, dangerously close to the edge.

"Tilly!" cried Julie. "Get away from there!"

SNAP! It happened so fast, Jumping Dog and one of the other Pawnee Indians were thrown to the ground. Dusty's rope had broken and the weight of the wagon began to carry the Indians to the edge of the steep trail. The other two Indians dug their feet into the ground with all their might and held on. One of them began to try to cut the rope, but it was awkward and he dropped the knife and went down. Tilly got caught up with the two Indians and rolled toward the edge. Jumping Dog reached out and pushed her back.

"Tilly!" Julie dove to grab her sister.

"Come on, Pride!" cried Caleb. If they lost Pride and the wagon now, it would be a disaster. Pride pulled hard as all the Indians grabbed the good rope and began to brace.

"Ten feet!" called Jumping Dog as he scrambled back. The other Pawnee Indians pulled mightily against the weight as they tried to steady the wagon. Finally the rope slacked as the wagon hit the bottom with a jolt and flipped over.

"It looks OK!" cried Julie as she looked over the clifflike hill.

"That was a close one," said Jumping Dog with a sheepish grin. For a moment, they could only stare at the little wagon now resting on its side, but seemingly intact.

Caleb looked at the wagon in amazement. Hopefully, nothing was damaged. "We'd better load up Dusty and Pride." He started to pile their belongings on the horses. Soon they had everything ready to make the descent. On horseback, it was dangerous, but much easier to make their way down to the canyon floor. The horses picked their way slowly along the treacherous trail. It was pretty obvious their wagon never could have made it down. They would have had to travel for miles out of their way to find a safe route. Once they got the wagon packed up, they turned to say good-bye to their Pawnee friends. "Thank you, Jumping Dog, for all of your help." Caleb held out his hand to shake and together they shared a smile.

"I wish you good journey." Jumping Dog then took out his knife and handed it to Caleb. "Take this."

"This knife?" It was long and graceful with turquoise stones set in the handle. "I can't," said Caleb, trying to give it back.

"It has brought me good luck. It is yours," said Jumping Dog. "Better hurry."

With barely a wave of good-bye, the Indians mounted their horses and rode back up the steep slope. They did not waste time with sentiment. Caleb and Julie marveled at the generosity of the Pawnee people. Some day they would return to thank them properly, for stopping in their camp had saved Tilly's life. The Indians had helped them on their journey without so much as a thought to their own safety. Caleb's father had always talked about the character of men. He was beginning to find out what that meant.

"Ready?" asked Caleb as he mounted Pride and studied a grove of ash trees in front of him. Julie boosted Tilly onto the back of the wagon, where Tumble sat barking in excitement.

"Let's go," Julie said as she climbed aboard and grabbed Dusty's reins. "Over to the right looks like the best way to the river."

★ ★ ★

"It's OK! It's shallow!" shouted Caleb as he urged Pride through the waters of Ash Hollow. "Hurry!" After a mile or so of navigating their way through the ash trees, they had entered the river. The wagon train was more than two hours ahead of them. They were falling behind, but the river was so pure up the bend that they took a few minutes to bathe and water the horses. Who knows when they would see the likes of these springs again? The water in Ash Hollow was famous and said to be the best around. Now they had to catch up.

Julie struggled a little with the wagon, but then Dusty found his footing and she was able to guide the gray horse through the gentle current, Tumble barking all the way. Dusty loved the cleaning Caleb had given him, and with newfound vigor, they crossed the mile-wide river with few problems. They pressed on, determined to close the gap with the wagon train, passing other pioneers who could not keep up. Many wagons over the years had broken down from the journey on the trail and had been cast aside like dead carcasses. There was even a lone man pushing a wheelbarrow stuffed with his belongings. As they passed the exhausted pioneer, Caleb noted the fixed, haunted look in the man's eyes. But the man walked on, his head no doubt filled with visions of gold, riches, or a new life. Dreams of the people from the east who had no idea of the rigors and hardships of traveling the trail drove them farther west. On they pushed into the unknown and into the teeth of danger. It was all some could do to keep their horses and wagons in a straight line, because of their lack of western experience. Caleb and Julie were learning this life quickly. They had to, for if they let up, they would not survive. They had traveled nearly four hundred miles in a little over a month since they had left their beloved home in flames. Not even halfway to the Bitterroot and their new home with their Aunt Sarah, they had been tested time and again. Caleb couldn't afford to let up, and the dying wish of his mother filled him with all the strength he would need. The muscles in his arms and the strength of his grip battled with his doubts and his fears, for who could say what perils lay ahead. They would be there, he thought, but he would not cave in to them. He vowed to never waver.

"You smell that?" Caleb pulled alongside Julie, who stood up on the seat of the wagon to get a good look ahead. The air was filled with dust and the stench of sweaty animals.

"Look, Tilly!" cried Julie as she hoisted Tilly onto her shoulders. There, far ahead against the setting sun, was the longest wagon train they had ever seen. "Wagons! There they are!"

11

WAGON TRAINS AND BUFFALO CHIPS

★ ★

I don't care how you say it, boy, you can't join up, and that's it!" The red-faced wagon master, Captain John Bellows, spat a stream of tobacco juice at Caleb's feet. Several other men circled on horseback around Caleb, Julie, and the wagon as the former Union officer chewed Caleb out for riding up behind the train. Sentries patrolling the rear nearly fired on them as they rode hard to catch up.

"I'm the leader of this here wagon train, and I am telling you we can't afford to take on three brats with no folks to take care of 'em. We got better than a thousand miles to Oregon and you'd be a danger to us all. Darn near got yourselves killed just now!"

"Sir, we would only go as far as the Bozeman Trail with your wagons, and then we'll split off. Maybe Fort Fetterman or Fort Casper," said Caleb.

"Look, boy, I can't guarantee half these folks are going to make it even that far. There's a heck of a lot of trouble with the Sioux up at Scotts Bluff and I got greenhorns who can't shoot and can't ride from places I never heard of. Tarnation, half of 'em don't speak good English. Last thing we need is to take care of you snot-nosed brats. Now get on back to Ash Hollow then to wherever you came from," ordered the Captain as he chewed off another chaw of tobacco.

"We can take care of ourselves," said Julie. "We've come weeks on our own so far!"

"Then you don't need us now, do ya?" sneered the Captain. "And we've got no use for you."

"I can outride any of you!" insisted Caleb. "I can shoot too."

"Hear that?" guffawed the Captain. "That's a laugh." All the men seemed to think that was particularly funny. "What about you, little missy? I suppose you're about as worthless as your brother here? You at least cook?"

"Yes, sir, I can." Julie narrowed her eyes and stared straight at the Captain. "I can also stitch you up next time you do something foolish and fall on your head, or whatever you men are prone to do," said Julie defiantly.

This caused a great roar of laughter from the men that did not sit well with Bellows. "Shut up!" barked Captain Bellows as he stared at Julie, trying to figure on some sort of answer. He settled on Caleb rather than take on Julie. "How old are you, boy?"

"Twelve, sir," answered Caleb.

"Twelve, huh? You think you can outride my best man?" muttered the Captain.

"Yes, sir!"

"This I gotta see. Corporal Posey!"

"Sir!" shouted a voice from behind the last wagon.

"Get your butt over here!" ordered the Captain. "And bring that excuse for a horse you call Devil with you!"

"Yes, sir!"

"Now, boy, I'll make you a little wager. You even keep up with Posey, I'll let you stay on. He beats you flat out, you and your sisters here head back, understood?" barked Bellows.

"Yes, sir!" Caleb smiled. "Pride will beat him."

"I know he can!" cried Julie.

"He'll eat Pride's dust!" yelled little Tilly as she bravely stood next to her sister.

"Pride, huh. We'll see," mused Bellows as he gave Pride the once-over. "Dad gummit, Posey!"

"Sir!" Posey galloped around the wagon on a screaming stallion so white, it glowed in the midday sun. The young Corporal's blue uniform with sparkling gold buttons and yellow-striped leggings clung perfectly to him, and his shiny black boots beat a brisk rhythm on the horse's flanks. Long blond hair flowed under a yellow-tasseled cavalry hat, its wide brim swept up on the left side. This was a real horseman. He gave a flick of the reins, and Devil reared up on his hind legs to his full height, his front hooves pawing at the air. Caleb had only seen a horse like this in books. An Arabian! He was big and strong, almost as big as Pride at the shoulder. Caleb swallowed hard as Posey let the snorting horse prance sideways. Devil, he knew, would be tough to beat. Arabians could run all day, and this one was young.

Pride had seen many battles and was at least fifteen years old, Caleb figured.

"This boy says Pride here can beat that crazy-looking horse of yours. You gonna let that happen, Corporal?" challenged Bellows.

"No, Captain!" Posey guided Devil alongside Pride. Instantly, Pride began to get agitated, for he was a warhorse that did not like a young stallion riding up on him. Pride reared up, and Caleb almost fell off the back. "Watch yourself there, boy," laughed Posey as he purposely swung his horse into Pride.

"All right." Bellows pointed to a tree some two hundred yards away. "Around that first tree and back. You fall too far behind, you and your sisters go. Got it?"

Caleb thought for a second and had an idea. A short race, anything can happen, but a long one? "Around that tree? That's too easy. What about that other one on the hill behind it? Might be more interesting," said Caleb as he pointed at another tree far in the distance.

"OK," muttered Posey confidently. "Don't matter much."

"Fine," growled Captain Bellows. "On your way back, take a shot at that stump over there. We'll see if you can shoot like you say."

"OK." Caleb looked across the trail at a burned-out stump some fifty yards away. He checked his Sharps to make sure it was loaded and put it back in its scabbard. Pride sensed something was up and he began to shift his feet in excitement. Posey lined up next to Caleb and yanked Devil in toward Pride. Pride, not to be messed with, lashed out with his hind leg and cracked the Arabian. Devil suddenly turned and bit Pride. Pride reared up hard. It was all Caleb could do to hang on.

"Wait for my shot!" Captain Bellows took out his Colt and pointed it skyward, then fired.

Corporal Posey spurred Devil hard, and the big Arabian took off like he was shot from a cannon. It was two seconds before Caleb could react. At first Caleb struggled, but Pride seemed to know his task and bolted on his own after the Arabian stallion. They were already thirty yards behind when Caleb settled in, and he could hear the jeering laughter behind him. "Let's go, Pride! Ya!" cried Caleb as he squeezed with his knees. It was nearly a half-mile to the tree and if he figured right, he might run the white Devil down.

On they raced over the prairie, and the big Arabian held the lead. Caleb winced as bits of dirt and rock were slung into his face, adding insult to injury. As he tried to control Pride, he thought about saving him for the finish, but Pride would have none of it. When Caleb tried to hold him back, Pride fought against the bit, struggling to gain more speed. He seemed to want to beat this Arabian stallion in the worst way. This was something Caleb had not known about Henderson's horse. He was as hardheaded as the gunfighter was. So, instead of trying to control the huge warhorse, Caleb simply squeezed again. "All right, Pride, go get him!" Pride stormed ahead, his proud blood pounding through his veins, willing himself to catch this white stallion. Posey shot a look back in disbelief as Pride surged toward him and he took out a crop and beat Devil, whipping the Arabian horse mightily to keep his lead. The Arabian rounded the tree first at a tremendous pace, his white tail flying straight behind him. Caleb rounded the tree seconds behind and shot after Posey and his horse. Posey whipped his horse like a madman and for a moment seemed to creep ahead. Posey tried to cut Pride off, but Pride veered to the side and pulled even with Devil. For some seconds it stayed like that, neck and neck. Then Caleb just gave Pride another squeeze, leaned a little forward, and relaxed his grip on the reins. Now Pride took it on his own. Smooth as glass, Pride flattened out his head, his black tail flying behind him. They left Posey and Devil several lengths in back of them as they closed in on the wagon train, the figures up ahead jumping up and down with excitement. The wind whipped and whistled as they pulled farther ahead. Now it was Posey eating his dust, as Pride pounded out a thunderous beat to the finish line.

Caleb let go of the reins and reached back for his Sharps. Calmly, carefully, he sighted on the blackened stump. Time seemed to stand still. He squeezed the trigger and fired.

"Holy sweet mother!" gasped Captain Bellows as Caleb shot past on Pride and scattered the wagon sentries who had gathered along with a growing crowd of pioneers to watch the race. "Did he hit it? Johnson! Check that stump!"

Ben Johnson, an older trapper dressed head to toe in

animal skins, sauntered over to the stump as Caleb walked Pride back to the group of onlookers. After some inspection, he walked back to the group, scratching his head.

"Don't see nothing, Captain," said Johnson. "Guess he missed."

"Missed, huh? Boy, get over here!"

Caleb slid off Pride and gave him a pat as he ambled over toward the Captain. *I can't believe it*, Caleb thought as he led Pride past the sentries. He had done well to win the race, but since he missed the stump, he figured Bellows would cut them loose. Posey trotted up on Devil and nodded to Caleb.

"Nice race, boy," said the Corporal grudgingly.

"What's your name, son?" The Captain eyed Caleb and ran his hand over Pride's sweating flank.

"Caleb O'Toole, sir."

"Well, Caleb O'Toole, that was one dandy of a race. Never thought I'd see the day the Devil would be beat. This is some horse you got here. Seen his share of battle, I see."

"Yes, sir." Caleb watched as Bellows inspected Pride, touching the big warhorse's wounds.

"N...V..." Bellows fingered the initials that were etched into the saddle. "Nebraska Volunteers, I take it? Where'd you get him?"

"A man gave him to me, sir." Caleb was careful not to mention Henderson's name.

"Gave him to you, huh?" Bellows stared hard at Caleb. "Well, Caleb O'Toole, you sure can ride. Too bad you can't shoot. Johnson!"

"Sir!" snapped Ben Johnson.

"You make sure this boy learns how to shoot that Sharps of his!" growled the Captain. "Caleb O'Toole?"

"Yes, sir?" Caleb brightened at the possibility of traveling safely with the wagon train.

"Johnson can hit the eye out of an eagle. You learn from this man. If you can shoot like you can ride, we'll keep you and your family around. Maybe make you a scout."

"Thank you, Captain, I will," said Caleb as Julie and Tilly ran up alongside.

"And you, what's your name?" Bellows asked Julie.

"Julie O'Toole. And this is Tilly."

"I told you Pride would eat Devil's dust!" exclaimed Tilly proudly.

"Ha!" laughed Bellows. "Well, Julie O'Toole, you say you can stitch a man's head?"

"I can!"

"Good. You can start with old man Peterson's head right now. The idiot got himself kicked by that ox of his. Posey!" barked Bellows. "Take her up to the idiot's wagon and see she fixes him up!"

Julie ran to get the doctor bag. "Wish me luck," Julie whispered to Caleb as she walked ahead with Posey and Devil. Caleb silently wished old man Peterson luck.

"Boy, until you learn to shoot, you need to make yourself useful," said the Captain.

"Yes, sir, I will. Anything," answered Caleb.

"Good." The Captain shoved another chaw into his mouth. "You can start by hanging behind in the back and collecting buffalo chips." Then Captain Bellows signaled and he and the sentries headed for the front of the wagon train.

"Buffalo chips, sir? What are…?"

"It's dried crap from a buffalo!" roared the Captain. "You see some, you throw it in that wagon of yours. It makes a good fire!"

★ ★ ★

Caleb stunk of buffalo dung in the worst way. His throat ached from the choking dust that kicked up from the wagon wheels. For a week, the wagon train crept across the desolate prairie, the oxen dragging the wagon train along the trail at barely ten miles per day. Sometimes they could only make two or three miles. Every morning, they would get up while it was still dark and build a fire with the buffalo chips. A breakfast of bacon, bread, and beans was mostly what they ate. The wagon master would give the word and Caleb would help the other pioneers hitch up all the wagons and rouse the livestock. Soon they would head out for another day on the trail. Wagons broke down and had to be fixed, and sometimes the weather would act up. The oxen were methodical, dependable beasts. Caleb had managed around twenty miles per day when they traveled with their horses alone. At the end of each day, Captain Bellows would order the wagons to circle so they could pen in all the livestock. Sentries would be posted to keep watch for Indians.

It was slow going, but Caleb was glad for the protection

they needed from the two hundred or so wagons along with several hundred earnest but tired pioneers. Along the way, Tilly fell in with the children of a family who came all the way from Europe. Dreamers who were headed to California or Oregon for the gold. Tilly played games with them like leapfrog or hoops or London Bridge. She led the other children to make bouquets from all the wildflowers and hand them out to the travelers. Julie was making a reputation for herself as a nurse and had stitched up more than a few fellow travelers who were injured along the trail. Sometimes she would help teach some of the children at night by the fire from books folks had managed to bring with them. And of course, Tilly wanted to hear her stories of King Arthur and medieval times.

But Caleb could not get the stink off him, for the prairie yielded no firewood, and buffalo chips were the only thing that burned well enough for the cooks that prepared their meals. He was so tired of the rock-hard bread, beans, and salted bacon. He longed for a real hearty meal, and today was the day he was to get one. They had made it to Courthouse Rock. In the distance, the huge sandstone rock looked like a war-torn castle. When pioneers made it this far, they knew their journey along the flat prairie was pretty much over. Rugged and difficult terrain loomed ahead.

Caleb sat from his perch halfway up Courthouse Rock and looked out on the vast landscape for deer or antelope. From several hundred feet up, he could see for miles around, and the silence of the desolate prairie filled his ears. He and Ben had ridden ahead to hunt. It was a relief from the relentless grinding and jingling of wagon travel. Far off he could see the dust rising into the midday sun from the wagon train. He figured the distance to be about five miles. Carefully he descended the rocky sandstone cliff as he saw Ben Johnson signal to him from below. The trapper must have found something.

An hour later, Caleb lay patiently in the tall grass in the shadows of Courthouse Rock, determined to bring back food. Johnson had shown him the signs and the droppings of some antelope, and there they crouched, downwind. Finally, an antelope grazing several hundred yards in the distance picked his head up, then moved to higher ground. Caleb had seen a few far away from the trail, but they were skittish and would not come near the ruckus of the wagons. Often, many of the pioneers would try to shoot at antelope or buffalo grazing in the distance for sport, an act that would drive Captain Bellows to sit the men down for a loud lecture. He despised the wasteful act.

Johnson had helped him in the days before to adjust the sights on the Sharps, given him pointers about wind and distance, and corrected him on how he should squeeze the trigger of the big rifle. They had grown close over the days of travel. With gentle hands, Johnson would refine Caleb's grip, encouraging him to use his own stance, find his own method of sharpshooting. The trapper had the soothing patience of his father. It was a comfort to Caleb in the places of his heart where he held the black sorrow of loss. "It ain't what you look like when you're shooting, it's where the dang bullet ends up," Johnson would say. He had a lever-action Henry rifle and let Caleb shoot it. It did not have the hard kick of the Sharps and Caleb soon could hit the bull's-eye from two hundred yards. The Henry rifle also held a dozen bullets, so if you missed, you could cock it and shoot without reloading. But the Sharps held only one. This antelope was a true test, and now it showed itself in plain sight.

Caleb took a deep breath and fired. The heavy recoil of the Sharps slammed into his shoulder. For a second, nothing happened, so Caleb quickly reloaded and sighted again. Then the antelope went down. "Got him!" Caleb cried as he mounted Pride. Together, the two of them rode across the prairie toward the fallen animal.

"Now that there is a heck of a shot!" Johnson clapped Caleb on the back. "Must be three hundred yards. Got him clean too, and that's what you want, so it don't suffer."

As they hoisted the antelope across Pride's back, Caleb felt a sense of satisfaction. He also felt some regret as he looked at the antelope, for he had taken its life. But it would feed his sisters and many others who wanted a good meal that night. And that made him happy.

★ ★ ★

"Three hundred yards, you say?" said Captain Bellows as he wolfed down the stew the cooks made from the antelope. "Pretty good shot. That settles it. Tomorrow we make Chimney Rock. Get Posey, and you, him, and young Caleb ride point."

"Ride point?" Caleb asked as he looked at his father's map of the territory.

"Scout ahead," said Johnson as he gnawed on a bone.

"I figure take your distance about two miles in front. Should be pretty safe for the next fifty miles or so, but when we hit Scotts Bluff, that's when things can heat up. And it won't be antelope that's shooting at you, boy!" Captain Bellows rose from the campfire. "We ride at dawn."

"Right, Captain," said Johnson. Then, seeing Caleb's confusion, he offered, "Scotts Bluff has some problems with the Sioux, mainly. Most of the Indians along here just want to trade for food, blankets. Peaceful folks. Crow, Cheyenne, Arapaho. Don't normally give the white people much of any trouble. Fact, they even go against the Sioux. But lately these years have seen it go bad sometimes all up Montana way."

"That's where we're headed." Caleb studied the map by the firelight. "Up to the Bitterroot Mountains on the Bozeman Trail."

"Bitterroot, huh," mused Johnson. "Jump off the Bozeman and into Yellowstone, Virginia City, then Bannack?"

"I guess so."

"Better do more than guess. You watch yourself good. That's a mean trip. Virginia City, there used to be some kinda war going on up there with all the gold and the thieves. Mining country. Heard the vigilantes are on the prowl, hangin' folks," said Johnson as he picked his teeth.

"We've got family there waiting for us."

"Young Caleb, don't know what your business is, what

you're runnin' from, but you watch yourself in these parts. My belly says you ain't out here alone, the way I see you checking back of you. Got an instinct for these things."

"We'll make it," said Caleb.

"The three of you alone out here are some easy pickings. You'll be all right with the wagon train, cover up your tracks and all, but this train ain't going north, it's going west, and whoever is behind you is going to know what I know."

"What?" Caleb asked warily.

"That Pride's got a funny front hoof, and that wagon of yours has a cut wheel. A blind man could track it." Johnson rose from the campfire and nodded toward Julie and Tilly who were asleep in the wagon. "You jump off to the Bozeman, they might just pick up your trail. That is, if you need to worry about that. I'm just sayin'. Meantime, we may have some Sioux to deal with once we get near Chimney Rock."

"Where's that?"

"Some miles ahead. It's a giant rock that shoots up and marks the trail west. Looks like a haystack with a chimney on it," explained Johnson. "Can't miss it."

12

A SCOUT IS BORN

★ ★ ★ ★ ★ ★ ★ ★ ★ ★ ★ ★ ★ ★ ★ ★ ★ ★ ★

But it wasn't Indians they ran into as they made their way past Chimney Rock. It was buffalo. Miles of the huge beasts in a herd so vast it took Caleb's breath away. Even using Johnson's telescope, they could not see the end to them. He had heard about the vast herds of buffalo that once roamed these territories. He also knew of their needless slaughter by white pioneers. Folks from all corners of the world were known to shoot them for sport without any regard to the future of these great beasts. Shot them from moving trains even, and left them to rot. Some buffalo hunters simply killed and sold their hides for pennies or a dollar, leaving the carcass. It was a source of trouble with the Indian nations. They relied on the buffalo as a way of life. The herds were dwindling. But what Caleb saw in front of him filled him with awe. The air was full of their rugged stench as they peacefully grazed on the prairie grass. Their bellows sounded like distant thunder. Posey sat chewing a piece of that prairie grass while Johnson sighted in on the lead buffalo. They were downwind of the herd. Caleb took out his Sharps and checked the breech. Then he aimed at a large buffalo some two hundred yards away.

"Figure we'll take maybe three," said Johnson to Caleb as he looked down the barrel of his Henry rifle. "Should feed us good for days. You on one?"

"Yes, that big one close in," said Caleb as he took a deep breath.

"All right then, go ahead and take him when I fire. They spook easy and once they scatter, look out."

The sudden crash of gunfire jerked them around in confusion. They had not fired on the buffalo. Half expecting to see Indians, they were surprised to see thirty or so of their own men from the wagon train riding toward the giant herd, firing at will at the huge beasts.

"Gall-darn fools!" shouted Posey as the pioneers advanced on the buffalo and proceeded to slaughter the animals with no discretion. "They'll stampede the herd!"

"Mount up quick," said Johnson. "This don't look good."

More men left their horses and advanced on foot with long rifles and even revolvers. They ran toward the herd, shooting the raging buffaloes for no reason other than having some fun. They clapped each other on the back as they brought down the beasts. Caleb knew there was no way they could eat or transport all the dead or dying buffalo, the carnage was so great. Caleb leaped on Pride and rode toward some of the pioneers who were bent on their slaughter, shouting at them to stop. Posey and Johnson tried to head some of the men off, but the pioneers ignored them and refused to back away from their sport. Great bleating moans could be heard from the wounded animals as they fled in panic. Caleb urged Pride into the herd where some of the men fired with glee, whooping and hollering, some in English, others yelling in languages Caleb had never heard before.

"Stop!" Caleb cried over the blasting of the rifles and the thunder of buffalo hooves. Some of the men looked at him like he was crazy. Men with no soulful feeling for the lives of these free-living beasts. To them it was a game. But the game turned deadly. The ground shook under the panic of the buffalo and, as quickly as they had scattered, the vast herd came together and circled around, thundering down on the firing pioneers. Suddenly, there were shouts of alarm as the stampeding buffalo charged the fleeing men. Caleb saw one man trampled like he was straw, his skull smashed. A horse went down and its screams were heard over the fury of the hooves. Two men tried to run and were swallowed up by the herd, never to be seen standing again.

"I'll ride back to the wagons!" shouted Posey as he spurred Devil. "This herd comes down on us there won't be nothing left! Try to head 'em around upriver!"

"Go on, Posey!" shouted Johnson as he and Caleb galloped their horses to the head of the herd. Together they tried to veer the front of the herd away from the path of the wagon train.

"Ya! Pride!" Caleb shot out of the herd toward the lead

buffaloes as Johnson scrambled on his horse to keep up. Together they tried to force the herd farther north to the river. Caleb pushed Pride within inches of one buffalo but the huge beast would have none of it. Suddenly it lashed out at Pride with its horns, but Caleb jerked his horse to the side just in time. Johnson nearly went down as another buffalo smashed into the side of his horse. Caleb looked around behind him as they crashed over the prairie, his legs gripping his warhorse tight, terrified he would get swallowed up by the thousands of storming animals in the herd. On he and Johnson rode with the lead buffaloes, and together they tried to veer them toward the Platte River. But the furthest buffalo ahead, the biggest of all, circled.

"Caleb! Put that one ahead tight against the river! They'll slow down! Go get him!"

"All right! Come on, Pride!" Caleb had never before herded on the gallop, but he was learning fast. He had to, for if they were not successful, the wagon train would be lost and many folks trampled or killed. Many including Julie and Tilly. He gave Pride a squeeze and took off toward the lead buffalo. Once alongside, Caleb was close enough to see the rage in the beast's eyes. *This one must be well over two thousand pounds*, thought Caleb, as time and again he tried to force it toward the river. Caleb stayed with the buffalo for perhaps a mile, side by side, blocking the huge beast from circling back. Pride seemed to sense that he could keep just the right distance, dashing in and pulling away, frustrating the buffalo, staying just far enough away from the horns, until finally the buffalo veered to the right toward the river. Caleb shot a look back toward Johnson, who rode like a madman in his animal skins, once crashing his horse into a beast beside him. Behind him, the thunder and rage of a thousand buffaloes tore a wide path over the prairie.

They rode for miles until the buffaloes stormed into the North Platte River, finally slowing down, the panic ebbing from the herd. They'd done it! As Johnson trotted his horse toward Caleb, he saw in the trapper's eyes the respect that one man gives another.

"Well, there you go," Johnson said simply. "Let's pray we took 'em all away from the wagons."

★ ★ ★

Caleb and Johnson arrived at the wagon train to the sound of Captain Bellows's booming voice. Fuming, the wagon master stomped among the pioneers who had attacked the buffalo, lecturing them about their foolhardy ways. Posey had ridden in hard on Devil and sounded the alarm. The wagons were bunched together in a tight circle to try to protect the women and children along with their livestock. Four men had been killed in the stampede and seven ended up badly injured. Julie was tending as best she could to them, assisting two of the other women who fancied themselves as prairie doctors. These brave women were not educated in medicine in any formal way like Dr. Sullivan, but were good at caring for the sick or injured along the trail. Julie held her own as they struggled to set broken arms and legs. The women nodded in approval as Julie carefully and skillfully sewed a man's torn ear back on to his head. The wails of the families of those killed could be heard. Gunshots sounded in the distance as Posey and Johnson returned to the wounded buffalo and mercifully put the injured animals out of their misery.

Caleb's heart was heavy as he unsaddled Pride and sorted out the events of the day, the sun just setting in the western horizon. Julie was building a fire near the wagon. Caleb sighed. The sight of so many slaughtered buffalo filled him with sadness. The scent of blood hung in the air like a punishment of the terrible deeds of the day. Many of the dead buffalo were cut up and handed out to the wagon party. Carcasses were stripped of their hides, the pioneers figuring they would need the warmth come winter. Still, scores of the magnificent beasts lay to rot on the prairie. Caleb went over to Dusty, the loyal gray horse nuzzling him as he fed him the last remaining oats they had.

"Hey, boy," said Caleb as he hugged his horse to him. "You've been doing all the work around here. You get us to Aunt Sarah's, you'll never have to do this again. You can just take it easy on her ranch." Dusty gave a soft whinny and pushed his nose into Caleb, looking to be scratched on his favorite spot on his head. Caleb noticed Julie reading a book by the fire. "What are you reading?"

"It was in Dr. Sullivan's bag. It's a medical book." Julie flipped the pages, lines of concentration appearing on her face. "I've found some things that come in handy. Common remedies and such. It says you can use a mixture of gunpowder and whiskey and spread it on a rattlesnake bite." She leaned over to toss another buffalo chip on the fire. The old Julie may have found that dirty task unsettling, but now she gave it no thought. She merely clapped the manure dust off her hands and then continued her reading.

"Where's Tilly?"

"She and Tumble are over at the Smiths' wagon. They're from England," said Julie with a laugh. "You can imagine what she's up to with their children. She's got them all playing her Once Upon a Time game." Just then, Ben Johnson ambled over with buffalo steaks and some long sticks. "Looks like we've got company."

★ ★ ★

"Why did they do it?" asked Caleb as he tested a piece of meat from the fire.

"Well, Caleb O'Toole," said Johnson as he gnawed on his buffalo meat. Julie held her steak over the campfire as the old trapper chewed away. "Don't rightly know why these people do what they do, killing the buff like that. Suppose they read all about it in books and once they get to these parts, just go crazy. Like the Lord put the buffalo out here just for their sport. Makes a mess with the Indians and all."

"I don't understand it, since if they keep on killing them, there won't be any left." Julie tried a piece of her steak. Her eyes lit up with appreciation. "This beats bacon and beans." Caleb was too busy eating to even reply, the juice running down his chin. All he could do was grunt in agreement.

"Heck, there used to be ten times more out here. I've been around for a while, as you can see from the snow on my roof," chuckled the trapper as he took off his beaver hat. His white hair glistened in the firelight. "I'm somewhere over fifty years old and for as long as I've been taking these folks over the trail, I've seen it over and over again. To them, everything out here is for the taking. Land, gold, buffalo. Don't matter. They just take it. Turns out a lot of them folks get took as well. But they keep on a comin'."

"My father said they were mainly city folks from back east and all over the world and they don't know any better," said Caleb as he dug into his buffalo steak.

"He's mostly right, but there's a lot of others that are good folk who just want somethin' better. Dern shame, though. For the Indian folk too. Seems no matter what they're given, it gets took away too."

"Do they ever bother you?" asked Caleb.

"The Indians? Not much. I just move in and move out, take some beaver or something. Trade with them sometimes. Once in a while, I get a bad feeling, like an itch for it in the middle of my chest."

"What do you mean an itch?" asked Caleb.

"An arrow."

"Have you always worked the trail, leading folks?" asked Julie.

"Pretty much. Though since the railroad got built, I go up north for the trappin'. Beaver and bear and such." Johnson chewed the last piece of his meat and stood and stretched by the fire. "I'll say this, Caleb O'Toole, I never saw the likes of what you did today from a young man yer age. Boy, you sure can handle that black of yours. And I am proud to have you alongside. Not a bad shot now too."

"I'm proud of you too, Caleb. I'm going to fetch Tilly and turn in." Julie squeezed Caleb's shoulder in affection. "Good night, Mr. Johnson."

"Night, missy," answered Johnson as he nodded to Julie.

"You may call me Julie or Miss O'Toole," said Julie, her eyes narrowing.

"Well, excuse my disrespect. I should say Miss O'Toole," nodded Mr. Johnson. Caleb couldn't help but smile as his sister walked off to the Smiths' wagon to get Tilly. With her medical bag in one hand and the heavy Colt in her pocket, Julie was becoming a woman to be reckoned with.

"Anyway, you did real good today. A father would bust his buttons to have a son like you."

"Thanks," said Caleb, glowing in the man's praise. "But it was Pride who turned the buffalo."

"Ha! I know better." Johnson ruffled Caleb's hair and jammed his beaver fur hat onto his snow-white head. "Well, I'm gonna turn in. In a day or two, we make the Bluff and something in my bones tells me we got trouble after today and what these gall-darn fools did."

"What kind of trouble?" asked Caleb as he kicked out the campfire.

"Sioux trouble," said Johnson as he headed off to his campsite.

★ ★ ★

Caleb rode in the deep ruts of the trail toward the split between the towering cliffs of Scotts Bluff, the wagon train a few miles behind. There must have been many thousands of wagons passing through over decades to make these grooves in the rocky trail, he thought. The sun beat down mercilessly, but even in the heat of the dusty prairie, he got chills from the glorious sight of the huge, fortress-like mountain of rock. It stood before him like a forbidden gateway to the unknown. Pioneers had talked of Scotts Bluff as the main landmark to the West. The landscape was changing, flat prairie turning to rocky hills and canyons. And in these hills, secrets lay hidden. Posey and Johnson rode beside him, ever on the watch for trouble, for trouble was known in these parts. As they rode along the trail through the vast split of the rock, Caleb couldn't help but reach back and take hold of his Sharps. On his hip, he wore Jumping Dog's knife and he touched it. The hilt of the large weapon gave him the slightest comfort as Pride surged forward, nostrils flaring and ears up, listening for some sound of danger.

"Don't matter how many times I pass through here, it gives me pause." Johnson grabbed his Henry rifle and racked a bullet into the chamber. Then he reached for his telescope and checked the hills. "Looks pretty quiet though, don't it?"

"Hold that thought 'til we get through Mitchell Pass," said Posey. "Caleb, why don't you take Pride up ahead while we scout along the sides of these cliffs?"

"Naw, I'll go." Johnson checked out the trail with his telescope. "I'll fire one if there's trouble. Two and you know what to do." The trapper kicked his horse ahead and soon disappeared through the rocks and scrub trees.

"I'll head left and you ride up on the right. Got that?" Posey nodded at Caleb as he moved toward the cliffs on the left of the trail.

"What's two for?" asked Caleb nervously.

"Run like the devil," said Posey over his shoulder.

★ ★ ★

Caleb took a deep breath and led Pride through the grassy hills toward the vast rock cliffs on the right, his senses alert for every sound. He reached for his rifle and checked to make sure it was loaded. His eyes were clear and sharp as he watched a hawk circle lazily in the sky. Caleb took a deep breath, his nostrils filling with the scent of dust and grass. Every fiber in his soul was alive, ready to warn him of the slightest danger. As he rode close along the huge rocky mountain, he could see initials carved into the sandstone, initials made by travelers passing through. Some were dated thirty years before. Pride suddenly jumped back in alarm and skittered on the rocky trail. Caleb pulled him back farther, curious to see what spooked the big warhorse. Then he heard the *rattle* of warning. Just to the side of the trail, a massive rattlesnake lay perfectly coiled and hidden in the grass. Caleb had seen many during the journey. At first, they were quite frightening. But as the weeks passed, Caleb accepted them as part of their travels, and he made sure to give the poisonous vipers a wide berth. *Don't bother them and they won't bother you*, he thought, *just don't get yourself bit by one*. He sat on Pride and watched the snake as it calmed and ceased its rattling, slowly disappearing into the hidden grassy world.

It had been an hour since he had seen either Posey or Johnson as Caleb worked the right side of Mitchell Pass. It was eerily quiet. The insect sounds buzzed faintly, and a gentle breeze and the whisper of prairie grass were Caleb's only companions. That and the steady breathing of Pride. Caleb paused near some trees and dismounted, stretching the ache from the miles in the saddle, weeks on the trail. He lifted his canteen from the saddle horn, popped off the cork, and took a long drink. As he stuck the cork back in, something caught his eye. It was ever so faint, the movement on the cliff. Was it an animal? A coyote? He shifted his gaze farther along the trail and saw another slight movement. Then another. The hair on the back of his neck stood up and he leaped onto Pride. Something was wrong!

The blast of two shots echoed through the canyon. Racing like a madman, Posey came galloping up toward Caleb, fear frozen on the man's face as he tore past.

"Run!" shouted Posey as he whipped Devil in a furious gallop. "Get back to the wagons! There's Sioux hidden all over the trail!"

"Where's Johnson?" cried Caleb as he rode Pride alongside Posey.

"They got him trapped!" Posey lashed Devil hard. "He's lost. Run, boy!"

"Is he dead?" shouted Caleb.

"He will be," yelled Posey. "Save yourself!"

Several more gunshots boomed in the distance. Then Caleb heard the loud report of Johnson's Henry rifle. He's alive! As Posey galloped back toward the wagon train, Caleb turned Pride and headed fast in the direction of the gunfire. Ben Johnson was fighting for his life, and all Caleb could think about was trying to help the trapper. "Ya, Pride!" Caleb rode like the wind toward the smoke of gunpowder, Pride's thundering hooves tearing up the trail.

Branches tore at Caleb's face as he pushed Pride hard through a cluster of pine trees along a dry riverbed. As he came to a clearing, he saw Johnson firing from some boulders a hundred yards away. Drawing closer, he could see his friend was bleeding from an arrow in his chest, struggling to reload his Henry rifle. Two Indians lay dead or wounded in the dirt in front of him. Dozens more Sioux were climbing down the cliff on the left, some firing guns while others shot arrows from their bows. Caleb grabbed his Sharps, leaped off Pride, and took cover in rocks. Crawling on his belly, he made his way to his right to try to protect his friend from behind. *THWACK.* Another arrow caught the trapper in the thigh and he crashed to the ground near the two fallen Sioux. Johnson's death loomed ever closer and he no longer had the strength to aim his heavy rifle. He reached for his pistol as a warrior leaped toward him with a tomahawk. Caleb aimed and fired just in time. The Indian grabbed his shoulder and went down. Caleb slid under a rocky overhang and fired and reloaded with precision. The advancing warriors began to scatter behind boulders for cover. Caleb ducked down quickly as arrows flew into the granite rocks just over his head. Johnson staggered toward his horse on the other side of the boulders, waving his pistol, signaling Caleb to move away. Caleb grabbed more bullets and ran back toward Pride, firing his Sharps as fast as he could. His heart pounded, but he also felt a strange sense of calm and purpose. Johnson fired his Colt at the Sioux hidden behind the rocks as he tried to get to his horse, pulling at the arrow in his chest.

Caleb leaped onto Pride and circled through the scrub trees until he got behind the Indians, firing quickly as he tried to draw their attention away from his friend. "Come on!" cried Caleb. "You can make it!" Caleb swung the Sharps and got off a shot as an Indian tried to run up and shoot an arrow into Johnson's horse. The Sioux warrior's leg buckled and he went to the ground. Johnson fired his Colt again and again as he struggled onto his horse and bolted from the ambush. Caleb turned Pride around and raced through the trees after Johnson.

"Go, boy! Let's get out of here!" Blood was pouring from the arrow wound in Johnson's chest, and he desperately gripped the reins. "Take the Henry!" He threw the big rifle, and Caleb caught it as they sped away from the Indians.

They were everywhere along the cliffs! Caleb could see all around him as the Indians exposed themselves, firing from their hiding places. "Go, Pride!" yelled Caleb as he brought the repeater Henry rifle to bear. Caleb kept up a steady fire as they raced back through Mitchell Pass toward the wagon train. Johnson, bleeding from his wounds, gripped his saddle horn and bent low. An arrow screamed by Caleb and tore off his hat. A flash of pain seared across his head and a trickle of blood blinded his right eye for a second, but Caleb brushed it away. He let go of the reins and fired the Henry to his left as an Indian rose to launch another arrow. The Sioux warrior went down, but Caleb felt the impact of the arrow as it grazed his left shoulder, tearing through his shirt. Another arrow hit Johnson in his side, and he struggled desperately to stay on his horse.

"Go on, Caleb, save yourself. I'm killed. Go on!"

"We'll make it!" Caleb grabbed the other horse's reins and ducked down. An arrow grazed Pride through his mane, but the big horse kept pounding his way through the pass. Caleb looked over his shoulder. Many of the Indians had mounted and were riding down hard after them. On Caleb and Johnson rode, just ahead of the Sioux warriors. It seemed the farther back through the pass they went, the more Indians appeared along the cliffs. It was an ambush of some planning. Time stood still as they rode like wind, until finally they could see the wagons. They had nearly circled at the entrance to Scotts Bluff, but left a small opening that was big enough to ride through. The rocky cliffs echoed with the Sioux gunfire from behind.

Caleb raced Pride down toward the wagon train, Johnson's

horse in hand. Bullets tore through the air all around him. Blood poured from his aching shoulder. Finally, they galloped through the opening in the circle, just as some men pushed two large wagons together, closing the entrance shut. Captain Bellows, his sword in his hand, gave a signal and a great roar opened up as the pioneers fired their long rifles at the pursuing Indians. Caleb let go of Johnson's horse and vaulted off Pride. He grabbed the Henry and the Sharps, looking frantically for Julie and Tilly through the smoke of the fight. There, some fifty yards away, he saw his sisters crouched under their little wagon.

"Are you all right?" Caleb ran to his sister and dove under his wagon with the two rifles.

"Caleb!" she cried. "I was so afraid. Posey said you went back to help Johnson. We thought you were killed! What happened?"

"There's no time!" yelled Caleb over the din of the gunfire. "Take Tilly and the horses behind the wagons in the center!" Caleb shot a look to the men who were desperately dragging wagons to the middle to protect the women and children.

"Tilly! Come with me!" Julie reached for Tilly's hand and ran to the safety of the wagons. Tumble scrambled out from under the wagon and took off after them.

Caleb fired the Henry rifle as a wave of Sioux Indians rode down from Scotts Bluff, some firing rifles, others arrows. Caleb cursed to himself as he missed the lead rider. *CLICK!* He was out of cartridges and quickly reached into his pocket to reload. Several Sioux warriors rode swiftly toward the

160

wagons, firing their guns at the inexperienced pioneers. Two arrows struck the buckboard near Caleb's head, and he scrambled behind the spokes of the wheel for cover as they raced past. Right behind them were six more warriors riding down on him as he frantically tried to load the Henry. *They don't fit!* Caleb thought as he tried to jam the bullets from the Sharps into the Henry. Suddenly, a Sioux with his bow drawn back galloped straight for Caleb. Caleb rolled under the wagon to his right and dove for the Sharps. He grabbed a handful of cartridges and slammed one into the chamber. Caleb fired just as the Indian shot his arrow. He missed, but startled the Indian. The arrow slid just past Caleb, nicking his neck, and stuck into the wheel of the wagon. Without thinking, Caleb slipped another shell into the rifle from the webbing of his fingers and fired. The warrior went down hard off his horse. Caleb reloaded, ready to fire again, but the Indian lay still. Caleb stared at the fallen Indian, realizing he may have killed him. He started to feel dizzy from the loss of blood, and he tore off a piece of his shirt to tie it around his wound. His heart jumped at the sound of Bellows's booming voice.

"Caleb!" roared Bellows. "Get that Henry going!" Captain Bellows tossed a bag of cartridges to Caleb as he shouted orders up and down the wagon train, impervious to the arrows and bullets whizzing through the air.

"Yes, sir!" Caleb caught the bag of bullets. He quickly loaded the Henry just as another wave of Indians began to circle the wagons. The big rifle roared in Caleb's nimble, strong hands, and another Sioux warrior went down. Just then, Julie appeared by his side under the wagon. "What are you doing? Go back with Tilly and the others!"

"Not on your life!" shouted Julie as she took out her Colt pistol. She fired on the Sioux warriors. "I'm not leaving you!" Julie set her teeth and fired alongside her brother.

On the Sioux Indians attacked and the pioneers answered with volleys of their own. Through the smoke and the confusion, Captain Bellows was able to maintain their defense and the brave men and women, these dreamers from all lands, fought like they had never fought before.

"I'm out of bullets!" exclaimed Julie.

"Here, take the Sharps," said Caleb weakly, the blood pouring from his shoulder and head.

Julie reached for the rifle, but there was no further need. The Indians had stopped firing.

"Cease fire!" ordered Captain Bellows. Gradually, the pioneers obeyed and stopped firing. The Sioux had backed away.

Caleb began to shake. His entire body trembled, his bloodied hands desperately holding onto the Henry rifle. He brought the rifle to sight in on the Indians, but his hands would not obey. "I can't hold the Henry," exclaimed Caleb. Caleb tried to focus on his sister, but his eyes betrayed him. He tried to reach out for Julie, but touched only air. Suddenly, everything went black.

13

FORT FETTERMAN

★ ★ ★ ★ ★ ★ ★ ★ ★ ★ ★ ★ ★ ★ ★ ★ ★ ★ ★

Caleb struggled to breathe, to gain some sense of his wits. All seemed lost in his nightmare of pain. He choked on the dust that kicked up in the blowing wind. Why was he in the wagon? Why were they stopped? He could barely lift his head he was so weak. His breath came ragged. He finally managed to ease himself up a few inches. In the fog of his mind, he could see men in black dusters coming toward him. The Blackstones! Caleb reached for his Sharps and weakly pulled back the hammer to check for a bullet. His movements were like lead, his reactions gone. The men in black were nearly alongside him. Caleb found a bullet in his pocket and chambered the round. His hands shook as he tried to lift his rifle.

"Julie," he called weakly to his sister. "They're here. Julie, the Blackstones!"

"Easy, Caleb," said Julie as she leaned toward him and took the Sharps from his hands. "There are no Blackstones." She reassured Caleb and stroked his sweating brow, cooling it with a wet cloth. "It's all right, they're Mormons. Those men in the black coats are leaders. Their wagons crossed over the river at Fort Laramie. They've been trailing us. They're all headed to Utah and the Mormon Trail. We're just outside Fort Fetterman."

"Fort Fetterman?" Caleb tried to shake himself alert and grasp where they were. "But, that's well over a hundred miles from…"

"From the attack in Scotts Bluff. I know. You have been in and out for days, and I thought we were going to lose you. You lost a lot of blood."

"I can't think…it's all a haze. What happened?" Caleb wondered as he tried to piece the events together. Gingerly he touched his bandaged shoulder and winced from the pain. His head was bandaged too, and he ached all over. "The last thing I remember is the Indians stopped shooting."

"Captain Bellows made a truce with the Sioux and gave them some of the oxen and some horses," said Julie as she checked Caleb's bandages. "We picked up a troop escort from Fort Laramie after that."

"What, a truce? Why did they take the oxen?"

"It was payment for what the settlers did to the buffalo. They attacked us because of the buffalo. We lost nearly twenty people, and the Sioux lost many as well." Julie saw in Caleb's eyes the pain of the battle.

"They let us go," Caleb wondered aloud. "After all that, it was because of the buffalo. People killed each other because of…I killed because…"

"I see he's up!" Captain Bellows walked up with some of his sentries who fell in step behind him. "Corporal Posey!"

"Yes, Captain Bellows!" snapped Posey.

"Bring me that Henry rifle!" ordered Bellows as he peered hard at Caleb, a whisper of a smile appearing on his weathered lips.

"Got it right here, sir!" Posey and other men gathered around Caleb.

Bellows grabbed the rifle and checked the chamber. "You men think anyone else deserves this rifle more than this brave young soldier here?"

"No, sir!" shouted the former soldiers.

"That is the most accurate statement I've heard this whole expedition! This young soldier deserves a medal for his action in battle, and if I had one, I'd give it to him!" roared Bellows. Then he took the Henry and put it in Caleb's hands.

Caleb felt the heft of the big rifle. "But, this is Ben Johnson's Henry, Captain Bellows." Then a wave of sadness moved through him as he remembered the trapper's wounds. "Did he make it?"

"No," said Julie as she tried to comfort Caleb. "He died the same day, Caleb. We tried to stop the bleeding, but he took an arrow in his heart."

"One of the last things old Ben said was for you to take this Henry rifle of his. He told us what you did for him and he was grateful to make it back with his hair, white as it was. Laughed about that. Wanted you to keep these too, since you got your hat shot off." Captain Bellows signaled to a sentry who brought over the trapper's telescope and the beaver hat and coat made out of animal skins. "Where you're going, you'll need 'em, though I could very well make a play for you to travel on with us, as you are a young man of some use. We make for Oregon in the morning."

Caleb ran his hands over the coat his friend had left for him. It was large and made from bear and beaver. Rabbit fur lined the cap and the flaps for the ears, soft to his touch. He would miss his trapper friend. The Henry rifle had saved them both. At least for a short time.

"Captain Bellows," said Caleb as he sat up in the wagon. "I thank you for letting us travel with you, but we'll make for Virginia City as soon as we can find provisions for the journey up the Bozeman Trail. We have family there."

"Sorry to see you go. You head to the fort and see Captain Vliet. He's an old friend of mine." Bellows stuck out his hand to Caleb. "He'll get you outfitted. I'll be there later today."

"Thanks, Captain." Caleb shook the man's hand. "We'll do that."

★ ★ ★

Caleb, too sore to ride Pride, sat in the wagon next to Julie as Dusty trotted down the road toward Fort Fetterman. Tilly sat with Tumble in the back. Fort Fetterman rose in desolation like it may as well have been the last place on earth. Caleb wondered how anyone would choose to live in such a dreary place. The gloomy landscape was bare, not a tree in sight, but in the distance loomed shadows of higher ground, and beyond that, the Big Horn Mountains. Pride was tied to the buckboard, prancing proudly. Part of his black mane had been shorn, stitches added by Julie to close the arrow wound. Julie handled the wagon through the troops who rode or walked among the wagon trains that lined the streets. Outfitter shacks were set up everywhere, piles of goods and furs stacked against sparse wooden structures, all to sell or trade to the pioneers heading farther west on the Oregon Trail or north up the Bozeman. Fort Fetterman was the last outpost along the Platte River, and folks were lined up. Caleb held Johnson's hat and coat, wondering how they would fit, as the garments were much too big for his twelve-year-old body.

"I can fix those," said Julie with a smile, having read his mind. Caleb returned her smile. Several soldiers walking along the road noticed them drive by. One of them whistled at Julie.

"Hey there, purdy girl," said the soldier. "You need any help with that wagon? We'll get you suited up proper, won't we, fellas?" The other two soldiers nodded in agreement as they watched Julie with a certain unmistakable admiration.

"No, thank you, sir, I'll do just fine." Julie winked at Caleb. "But I am sure that whistle was meant for your dog, and I am guessing he will be along shortly, for I cannot imagine you would be so crass as to summon me that way." This got a rise out of the two soldiers, who whooped and hollered, teasing their friend. The whistling soldier spit out a wad of tobacco, stung from Julie's retort.

"Good one," Caleb chuckled.

"The fool," sniffed Julie. "One day he'll learn we women don't appreciate that sort of thing. Man doesn't know who he's dealing with."

"That's for sure." Still, he remembered just some months ago when he thought of his sister as just a girl, himself just a boy. But all that they had been through was changing that. As they drove down the road to the fort, they noted many Indians. They were trading with the settlers and travelers. Some were mounted on horses as they ascended the hill that led to the entrance of the fort. Caleb figured they were scouts for the army, as some were dressed in old Union Civil War jackets. Goods and supplies were being loaded onto war wagons. Cannons were lined up as if the troops were outfitting for a great campaign. Caleb wondered what battle they were preparing for. "Over there," said Caleb as he spotted the command office. Two soldiers walked over to the wagon as they pulled up.

"You Caleb O'Toole?" asked one of the soldiers. He was a handsome young man of about eighteen. He smiled some white teeth at Julie.

"Yes, sir," said Caleb as he eased himself off the wagon.

"Captain Vliet says to outfit you for the Bozeman Trail. I'll load you up while you go inside." The soldier pointed to the commander's office. "Go on in, he wants to meet you. What kind of cartridges you need? I see you got a Henry."

"Forty-fives for the Henry. I can take fifties in the Sharps," said Caleb.

"How about that Colt, ma'am?" The soldier eyed the handle of Julie's pistol sticking out of her pocket. "Pretty hefty gun there."

"It's a forty-five, sir," said Julie, smiling at the handsome young man. "I can handle it."

"Coming up," said the soldier admiringly to Julie. Then he nodded to Caleb. "Might want to convert the Sharps to forty-fives so everything shoots the same bullet. Easier that way. Pull up over there and I'll load you." He pointed to a wagon stocked with goods on the far end of the fort.

"Go on," said Julie to Caleb. "I'll stay here with Tilly." She drove the wagon across the fort to the stack of supplies.

★ ★ ★

Caleb stepped onto the wooden porch of the command office and peered through the window. Inside he could see the man who must have been Captain Vliet sitting at his desk. As Caleb turned toward the door, he heard Captain Bellows's booming voice.

"Henderson! William Henderson? Same one they jailed at Leavenworth?"

Caleb pulled back his hand just as he started to knock on the door. He ducked out of sight quickly, listening quietly, watching to see if anyone noticed him.

"That's the man," said Captain Vliet, who shuffled some papers on his desk. "Just dug out these wires I had filed away from weeks ago. Thought the names sounded familiar, these O'Tooles. Says here Henderson killed some folks in Great Bend and Dobytown, then stuck the Sheriff down in Cottonwood Springs in his own jail. Maybe he lost his mind after Leavenworth."

"Got to tell you, I did get a feeling about that big black horse Caleb is riding. Got N.V., Nebraska Volunteers, burned in the saddle. Must be Henderson's horse. Could be he got killed, that's why the boy's got him. But Henderson losing his mind don't make sense to me. I rode with the man years ago. Best fighter I ever saw. Heard he went after those who killed his family, caught up with a few. But the man's mind was as strong as they come. Must be some mistake," said Captain Bellows.

"Well, says these O'Toole children are riding with him. I got a handful of telegraphs from that Dobytown Sheriff, uh, Blackstone I think, saying to wire them if they show up around here. Supposed to be heading Montana way." Captain Vliet waved the papers in his hand. "You say this Caleb O'Toole is headed for Virginia City?"

"That's my understanding. Apparently, they have family there. My man Johnson said they buried the mother and father in Great Bend."

"Don't make sense they'd be riding with Henderson," mused Vliet. "And, Lord, Virginia City of all places. There's a lot of Sioux between here and there, not to mention they got problems with the Nez Perce up that way near Bannack. I tried to hold back a train of six wagons just last week. Folks from somewhere back east heading up for the gold, the fools. That's wild country up that way."

"I hear Colonel Gibbons rode up with his men to deal with the Nez Perce," said Bellows.

"That's right. Sioux must have burned down some wires so we haven't heard anything from up that way. Anyway, I maybe oughta keep those O'Tooles here in the fort until I hear back from Sheriff Blackstone of Dobytown. Might be a few days until the wires are up. I got patrols coming through here to fix it all. Don't have the manpower to escort anybody north. Tarnation, half my men want out of here. But, we'll outfit 'em, see they're supplied. If everything checks out, maybe they can hook up with another wagon train heading north."

"Appreciate it. Boy did a lot for us. I expect he'll be coming around any minute," said Bellows. "Meantime, Captain, please tell me you have some of that famous whiskey of yours."

"Captain Bellows, you old warhorse, got just the thing," chuckled Vliet as he pulled a bottle of whiskey from his desk.

★ ★ ★

Caleb walked swiftly to the wagon. There was no way they could stay at Fort Fetterman. There was no telling how close the Blackstones were, or even if they were still pursuing them. Caleb figured they would likely go after Henderson, but he couldn't afford to take that chance. They had to leave now. The soldiers had gone off somewhere and there was no one to stop them.

"Let's go. Hurry." Caleb went quickly to untie Pride.

"Caleb, they haven't finished loading us yet," said Julie. "We've got the ammunition, but we still need food and grain."

"If we don't leave now, we're stuck here for days." Caleb struggled to saddle Pride. His shoulder was killing him, but he shrugged off the pain. "They're tracking us through the telegraph wires."

"Who's tracking us? The Blackstones?"

"Yes. I heard that Captain talking about what happened in the Dobytown saloon. We have to go right now. Where's Tilly?" Caleb looked around for his little sister. She and Tumble were nowhere to be found.

"She's with that soldier. She has him promising to give her sweets," said Julie.

"We've got to get out of here before Captain Vliet sees us. Once he does, he won't let us leave."

"I'll get her. You see if you can find any food. Those soldiers were unloading that wagon over there next to the stables. Sacks of grain, I think. Be right back." Julie ran off around the barracks.

Caleb waited until the two troopers disappeared into the stable with the horses. He trotted over to the barn door and peered inside. The men looked occupied with the horses. Caleb went over to the wagon, and with his good arm, pulled himself aboard. Taking a look to make sure no one was watching, he began rummaging through the supplies. He found hardtack, beans, grain, and salted bacon. *Well*, he thought, *they said they were going to outfit us. Might as well give them a hand.* He picked up a case of beans in one hand

and gingerly grabbed some hardtack with his wounded arm, then ran back to the wagon. After he added some bacon and some grain, Julie came running around from the side of the barracks with Tilly and Tumble. Just then, a large platoon of soldiers rode into the fort.

"That was quick," said Caleb as he mounted Pride.

"That was a nice young man, that soldier," offered Julie with a smile.

"Look!" Tilly held up a handful of licorice as she climbed aboard the wagon. "He gave this to me!"

"You would be surprised what a smile can do, Caleb," winked Julie. "Must be some awfully lonely soldiers in this fort. Let's go." She gave the reins a shake and Dusty tugged the wagon around in a circle and headed toward the fort's entrance.

"Slow." Caleb urged Pride forward and nodded to the soldiers on horseback. "Captain Bellows and that commander are still sharing a drink. Let's not attract attention."

Caleb rode Pride out of Fort Fetterman and headed north on the main road. Fur traders, their skins piled high on mules, trotted past them. Julie drove right behind Caleb as they passed shabby wooden shacks. The Mormon wagon train was just ahead, the leaders standing guard like military men while the travelers bought and traded goods for their journey west. They kept apart from other pioneers, preferring not to engage. Caleb noticed a woman bending over one of the men, dabbing a great wound as she sewed a gash in his head.

"Caleb!" cried Julie. Caleb turned Pride around and rode to the wagon. "Wait!"

"What's wrong?"

"I need some more thread. I used the last of it stitching Pride up." Julie pulled Dusty to stop and grabbed her medical bag. "I'll just be a second."

Caleb had yet to see his own wound; he had been so intent on getting his supplies and then leaving the fort. Carefully, he peeled back his shirt. His raw, red shoulder had been neatly sewn. He ran his fingers along the stitches as he gazed in wonder at his sister. She and his mother were known for their sewing, and it was apparent in her ability to take care of his shoulder. Pride's wound had the same pattern of thread. He watched as Julie began an animated conversation with the Mormon prairie doctor. She opened her medical bag and displayed several instruments. Caleb shook his head in wonder as Julie made her trade, then offered her hand in gratitude.

"All right, we can go now. I have thread, more needles, disinfectant, and even chloroform, though I hope we don't need that, since I don't know how to do it. Might come in handy, though." Julie jumped aboard the wagon. "All it cost me was a tooth puller and a surgical knife, oh, and the bacon."

"But we need the bacon," protested Caleb. He figured they had at least weeks of travel over another four hundred miles.

"Well, we have the beans, which should last for a while." Julie reached for the bacon in the back of the wagon. "Besides, I have faith in you. From what they say, there's more game farther north. The way you shoot, we should be fine."

14

THE BLOODY
BOZEMAN TRAIL

★ ★ ★ ★ ★ ★ ★ ★ ★ ★ ★ ★ ★ ★ ★ ★ ★

Caleb fired and the deer dropped in its tracks a hundred yards away. Caleb put the Sharps back in its scabbard and eased Pride over to the fallen deer. The Henry rifle he left behind with Julie for protection while he hunted. Julie was right. He had done well. They'd had no problem finding game, for deer and antelope were plentiful. Caleb settled into hunting like a natural, having learned from Ben Johnson about wind and distance. A sharpshooter during the war and a trapper, Johnson had been a man who knew his business, and Caleb had been a good student. Now Caleb wore the trapper's animal skins and hat. Julie, true to her word, had cut and sewn them to fit Caleb. He blended into the land like he was born to it. And the land of Wyoming Territory was changing as they traveled along the Bozeman Trail. The mountains of the Big Horn loomed in the distance. Great splashes of red rock and pine trees replaced the monotonous prairie and the region was taking on a more majestic beauty.

Canyons cut by rivers provided them shelter as well as good fishing. Tilly even managed to pull in a big trout using a hand line that Julie had made her, gleefully dancing at the water's edge in celebration.

It must be the middle of August, Caleb thought as he sweated over the task of cleaning the deer. Jumping Dog's knife was razor-sharp, and he had no trouble with cutting away the tough hide. The days of their journey on the Bozeman Trail had been uneventful, and they were making good time, except for a day wasted on having to fix the wagon wheel. There had been trappers and friendly Indians, but so far the hundred miles up Bloody Bozeman had been pretty tame. In their effort to catch the small wagon train he had learned about from over-hearing Captain Vliet, Caleb had forced them to make close to twenty miles a day. There had been no sign of the wagon train, but Caleb could tell from the droppings of the animals that they were closing the gap. They hit the trail north hard in the effort to put as much distance as they could between them and Fort Fetterman, and any farther delay would have brought the Blackstones that much closer. Visions of the murderous brothers appeared in Caleb's sleep and he could not shake the feeling that somewhere he and his sisters were being tracked, dogged. So far, they had been lucky. He wondered if their luck would hold as he bent down to the deer and hoisted a hind leg onto the back of Pride. He felt bad about leaving the rest of the deer, but he had no way of keeping it fresh enough to eat. The coyotes or wolves would make short work of the remains, he figured. Or the buzzards that circled in the sky. He watched the large birds arcing lazily, waiting for their turn to eat. That's when he noticed the smoke.

Caleb rode Pride fast through the canyon and splashed across the river. He wasn't worried about Julie and Tilly, for they were a mile or so back on the trail. He held on to the deer as he charged up the hill and pulled Pride up behind the rocks. Then he took his telescope out and searched the horizon. The smoke rose above a cluster of trees about half a mile ahead and some distance off the trail. He urged Pride closer to get a better look. As he entered the tree line, he stopped and raised his telescope. There! Over by a ravine to the right of the trail, he could make out several burning wagons. Whatever had happened, he figured he needed to get back to his sisters, for whoever was out there may have heard him shoot the deer.

"Let's go, Pride!" Caleb tossed the deer to the ground, turned Pride around and galloped back on the trail to Julie and Tilly. He would hunt another day. Making sure his sisters were safe was his main concern. He headed toward the rocks where they agreed they would meet after the hunt. In a few minutes' time, he spotted Julie racing toward him in the wagon. *She must have seen the smoke as well*, he thought as he rode up to his sister.

★ ★ ★

"See anything?" asked Julie as she peered out from the trees where they lay hidden.

"It looks bad," Caleb said, looking through his telescope.

"It must be the wagon train we've been looking for. Six wagons all burned. I see bodies with arrows sticking in them lying on the ground. No one's moving. Must have been the Sioux."

"Should we try to help? Someone might still be alive."

"Maybe. I don't see any Indians. They took the horses, so I guess they're all gone. But keep Tilly away. She shouldn't see this." Caleb brought Pride around and took out his Henry rifle. Julie pulled out her Colt as she climbed aboard the wagon.

As they approached the burning wagon train, Julie stopped Dusty fifty feet away from the closest wagon. "Tilly, you stay here with Tumble and hide way down low so I can't see you, OK?" Tilly nodded and grabbed Tumble and hid under a blanket. Caleb dismounted, and together they walked toward the smoking ruins.

It was a massacre. No one had survived. Ten men, five women, and several children were all strewn about, arrows sticking from their bodies. Two horses lay dead. It must have happened that morning, for birds had gotten to some of the corpses and flies buzzed all around them. "Caleb!" cried Julie as she stared down at a woman who lay dead. "It's that same woman from before, the one who wouldn't help Tilly."

"Bess." Caleb looked at the badly burned corpse of the pioneer woman. So this had been their fate. All their dreams destroyed in a murderous attack by the Sioux. They had journeyed all this way, only to the violent end of their lives instead of the gold they were seeking. "That's the wagon master," said Caleb as he walked over to the body. He turned white as he looked at the mutilated corpse. His chest had been slashed open.

"They took his heart, Caleb." Julie turned away from the body, and together they looked around at the bloody scene of the massacre.

"Look!" Caleb pointed to a trail of blood that led away from the camp. "One of them might have escaped." The blood led to a ravine some fifty yards away. It was possible someone survived and lay hidden in the rocks. "Keep watch here with the Henry rifle. I'll see if they're still alive."

"Be careful, Caleb."

Caleb followed the blood trail through the rocks and into the ravine. It looked as though the wounded victim was dragging himself forward. As he lowered himself toward the small creek below, he saw boots sticking out from behind a boulder. In the creek below, an Indian pony stood along the water, drinking. Carefully, he advanced on the body, clutching his Sharps, looking from side to side for any movement, any sign of a Sioux warrior. The man was dead, several arrows sticking out of his back and leg. *There is nothing I can do for the man*, Caleb thought as he turned back toward the wagons. Suddenly an Indian leaped from the rocks above, emitting a violent war cry.

Caleb turned with his Sharps and tried to fire, but the warrior was too quick and landed on him. Together they went crashing down the rocky slope, rolling over and over, locked together in a fierce struggle. Desperately, Caleb tried to shake the Indian off and bring his rifle to bear, but the warrior had him by the throat and wrapped his legs around Caleb, trying to choke him. Caleb threw his elbow back and connected with the Indian's jaw with a solid crack. The Sioux warrior was young and fast, and he fought like a wildcat. Caleb could see that the Indian was bleeding a little from his side. The warrior had no weapon of his own, but he picked up a rock as they tumbled to the ground toward the water and smashed it against Caleb's head. Caleb fought off the blinding light of pain as he held on desperately to his Sharps, but the Indian had the upper hand and pried it away from Caleb. Caleb lunged at the Indian before the warrior could turn the rifle on him, and reached frantically for the trigger. Just as the Indian swung the barrel toward him, Caleb brushed the rifle aside, found the trigger, and pulled. *BOOM!* The Sharps exploded, but the bullet went wide of Caleb. The Indian pulled back the hammer and tried to fire again, but Caleb knew the Sharps was a single-shot rifle and the trigger clicked empty.

The Sioux warrior, seeing that he could not fire, swung the Sharps at Caleb's head, using it as a club. Caleb ducked, and in an instant, pulled out his knife and buried it in the Indian's side. Together they tumbled farther down the hill into the shallow water of the stream. A great breath escaped from the Indian's lips as Caleb held the knife into the warrior's side. Still the struggle continued, and they fought hard for their lives. Finally, the Indian weakened and he lost his grip on Caleb. As the young warrior stopped his struggles, Caleb raised the knife over his head, poised to deliver the final cut. Suddenly, his foe began to chant, as if knowing he was going to die. Caleb brought the knife to the Indian's throat and held it there. He could easily kill him, but something stopped his hand. The Sioux was just a boy, like him. A warrior boy, like Caleb.

★ ★ ★

"It's really bad, Caleb," said Julie as she examined the knife wound on the Indian. "It's a wonder he's still alive." Julie studied another wound near the boy's ribs. "It looks like he was shot here too, but it's only a crease."

"What should we do?" asked Caleb. "I guess we could just leave him. Maybe his people will find him. We had better be long gone if they come back looking for him."

Together they looked at the Sioux boy tied up in their wagon. They had carried him from the ravine and ridden to shelter for the night some distance up the creek from the burned-out wagon train. The boy's pony was tied behind. Tilly and Tumble lay near the fire on blankets, finishing the last of the beans. The sun glowed red as it set in the west.

"If we leave him, he'll surely die. Boil some water."

"What are you going to do?

"Try to stop the bleeding. I saw Dr. Sullivan do it on Henderson. She sewed him from the inside out."

"But she's a real doctor," protested Caleb. Then he touched his shoulder and the stitches she had done on him. "I'll cut some branches. Be right back."

Together Caleb and Julie prepared to help save the young

181

Sioux. Barely conscious, he did not struggle as they shifted him in the wagon. Julie cleaned his gaping knife wound and took out one of the instruments in her bag. As she increased the pressure and tried to pry the wound apart, the boy began to writhe in pain. Even tied up, he moved too much for her to continue her work. Unless he lay still, it would be impossible to help him.

"Hand me that bottle of chloroform." Julie tore off a piece of cloth from her shirt. "Soak this in it."

"Like this?" asked Caleb after he shook the smelly fluid onto the cloth.

"The book says to put it over his nose and mouth." Julie held the burning stick over the little medical book. "Go ahead, Caleb."

Caleb reached over to the Indian's face and stuck the cloth over his nose and mouth. Instantly the boy began to choke and struggle. "Hold him!" Julie grabbed the Indian's legs and held them down, half sitting on the boy. Caleb held the cloth on hard and soon the boy relaxed, passing out from the anesthetic.

"Well, that worked out pretty well," said Julie. "Hold the torch over him so I can see." Julie used the instrument to spread the knife wound. She carefully washed the wound with the clean pieces of cloth they had boiled. "See these in here?" Caleb saw the blood seeping deep within the wound. "These are veins. I watched Dr. Sullivan sew them up before she stitched the outside. Hand me the needle and thread."

Caleb watched in wonder as his sister, by instinct rather

than knowledge, performed the kind of surgery doctors did in battle. Whether it would work or not remained to be seen, but it was the Indian's only chance. It seemed to take hours as Julie patiently sewed up the boy. Once, Caleb had to give the Indian more of the anesthetic, but there was little struggle left in him. At first Caleb was queasy from the sight of all the blood and tissue, the damage he himself had inflicted while fighting for his life. After a while, he was used to it. Julie was not the least bit affected by the gore. To Caleb, she seemed as at home doing this as she was making a quilt. Finally, she was done. They let the Indian rest while they cleaned up the instruments.

"Now we'll wait and see." Julie stretched and headed over to Tilly and the blankets by the fire. Her shirt was a tattered, bloody mess and she had torn off more pieces of cloth. "If he's not dead by morning, he has a chance. Good night, Caleb." She slipped off the bloody shirt, buried herself in the blanket, and pulled sleepy Tilly next to her. "You might give him some water every now and then."

"All right. Good night." Caleb reached for the Henry rifle. "I'll take the first watch."

"Thank you, Caleb," said Julie as she closed her eyes. "Wake me in a few hours."

Caleb checked the boy one more time. *Well, he is breathing,* he thought. *We'll see what the morning brings.* Then he sat by the fire and listened to the night sounds, for wolves, mountain lions, coyotes, bears, Indians, anything that seemed unusual and dangerous. *Nothing,* he thought as he relaxed his hand on the Henry's trigger, *just the crickets.*

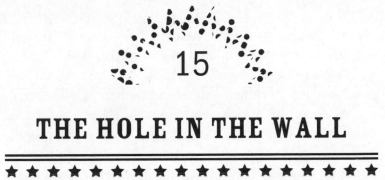

15

THE HOLE IN THE WALL

★ ★ ★ ★ ★ ★ ★ ★ ★ ★ ★ ★ ★ ★ ★ ★ ★ ★ ★ ★

Caleb looked up at the blazing sun and wiped his tired brow. He didn't know how they could go on after the last few days of rough, slow travel up the Bozeman Trail. They named the Sioux boy Patch, since he had survived that night and wore Julie's stitches like a patched-up doll. To make the travel easier for him, they had cut boughs of pine and made him a bed in the back of the wagon. The Indian would not speak and could not understand them, but Julie and Tilly took great care of him, feeding him, soaking his brow, making sure his bandages were clean and as fresh as they could. Julie went on and on, quoting from her medical book and talking of Dr. Sullivan. She vowed to return to see her one day, even tickled the thought of studying medicine just like her. One day.

They kept Patch tied up for his own good, lest the boy struggle and open his wounds. Caleb was in charge of taking him out a little ways from the wagon, away from his sisters, so the boy could relieve himself in private. He led him by a rope and held his Henry rifle on the Indian as he did his business. He felt bad about having to do that, but he could not trust Patch, even injured as the Indian was. Then he would lead him back and tie him up in the wagon. They didn't know if Patch hated them and wanted to kill them, or if he realized his life had been saved. It was hard to tell what Patch was thinking. But he was getting stronger during the days of travel. Mile after slow mile disappeared under the plodding hooves of faithful Dusty, and still there was no sign of the Sioux warriors.

"Here, Patch," said Tilly as she climbed onto the wagon to offer him some beans. She spooned out some beans and held it near Patch's lips. At first the boy just stared at Tilly, then he finally smiled, for the first time, and accepted the food. "Good!" She spooned out some more and Patch ate hungrily.

"He's feeling better," said Julie. "I figure in a day or two, we should let him go."

"Will his stitches hold up?" Caleb began to load the Henry rifle.

"I don't know, but the farther we take him, the farther he would have to get back to his people." Julie checked their supplies. "There are just two cans of beans left."

"I'll go look for some game. Do you want the Henry?"

"No, I'll be fine. I don't want to tempt Patch with it," Julie said.

"OK." Caleb jumped aboard the wagon and faced the Indian as Tilly fed him. "Patch, in a day or two we will let you go." Patch looked at Caleb as he chewed on the beans and shook his head. "Let's see," mused Caleb. Then he pointed to Patch and tried to sign, gesturing to Patch's horse and then back to Patch. After much effort, the Indian's face brightened and he nodded his head in understanding. "In one or two days," said Caleb as he counted his fingers. Then he pointed to the Indian's stitched wound and smiled. A look of relief crossed the Indian's face and he smiled back at Caleb. Caleb stuck out his hand and touched Patch's bound hands and wrists, and then he turned and jumped off the wagon.

"I should be back soon." Caleb took a look behind him as he mounted Pride. "I saw some tracks about a mile back. I'll double back and head east a little, and then I'll circle around."

"One if there's trouble," said Julie as she touched the handle of her Colt.

"Two, you know what to do." Caleb turned Pride around and headed south.

★ ★ ★

Caleb sat in the grass with his telescope and studied the horizon. It had been three hours and he had not seen a thing. He traveled east for a few miles, then back north, always keeping an eye on the landmarks he picked for the location of the wagon. He could not see the trail. In the distance, the Big Horn Mountains loomed in their majesty. Great canyons, giant gouges in the countryside, peppered with blazing red rock, beckoned in their timeless beauty. Plateaus against the brilliant blue sky revealed none of the deer or antelope that accompanied them on their journey north. Finally, Caleb turned back toward the trail. Though he felt defeated, he was confident he would find something the next day. "Let's get back, Pride," said Caleb as he put away the telescope and slipped the Henry into the deerskin scabbard Julie had made for the rifle.

Caleb sensed there was something wrong as he trotted Pride in the direction of the hollow in the trees where he had left Julie and the wagon. He could see hoofprints and fresh horse dung on the trail. Julie had not fired a shot. Worried, he broke Pride into a gallop as he got within a mile of their hiding place. He stormed into the camp, his Henry out and ready. His sisters and the wagon were gone! Panic began to seize him as Caleb brought Pride around in a circle, studying the ground, trying to read what now looked to be fresh tracks of at least three other horses.

"Julie!" called Caleb. "Tilly!" Caleb's blood ran cold as he saw that hoofprints had overrun the wagon's tracks. He leaped off Pride and ran his hands over the tracks of their wagon, noticing the cut in the wheel, the slice of a line. His greatest fear had been that they would somehow be separated from him, and now it had been realized. Julie and Tilly had been taken. His heart pounded in his ears. What was he to do? He began to feel more and more helpless as seconds ticked away. Caleb slowed his breathing and his senses began to return. He had to think, stay calm. He would track them! The weeks with Ben Johnson had taught him well, and he would put that knowledge to use. Caleb forced himself into action. He raised the Henry to fire a shot to signal his sister, but then stopped. Whoever was with them should not be alerted. It was better to be unseen, and he might need the advantage of surprise. Determination filled his heart as Caleb swung his leg over Pride and raced out on the trail. It would be dark in a few hours. He had to find them. There was no telling how far they were ahead, where they were, or exactly where they were going. He knew it was north, and from the look of the horse hooves, they were moving fast. "Come on, Pride!" Caleb broke the big warhorse into a run for his sisters' lives.

Caleb raced along the Bozeman Trail at breakneck speed as he tried to follow the wagon tracks. Pride tore up the earth with his giant, flying hooves. He figured he must be at least an hour behind, but Pride was making up ground fast. Vast mountains loomed on his left. He searched the trail as the sun dipped below the mountain peaks, his heart pounding and his legs aching as Pride covered the miles beneath him. Suddenly, the trail veered toward a grove of pine trees that grew scattershot on the mesa before him. The wagon tracks deepened in the sand as he took Pride down farther into the cut in the earth. All at once, the wagon tracks disappeared. Caleb brought Pride up quick and looked frantically for the tracks that seemed to have vanished into thin air. Then he saw what appeared to be chopped tumbleweeds between a rocky outcropping and some pine trees. He jumped off Pride and examined the tracks alongside the weeds. The tracks turned straight into them. Caleb moved the tumbleweeds and saw the cut wheel tracks and the hoofprints of the horses. A hidden trail! Quickly he tore away the bushes and the weeds, and then he walked Pride through the dense pine patch until he entered a cathedral-like bowl with boulders stacked high on either side. A stone archway lay before him that was just tall enough for a man and a single horse to get through. There, resting near the stone-walled cathedral, was his wagon.

Caleb looked into the wagon and found that everything still remained. There was no sign of Dusty or the Indian horse. No sign of Julie and Tilly, Tumble or Patch. Caleb studied the ground before him. He knelt and saw the tiny footprint of his little sister, Tumble's paws alongside. They led directly through the archway. Caleb mounted Pride and walked the big horse slowly through the stone arch. It was hard to see at first, and since the sun was setting, his task was all the more difficult. To Caleb, the stone cave smelled like death. He tried to shake the image from his mind as he continued through the passageway. Caleb leaned low over Pride, trusting that the big warhorse could see better than he could as they picked their way along the cave. After some distance, light appeared at the other end of the passageway.

Caleb walked Pride slowly out of the cave and stopped. Before him lay a tremendous ravine. He held his breath as he looked down over the sheer rock cliff. *Lord*, thought Caleb, *it must be five hundred feet down*. He stared in wonder at the sight of such awesome country, its deep red rocks disappearing into the blue river below. Reaching into the saddlebag behind him, he took out his telescope and searched the hills and rocks around him, realizing that this was a place that was meant to be secret. And if that were true, he was certainly not wanted here. As he scanned farther down the ravine, he saw a man with a rifle climb down from a rocky ledge. As he followed the man's descent, he spied a small cabin a half-mile down the winding trail. There, next to the river, several men sat around a growing campfire. Horses stood in a wooded area off to the side, feeding. Patch's pony! And tied to a tree nearby, Dusty!

Caleb followed the rocky trail down the side of the cliff, his Henry rifle at the ready. Pride slipped a little on the loose rock. The footing was bad, and just a few feet to his left, there was a drop of several hundred feet into the river. It was hard going, the sun completely down. A huge moon surfaced behind the rocky ravine on his right. His mind raced as he tried to imagine what he would do if he were seen and how he would deal with the men if he found his sisters. He felt for his knife and the big blade bounced against his hip. He knew from riding with Ben Johnson that his clothes hid him well. By the time Caleb reached the bottom of the ravine, the moon hung in the night sky like a beacon. Caleb slipped into the trees and tied off Pride. Then he crept over the rocks to the cabin, careful not to make a sound. Just the other side of the cabin, a second structure laid half-built, dark on the inside. Caleb sneaked along the ground some fifty feet away and slowly made his way to the second cabin. *I'll check that first*, he thought as he laid next to the structure, holding his breath, his heart beating so fast he could feel it in his ears. Slowly, he slithered to the window and peered inside. There, next to the moonlit window of the opposite wall, lay Patch. He was bound hand and foot, gagged, in pain and alone.

"Wolf, you three fools bring me two girls and an Indian? That ain't much of a haul!" Caleb's head snapped around at the sound of a man's voice coming from the main cabin.

"Well, Jake, just what do you think we ought to do with them?" another voice rang out.

"Ain't made up my mind yet," said Jake.

Caleb crept silently to the main cabin. Lantern light revealed a gap in the side of the wooden shack, and he peered inside. There were four of the toughest-looking men you would ever want to see. These must be some of the outlaws that Caleb had heard about from the newspapers, men who rode the trails, robbing pioneers and trains. Julie and Tilly sat off to the side, bound and gagged. Tumble was tied to the stove near Tilly.

"I bet we could get some money for 'em," said a rough-looking man with a black droopy mustache, slouched against the wall. "I mean, we can't rob any of the trains, they ain't running yet. And I tell you, it's daggone boring around here. I say we head south and sell 'em. Mexico maybe. Trains might be moving again after that. We hit one on the way back and ride back here to the Hole."

"Larson's got himself a good idea, Jake. The little one is like a fairy princess. Raise a fair price down in Mexico," said a scurvy-looking man who sat on the edge of a wooden table, staring at Tilly. His bowler hat sat ridiculously on his hatchet-like face. His fingers played freely with his pearl-handled Colt, twirling it round and round, as his glazed eyes turned to Julie. "We should keep the older one here for a while, though. For the cookin' and cleanin' and such."

"He's got a real good point there, Jake. Trigger and I go head Mexico way. You keep this older one here," said Wolf.

"Maybe. Though you boys have gotta take good care of her or she won't be worth beaver crap in Mexico." Jake, the apparent leader of the group, dapper in a worn suit, rose from his chair, walked over, and yanked Julie close to him. "What do you think there, girl?" he said as he slipped off her gag. "You could be my Hole in the Wall maid. You can start cleaning tomorrow, scrub some floors, cook us dinner."

"I would rather die." Julie leveled her fiery gaze at Jake. "Men like you disgust me." This brought a big laugh from the men. Even Jake appreciated the boldness that Julie displayed.

"I just wonder who you belong to, girl. Someone has got to be out there looking for the two of you," mused Jake.

"I told you. No one is looking. We're on our own. Our folks were killed a few days ago by the Sioux. We got away."

"She may be right," said Larson. "We saw some wagons still smoking back on the trail. We watched these three for an hour before we took 'em. No one showed up."

"Her folks got killed by Sioux and she saves a gall-darn Indian?" Jake scoffed. "Story's full of holes, girl." He slipped the gag back over her mouth and shoved her hard to the floor, where she landed painfully next to Tilly. Caleb tightened his grip on his rifle. He bit his lip as he watched his sister stand up to the outlaw, grateful she had not revealed anything about him. There were too many for him to fight. Even if he fired first and fast, surely he could not get all four before one or two of them would shoot him down. He relaxed his grip and calmed himself so his mind would stay clear.

The men sat gnawing on meat, drinking from a whiskey bottle. One threw a scrap to Tumble, who refused to eat it. The man lashed out and kicked Tumble with his boot. Tumble let out a painful yelp, bared his teeth, and tried to crawl toward Tilly.

"Tell you what," said Wolf as he took out his Colt and checked it. Dead eyes peering out of his wolflike face sized up Tumble. "When I'm done eatin', I'm gonna take that mutt out and shoot it. Worthless dog darn near took my leg off today."

"Should have shot it dead on the trail." Trigger gave Tumble a second kick and laughed as Tumble strained against the rope to take a bite out of him.

"Joe Wolf, you have to be the biggest fool. Firing off your gun to kill a dog is a right stupid idea. You'll bring whoever owns these kids around to the Hole, maybe some Indians too," said Jake as he took a swig from a bottle of whiskey. "You put the dog in that sack and throw him in the river and drown him. Besides, you should be out there anyway. It's your watch tonight."

"Dang it, Jake, ain't no one out there. I checked. Ain't nobody can even find the Hole in the Wall."

"You do what I say or you go find yourself another outfit to ride with," ordered Jake.

"OK, boss, whatever you say." Wolf picked up the sack. "Come here, you dern mutt." Wolf took out his knife and cut Tumble's rope. Then he grabbed him by the scruff. Tumble immediately latched his jaws onto his sleeve as Wolf tried to cram him into the sack. "Get in there, daggone it. Time to meet yer Maker!" Tumble tore the outlaw's sleeve off as he tried valiantly to break free. Wolf took out his Colt and smacked it against Tumble's head, then shoved the dog into the sack and tied it shut. "Dang tough little beast."

"What do we do with the Indian boy?" asked Trigger as he chuckled at Wolf's struggle.

"Hang him in the morning," said Jake as he took another swig of whiskey.

★ ★ ★

Caleb followed silently some fifty feet behind, staying hidden in the shadows of the rocks as Wolf walked to the river with Tumble in the sack. On the way, the outlaw paused to throw some more wood on the fire, dropping Tumble close to the flames. "Ought to just burn you," he mumbled as he picked up the sack. Caleb figured Tumble must be out cold from being hit on the head, for there was no movement inside the sack. As Wolf neared the river, Caleb sneaked up from behind, gripping the Henry rifle like a club. Wolf took hold of the sack with both hands. "Meet yer Maker, dang dog."

Wolf tossed the sack about ten feet into the river. "There you go!" Wolf laughed as he turned back toward the campfire. *SMACK!* With all his might, Caleb swung the heavy rifle and connected squarely with Wolf's jaw. Wolf went down in a heap, half in the river, unconscious. Instantly, Caleb waded out into the cold river and felt around for the sack. The water was only a couple of feet deep and it didn't take long before he kicked it with his foot. He yanked Tumble out of the water and carried the sack to shore, hiding it in the rocks. No time to see how Tumble is, he thought. Besides, it would be better to keep him inside the sack. He opened it a little to make sure air could get in and then he went back to Wolf. With all his strength, he dragged the man behind the rocks to hide him. A summer of rugged life on the trail had made him strong.

Caleb had to move fast. First he ran to the horses. He found Dusty and Patch's horse and led them around the cabin into the trees and tied them off. Then he returned and led the other horses away from the cabin, several hundred yards up the river, and smacked them on the flanks, the way Henderson had done it the many weeks ago in Dobytown. The horses scampered farther upriver. It would buy him some time if his plan went well, he thought as he ran back to the cabins.

Caleb could still hear voices arguing and laughing in the main cabin as he crept silently to the campfire. Several torches that had been dipped in pine pitch were stuck in the dirt nearby. He set the Henry behind a rock and gathered some kindling near the fire and tucked the wood under his arm, then snatched up a burning torch. Careful to keep it lit, he jogged a couple of hundred yards or so away from the cabin and back up the river. He stopped and set the kindling down, picking up twigs and leaves and sprinkling them over the kindling. Then he set the torch on top and blew on the flames until the fire spread. Satisfied it was burning strong, Caleb reached into his pocket and took out a handful of bullets. Carefully, he placed them into the flames. He had to hurry. He had exploded bullets this way before behind the schoolhouse, even gotten himself into trouble with his father for it. He knew they wouldn't shoot off like they would from a gun, but the noise of the shots would prove a distraction, an important piece to his plan. He ran as fast as he could back to Patch's cabin. Grabbing his Henry, Caleb crept quickly to the window. Patch was lying on the floor. It was hard to tell in the moonlight, but it looked like his eyes were closed. Caleb climbed into the shack and crawled over to him. Softly, Caleb shook Patch's shoulder and the young Sioux instantly awoke. Terrified, he backed to the wall. Caleb put his fingers to his mouth to signal to Patch to be quiet. Patch nodded his head. Quickly, Caleb took out his knife and cut the ropes that bound him. Then he led Patch out of the cabin and they headed into the trees to the horses. Caleb helped Patch onto his pony. Patch raised his hand in a gesture of peace. Caleb nodded to the Indian and raised his hand in a sign of farewell, then he pointed toward the dangerous path along the cliff to the stone archway. Quietly and swiftly, Patch and his pony disappeared through the trees and rocks.

Caleb raced back to the cabin. If the plan worked, they could get away; if not, their fates would be sealed forever in the Hole in the Wall. Caleb hid near the side of the cabin and held his breath. Suddenly, several blasts broke the silence of the night as the bullets ignited and exploded up the river. Jake, Trigger, and Larson ran from the cabin, guns drawn. Caleb hid in the rocks and drew a bead on them with his rifle.

"They took the horses!" yelled Larson as he searched around the campfire. The bullets continued to explode, echoing through the ravine.

"Wolf must be holding them down!" shouted Jake. "Trigger. You stay with the two girls. Whoever's out there must be after them! Keep a gun on 'em. We'll head up the river. If they get through us, shoot 'em."

"Right, boss!" Trigger headed back inside, his pearl-handled Colt dancing in his hands.

"Larson. Let's go!" Jake yelled as he and Larson ran toward the gunshots.

Caleb sneaked up close to the window and carefully peered inside. Trigger, his Colt drawn, stood by the door and looked out. Then he advanced on Tilly, reaching out his free hand like a sidewinder, and removed her gag.

"What do you think there, little princess?" said Trigger. "Lordy, you are like a fairy girl. You like fairy tales?"

"Yes," said Tilly meekly. "And a knight is coming to rescue me."

"Ha!" laughed Trigger as he holstered his pistol. "That's a

good one. Well, you want to come with Sir Trigger to Mexico? I bet you'd bring a thousand dollars, I do."

"No!" yelled Tilly. Suddenly, she kicked out with her foot and connected with Trigger's shin.

"Son of a...!" exclaimed Trigger as he danced on one leg. Julie sprang like a cat and cracked Trigger's other leg with a thunderous kick. Trigger backhanded her across the face, knocking her back against the wall. Blood spurted from Julie's lip as Trigger grabbed her and slammed her against the wall.

"Hold it!" shouted Caleb as he pointed the Henry at Trigger.

"Caleb!" exclaimed Julie, her gag slipping down as she struggled in Trigger's grasp.

"Well, well," Trigger hissed as he let go of Julie. "Looks like we got ourselves a family reunion. Careful with that rifle, boy. Kind of big for you, ain't it?" Trigger shot his hand out like a rattlesnake and grabbed his Colt. Like lightning, he swung it toward Caleb.

The Henry fired and blew Trigger against the wall, shattering his shoulder. Caleb ran around to the door and burst into the room. Trigger tried to reach out for his pistol, but Caleb kicked it away. Then he smashed the Henry into the side of Trigger's head. The outlaw went limp.

"Come on, we've got to hurry!" Caleb took out his knife and carefully slashed Julie's ropes, freeing her hands. Then he went to Tilly and cut her ropes.

"Oh, Caleb," exclaimed Julie as she ran to Tilly and

scooped her up. "Lord, I was praying you would come! How did you manage…?"

"There's no time!" Caleb rushed them out the door. "They'll be back once they figure it out. I'll explain later. Let's go!"

"I'll just take this with me." Julie grabbed Trigger's pearl-handled Colt.

Quickly, they bolted from the cabin and ran over to Dusty. Julie grabbed onto Dusty's mane and vaulted onto his back. Caleb boosted his little sister up behind her.

"Head back up the trail to the cavern. Be careful. The moon is full and it's light enough to see, but it's a sheer drop on the right. I'll meet you on the other side by the wagon."

"We'll be OK." Julie took the rope that was tied around Dusty's neck and urged the horse forward.

"Tumble!" cried Tilly over her shoulder. "The man was going to throw him in the river!"

"Don't worry, Tilly, I'll get him. Go on!" Caleb turned and ran back to where he had hidden Tumble.

Caleb grabbed the sack and hefted Tumble over his shoulder as he picked up his Henry. Shouts from the outlaws told him they were on to his trick. They would be back in no time, most likely with their horses. Caleb ran to the campfire. He quickly grabbed another torch in his left hand and shifted the Henry into the crook of his elbow, then ran up the trail to Pride as fast as he could, his arms aching from the effort. If the torch would stay lit, the final part of his plan would fall into place.

Pride snorted and stomped his hoof as Caleb ran up to him. "Easy, boy," said Caleb as he stuck the burning stick into the earth. With both hands, he lifted the sack with Tumble onto the saddle and tied it off to the saddle horn. He stuck the Henry into its scabbard. He could hear the outlaws shouting as they rode back to the cabin. They would be on him in less than a minute once they discovered the wounded Trigger. He quickly grabbed the torch, mounted Pride, and headed up the trail. He let Pride have his head, for he knew the horse could see better than he could. Two hundred feet below, the dark river roared. Caleb silently prayed that Julie had made it safely. The outlaws were racing up the trail just two hundred yards below. Caleb saw torches light up in the moonlight sky. They were on him now and closing. Caleb had to double his speed. He gave the reins a shake, urging the warhorse faster. Pride skittered for a moment on the rocky trail, nearly tossing Caleb to the river below. He yanked Pride to the left as the big stallion found his footing. They picked their way forward as fast as they could until they finally made it to the rocky cavern.

"Julie!" yelled Caleb as Pride led him through the stone passage.

"Caleb!" shouted Julie from the other side. "We made it!"

"Hitch up Dusty! They're coming! Hurry!"

Caleb burst out the other side as Julie brought the wagon around in a circle. Quickly, he dismounted and stabbed the lit torch into the ground at the entrance to the cavern. "Take Tumble!" he said, pointing to the sack hanging on the saddle horn. Julie ran over and lifted the sack with Tumble in it, then put it into the back of the wagon. Caleb took out his knife and started hacking up the tumbleweeds. "Quick. Pile these weeds into the cavern!"

Julie and Tilly frantically dragged the tumbleweeds and stuffed them into the stone passageway. Caleb could hear the whinny of the outlaw horses as they entered the other side. He took the burning sticks and began to light the weeds. "Go! Get out on the trail and head north." Caleb hit the dirt as the outlaws fired through the cavern, gunshots ricocheting off the cavern wall. Then he leaped up and grabbed the Henry as the weeds caught fire.

"I'm not leaving you!" cried Julie as she grabbed the pearl-handled Colt. Julie lay on the ground and fired into the cavern. Caleb hit the dirt right beside her and let loose with his Henry. Smoke from the fire began to pour into the cavern as they fired side by side at the hidden outlaws.

"All right, let's go!" Caleb tossed some bullets onto the burning weeds, hoping they would explode and buy them some time. Then he sprinted to Pride and quickly mounted the big black stallion. Julie leaped aboard the wagon and grabbed the reins. With Caleb in the lead, they tore out as fast as they could. They could hear the gunshots behind them as the outlaws continued firing. They had to move fast. They had half the night ahead of them. Tracks would be hard to see in the moonlight. Caleb led them to the trail and jerked Pride north as Julie drove Dusty and the wagon right behind him. It was hard going at first, and the shadows of giant boulders obscured the trail at times. Rocks and ruts tossed the wagon to and fro, but Julie managed to hang on. Tilly took Tumble out of the sack and put her arms around him, willing the mutt to live. But there was no movement from the little dog. Up ahead, the trail split. The main road veered left. A smaller one headed east. In an instant Caleb chose the eastern route, hoping to fool the outlaws. He figured as long as he kept the mountains on his left, he could always find his way back to the Bozeman Trail. The eastern road cut through vast walls of rock. The road was narrowing as the sheer walls converged on the trail. Just as Caleb feared they would meet a dead end, the trail widened and they shot through into a giant ravine.

Two hours later, the trail burst from the ravine and opened out to a vast prairie. Pride could run forever, it seemed, but Dusty, sweat flying off his gray hide from pulling the little wagon, was beginning to tire. The moon shone bright over the mountains to the west as they rode like the devil back toward the Bozeman Trail. The sun began to rise in the east as the horses pounded a mighty beat. *We must have fooled them*, Caleb thought. *Surely they would have caught up to us by now.* Caleb prayed they had outrun the outlaws as he looked over his shoulder. His heart caught. There, just a half-mile behind, were three riders bearing down on them fast.

"They're on us!" Caleb reached for his Henry rifle. "Pull up! It's no use trying to outrun them. We'll make a stand here!" Caleb reached for the Sharps rifle and tossed it to Julie as she pulled Dusty to a stop. Then Julie grabbed her pearl-handled Colt and climbed into the back of the wagon.

"Tilly, stay down!" Julie said as she pushed her little sister's head lower. Quickly, she brought the Sharps to bear as the outlaws rode down on them. Caleb leaped off Pride with his Henry rifle and dove into the back of the wagon. Together he and Julie sighted in on the advancing men.

"Wait till they get a little closer!" yelled Caleb as he saw the outlaws draw their rifles. "Shoot at the one on the left, then reload quick! I'll try to take the other two."

"OK!" Julie peered down the barrel of the Sharps. "You say when!" Julie moved her hand over to the Colt and brought it next to her. If they got in close, she thought, she would switch to the pistol.

Suddenly, two of the outlaws split off wide. Caleb grabbed the telescope. At barely two hundred yards away, he could see that Jake was in the middle. He figured if he could hit him, the others would be without their leader, so he took a deep breath. Jake fired from the middle, Larson from the left. Wolf took his horse out wide to the right. The three outlaws, guns blazing, galloped toward Caleb and his sisters.

"Not yet!" Caleb forced himself to wait. He carefully drew a bead on Jake as he closed to within a hundred yards. "Ready?"

"Ready!" shouted Julie as she sighted in on Larson.

All of a sudden, the three outlaws stopped dead in their tracks. Quickly, Larson and Wolf rode back to the center toward Jake. Caleb held his fire, puzzled that they had ceased their attack. Then a great rumble of hooves shook the ground behind him. Caleb turned, half expecting to see a herd of buffalo. His heart jumped at the sight before him, for more than a hundred Indians rode down on them from the north. War cries filled the solemn prairie air as the Indians swept toward them. Julie dropped the Sharps and hugged Tilly next to her. Caleb dropped his Henry and put his arms around his sisters. There was nothing they could do. If this was how their lives were to end, in an attack by the Sioux, then so be it. The hearts of the three O'Toole children beat to the pounding of the horses as the Indians overwhelmed the wagon.

16

TOUCH THE CLOUDS

★ ★ ★ ★ ★ ★ ★ ★ ★ ★ ★ ★ ★ ★ ★ ★ ★ ★ ★ ★

Caleb, Julie, and Tilly lay in the wagon, clutching each other, as the Indians surrounded them, the dust swirling as the Sioux warriors came to a fast stop. They lined up on either side of the wagon and faced down the outlaws. Not a word was spoken, not a war cry was heard. Julie and Caleb peered over the wagon. Wolf, Jake, and Larson sat on their horses a hundred yards away. The Indians stretched out wide to either side, and the line of one hundred Sioux warriors walked their horses slowly toward the outlaws. Suddenly, the three bad men turned and galloped away in the opposite direction. Then the Indians turned and faced the wagon. The leader motioned for several fierce-looking warriors to follow him. They trotted their ponies toward the buckboard, rifles held in their iron grips. Then they stopped and studied Caleb and his sisters, speaking among themselves for several moments. Caleb wondered if they were deciding whether or not to kill them. The leader then motioned toward their guns.

Slowly, Caleb handed him the two rifles and the Colt. Then the Indian turned his horse and signaled them to follow.

"They want us to follow them," said Caleb as he jumped off the wagon. Pride was about fifty feet away, and Caleb made his way through the Indians to the big warhorse. Some of the Indians circled around him, curious, murmuring to each other while Caleb mounted Pride.

"We've got no choice." Julie climbed into the driver's seat and picked up Dusty's reins.

They rode west for an hour along a game trail some distance closer to the Big Horn Mountains. They were still near enough to the Bozeman Trail, so they could get back on it when they had to. As the game trail wound closer to the mountains, they turned north and the ride became a lot rougher for the wagon. The jostling of the buckboard managed to rouse tough little Tumble from his terrible ordeal. He nuzzled onto Tilly's lap for comfort. Just as the going seemed impossible, the trail led into a clearing near a river. Sioux tepees surrounded the banks on either side. Caleb led Pride through the camp as Julie followed with Dusty and the wagon. Indian warriors surrounded them, and many women and children walked alongside, curious about them, as they were led to a large tepee. Then the biggest man Caleb had ever seen stepped from the tepee. He rose head and shoulders above all the others, and his torso rippled with muscle. *Touch the Clouds!* Caleb gasped to himself. It was the great Sioux war Chief. The one who had his people lay down their arms in peace. Like Red Cloud, he vowed never again to fight in what the white man called the Indian Wars. As Caleb neared the huge man, the Sioux Chief held out his hand and gripped Pride's bridle.

"I am Touch the Clouds. You are welcome here," said the Chief. "Climbing Rat has told us of his story. How you set him free from those men who wished to kill him. He wishes to express his thanks." Then Touch the Clouds called out to someone over his shoulder. After a moment, Patch slipped from the tepee and stood next to him, dwarfed by the big Chief.

"I am Caleb." Caleb sat next to Touch the Clouds. Other Sioux Indians sat attentively in the big tepee. "These are my sisters, Julie and Tilly. Patch, or Climbing Rat, was too hurt to leave alone so we took him with us. We called him Patch because Julie patched him up."

The Chief explained this to the others in his language. "Sitting Bull is leader of his people. Climbing Rat wishes to say that he had not intended to harm you when his warriors attacked the white wagon train for shooting his brother, Listening Bird. His brother was scouting for game and was killed that day." Touch the Clouds spoke in very good English. "He only wanted to touch you and try to run away, not fight you. It is called *anho*."

"Please tell him I am sad about his brother." Caleb accepted some food and water from one of the women. Touch the Clouds spoke quietly to Patch, who then looked at Caleb and smiled his appreciation. It seemed they all shared the good and the sorrow of life. "What is *anho*?"

"Counting coup. When a young boy is the first to touch an enemy in battle, it brings great honor to him and his family," said the Chief. Patch spoke at length, demonstrating painfully to the other Indians in the tepee the battle he had with Caleb. "He says you grabbed him out of the air and he had to fight for his life. He says you are a young warrior of much strength and you killed him with your knife. He was singing his death song."

"Tell him he fought very hard and that I had been lucky. He may have killed me if he had not been shot before our fight." Caleb pointed to his side where the bullet had passed through Patch. He thought if he showed respect, he would be given the same treatment in return. He felt the Sioux were not evil. They did not usually kill for no reason. It was his father's voice, the teacher voice that called out to him once again. "Tell him he is very strong too."

The Chief spoke with Patch and the others, explaining what Caleb had told them. There was much nodding of heads and murmuring. "They say they have heard the Lakota talk of a young white warrior on a black horse who rides and shoots like an Indian. They have heard of this boy from Scotts Bluff who rode with no hands and fired on our brothers in the south. They say he has the roots of a warrior. Are you this boy?"

"Yes," Caleb nodded his head carefully, unsure of where this was leading. The Indians talked among themselves. Several of them spoke to Patch, offering congratulations. Patch smiled as if he were given a great honor and began to speak animatedly. The others paid rapt attention to his story.

"He says he is honored to have fought with the young white warrior. He says at first he wanted to kill all of you for letting him live. He was afraid that the girl did some bad magic that made him die again," said the Chief.

"It was something from my bag to make him sleep so I could stitch him up," explained Julie as she pointed to Patch's stitches. She pretended to sew with her hands. Touch the Clouds spoke and someone brought in Julie's medical bag.

"We want to see how you made Climbing Rat sleep."

"I don't know if that's a good idea," Julie protested. But seeing how serious the Indians were, she reached into her bag for the chloroform and poured some onto a cloth. Then she went over to Patch. Patch immediately covered his face in fear, refusing to participate. At first, no one moved. Then one of the men stepped forward.

"Do this thing on Running Deer," commanded the Chief.

"Well, all right," Julie said hesitatingly. She motioned for Running Deer to sit. When he did, she placed the chloroform against his mouth. Running Deer gasped at first, then he breathed from the cloth. After a moment, he stood and looked around as if nothing had happened. All the Indians looked confused about the powers of the sleeping medicine. Then Running Deer took a step and began to stagger to the side, crashing into a heap. He tried to rise, but his legs would not cooperate. He was conscious, barely. "When he is like that, I then can do the stitches." She sat Running Deer up and pretended to stitch his side like she did Patch's. Running Deer sat slack-jawed, a rather comical expression on his stern face. Patch began to speak at length with the elders. There was much discussion among them.

"Climbing Rat wants to know if his debt is paid," said Touch the Clouds. "It is important to him, so when he returns to his people, he can tell them of his story. We are taking it under consideration. It is not so easy to know. In time, it will be decided."

"Thank him for bringing you to help us. I feared between your tribe and those outlaws, our lives would end here," said Caleb.

"Not all Sioux will kill like that. I do not wish to make any more war with the whites. I see things that my brothers are unwilling to see. Some of my people still wish to kill all whites. Drive them from their lands. But what for? They will keep coming, and there is no way to stop this change."

Suddenly, there was a round of barking outside the tent. It sounded like a half-dozen dogs were at it. An old Sioux woman came running into the tent and began to gesture wildly, speaking animatedly with the Chief. Then she threw up her hands and ran out.

"She says your dog is chasing all the other dogs in our camp."

"Tumble!" cried Tilly as she ran out of the tepee.

"It might be good to tie him up," explained the Chief.

"Seems he's feeling better," chuckled Julie as she packed her bag. "I'll go."

Touch the Clouds folded his massive arms in front of him. "The elders want to know how it is that three white children are alone. It is not a place to be alone in this country. There is a name the whites use for this trail they made. They call it Bloody Bozeman."

"We are heading to the Bitterroot Mountains. Our own mother and father are dead. We have to meet my mother's sister in a town called Virginia City," explained Caleb.

Touch the Clouds conversed with the elders for a while. One old man in particular seemed to have the final say. Touch the Clouds nodded his head and turned to Caleb. "You will ride with us. You will be safe. It is many miles and many days. We are going on our last hunt before the winter to this place your government wants to protect. You must go through this place before Virginia City. The lands are rich and full of game. It is a sacred land where water shoots to the sky. We will get fat and take skins before we go south for the winter."

"What is this place?" asked Caleb

"Mi tse a-da-zi," said the Chief. "Your government calls it Yellowstone."

★ ★ ★

For nearly three weeks, Caleb rode Pride along the hunting trails, surrounded in the safety of Touch the Clouds's people. During that time, they had not seen a white man for three hundred miles. There was no end to the amount of game they found along the route to the huge mountain pass. They were some distance south of the Bozeman Trail, but nearing Yellowstone. Sometimes Caleb rode alongside the great Chief and listened to stories of the Indian's life. Though Touch the Clouds supported his fellow Sioux Chiefs in their wars with the white men, he told Caleb he would no longer participate in them.

For days, Caleb and his sisters traveled in the company of the Indians, and he and his sisters were the better for it. Julie and Tilly had been given new clothes by the Sioux women. Julie's own clothes had become a tattered mess, and she was grateful for the soft doeskin dress. She wore this on top of buckskin trousers. She preferred to wear pants as they were practical and tough and more suited for the rugged terrain than her dress and shirt. Tilly wanted to look like her sister, so she was given matching clothes. Together they looked like a pair of golden dolls. A great deal had been made of their long blond hair, and they let the Sioux women cut little locks of it for their keeping. The Indian women were fascinated by the golden color and loved to run their hands along the fine hair. There was excitement as the Sioux warriors and all the women and children prepared for the buffalo hunt.

"You will see how we hunt buffalo on the jump," said Touch the Clouds as he and some hunters rode up to Caleb. "Come."

Caleb watched from the tree line as the Sioux hunters rode alongside a small herd of buffalo about a half-mile away. They dashed in and out among the huge beasts. They did not shoot their arrows or fire their rifles, but instead drove the rampaging buffalo along the plateau that led to a cliff. Hundreds of feet below by the river, the Sioux women waited with spears and knives. They were given tasks to perform once the hunt was over. Caleb held his breath as the poor bleating animals were driven to the edge of the cliff. Suddenly, the hunters stopped, but the huge animals continued their flight straight off the cliff, perishing either from the fall or speared by the Indian women below.

"This is the best way to hunt the buffalo. That is why we call it Buffalo Jump. It is quick and it saves our arrows and our ammunition," said Touch the Clouds. "Now the women do their work."

Caleb, shocked by what he had seen, urged Pride down the trail to the river. The women were working furiously, killing the wounded buffalo and skinning them. They were efficient and quick, for they did not want the meat to spoil. Nothing was wasted. For several days, they labored hard. Caleb and Patch cut and shaped the buffalo bones, sharpening them to make tools and weapons. Julie and Tilly helped the Indian women build small fires and learned to dry the meat. The buffalo steak was cut into large, thin pieces and draped on wooden racks over the small fires like clothes drying on a line. The smoke billowed and kept the insects away so they could not contaminate the meat or lay their eggs in it. The steaks were slowly dried in the hot sun and preserved to make jerky to be eaten in the cold months ahead when the Sioux would travel to their winter grounds. When all the work was done, preparations were made for a grand feast. Tales would be told of the great hunt.

★ ★ ★

Caleb woke to a fierce licking from Tumble. "Tumble, cut it out," he laughed as the scrappy little dog climbed over him, forcing him to leave the comfort of his bearskin blanket. The first chill of an early fall filled the air as he went outside and stretched in the morning sun. Caleb figured it must be September by now, but he had lost track. As he looked around, he noticed the entire camp was being dismantled. The Indians were packing up and preparing to make a move.

In the distance, fifty Sioux warriors from a different tribe were fanned out on horseback in a line along the forest edge. Caleb went over to Pride and stroked the stallion's mane. The air crackled with danger. Even from this distance, he could see the painted faces of the warriors among the trees. They looked ready for battle. Touch the Clouds and some of his men rode out to meet them. After a few moments, the Indians advanced on the camp with Touch the Clouds. As they got closer, the hair stood up on Caleb's head as he recognized the man who rode next to Touch the Clouds. *Dear Lord*, Caleb thought as he took a deep breath. It was Sitting Bull himself! He recognized the Chief from newspaper photos. Tales of the Battle of Little Big Horn and the massacre of Colonel George Armstrong Custer and the 7th Cavalry reached far and wide. Touch the Clouds pointed to Caleb as he spoke with the famous war Chief. Caleb shivered as the barrel-chested Sitting Bull stared coldly at him.

The two men rode up to Caleb.

"Our brother Sitting Bull has come for Climbing Rat. They are heading to Canada. I have told him of you. He says he will put his sign on your wagon. You will go in peace," explained Touch the Clouds.

Caleb swallowed hard as one of Sitting Bull's warriors rode over and painted a red outline of a buffalo on their little wagon. Just then, Julie and Tilly emerged from the tepee.

"What is it, Caleb?" asked Julie as she rubbed the sleep from her eyes.

"It's Sitting Bull. He's come for Patch."

"Oh Heavens!" Julie sucked in her breath and pulled Tilly tight to her.

"Do not worry, you are safe. He says we must leave now," said Touch the Clouds. "There was a battle in a place called Big Hole. Many of the Nez Perce were killed. Many women and their children."

"What happened?" Caleb began to saddle up Pride. The Sioux had taken down all their tepees. They would be moving in minutes.

"It is heard that this man, Colonel Gibbons, planned the attack. Joseph is the leader of the Nez Perce, a good man who wants peace. He only wants to hunt and keep his land. The leaders in Washington want me to help drive Joseph's people out of their land. This I will not do. We will leave for our winter home." Touch the Clouds gazed sadly across the intense beauty of Yellowstone. "The Nez Perce are moving through here, maybe to Canada. The white soldiers are trying to find them. There will be more killing. It is not safe for

Indian or white. Go west to where the water shoots to the sky, and in a few days you will come to a river. Ride north, and you will find the road to Virginia City. It is best we leave now."

★ ★ ★

Caleb stood next to Julie and Tilly as Touch the Clouds's people rode past them and headed east. The O'Tooles' little wagon had been filled with food and animal skins as a final gesture. Patch rode up quickly and held up his hand in farewell. Caleb walked to his horse and held out his hand, offering it to Patch to shake.

"*Toksha.*" Caleb pronounced the Sioux word for farewell as he shook the Indian's hand.

"*Toksha!*" said Patch. "*Le mita cola.*" Caleb learned this phrase meant "friend."

"*Le mita cola,*" said Caleb, waving as Patch turned his horse and rode away. Sitting Bull and his warriors then surrounded Patch, and together they galloped north. In a moment, they were swallowed up by the forest.

17

THE FLIGHT OF
THE NEZ PERCE

★ ★ ★ ★ ★ ★ ★ ★ ★ ★ ★ ★ ★ ★ ★ ★ ★ ★ ★ ★

Caleb and his sisters rode through the Yellowstone forest on a narrow beaten trail, awestruck by the wild, untamed land. It was hard going. After three days, they passed a vast lake and pools of lily pads. Eagles sailed overhead. Moose and elk grazed in the fields of purple fireweed. As they approached a clearing, the smell of sulfur became overpowering. Then, from a mound of yellowish mud, came a loud, gurgling, hissing sound. A great roar followed, and they rode quickly away from the large circle of mud to a safe distance. Suddenly, boiling water spilled from a hole in the ground. They stood and watched in disbelief as the roaring geyser spewed its smelly stream from the bowels of the earth ever higher and higher. It seemed impossible that so much water could shoot so far into the blue sky.

"It smells like rotten eggs!" exclaimed Tilly as she held her nose and made a face.

"It's sulphur gas from the geyser, Tilly," explained Julie. "It's like the hot springs in Kansas."

"Well, it stinks!" giggled Tilly.

Finally, the great geyser died down to a few gasps of steam. They continued their journey, marveling at the beauty of the new federal park. There seemed to be no end to the game. Deer and buffalo shared fields with coyotes. A great, golden grizzly bear, her cubs near her side, eyed them warily only fifty feet away by a river. For a second, the bear rose to its full height, nearly eight feet, perhaps to warn Caleb and his sisters of her power. Satisfied she was safe, the bear continued to teach her cubs how to fish. And there were plenty of fish to be had. They flipped and flopped in the rivers. Caleb had the feeling that he could just dip his hands in the cool stream and pull out a trout.

★ ★ ★

Two days later, Caleb took a bead on the horizon as they moved on through the scenic wonderland. It was getting close to dark and they decided to make camp near a rock-lined river that led into a grove of pines just a short way from a small geyser. Carefully, they tucked the wagon out of sight into the cover of the trees. Tilly ran to the river and began to splash around.

"It's hot!" she cried delightedly. "Feel it!" Tumble took the opportunity to do a little barking. Two elk grazing in the distance lifted their heads, curious as to what the commotion was all about.

"Ohhhh. This is nice!" said Julie, dipping her hand in the water. "Tilly, guess what?"

"What?" answered Tilly as she splashed in the geyser-heated water.

"It's bath time! Caleb, you go down the river. Tilly and I are going to take a bath," she said modestly.

Caleb picked up their map and his Henry and hiked farther downstream. After a few minutes, he stopped and took a short look around, eyeing the clear water of the river. He also could use a soak. Gingerly, he stripped off his clothes and sat down in the luxurious, healing waters. He picked up the map and studied it. Virginia City would be a week's ride, if he figured it right. There they would go to the bank for the money that had been wired. Their Aunt Sarah was some distance farther west. They had come close to a thousand miles. The September nights were getting chilly. *Just a few hundred miles farther*, thought Caleb as he leaned back into the stream. The water drifted over his aching body. It felt good. He shut his eyes and drifted into a relaxing sleep.

★ ★ ★

The blast of a gunshot jolted Caleb into action. He scrambled into his clothes and grabbed his rifle and the map. There was no second shot, so he hoped that whatever happened, Julie had it under control. Caleb raced back up the river, leaping over rocks and fallen trees. Tumble barked in the distance. As he closed in on the camp, he could see a mule, loaded with animal furs and traps, grazing nearby. The jagged-toothed, steel traps clanked together as the mule shifted away from

Caleb. He chambered a round in the big Henry and quietly approached through the trees. Just ahead was a scene that almost made him laugh. A trapper lay on the ground with his hands covering his head. Julie, holding her Colt and dripping wet in her Indian clothes, had a bead drawn on the scraggly man. Tilly stood next to her sister, bravely holding a stick and pointing it at the trapper as Tumble held the man's trousers in his teeth.

"Lucky I didn't shoot you dead," said Julie to the trapper.

"Everything all right?" Caleb relaxed his grip on the Henry.

"Keep a gun on him while I dry off. He was sneaking around, spying on us."

"Well, I don't mean no harm," said the trapper. "I saw your camp and thought I'd just wander over. Pretty hungry."

"Just stay right there." Caleb held the rifle on the man.

"Easy now, friend." The trapper got to his knees. "I ain't armed or nothin'."

"He was snooping around, Caleb." Julie said as she squeezed the river water from her hair. "I saw him over by Pride, looking at the rifle."

"You out here alone with no gun?" asked Caleb.

"Funny thing about that. I had a run-in with a grizzly last week. Dern thing was as big as a house. Knocked me clean into the river. Lost my rifle. I see you got a Sharps there. Say, don't suppose you'd trade for it."

"My guess is he was going to take it," said Julie.

"No, no. Just lookin'," said the trapper. "Any other folks riding with you?"

"No. It's just us," said Caleb

"I see that saddle on the black and the N.V.; that be Nebraska Volunteers?"

"That's right." Caleb went over to Pride and checked the Sharps. Something about the man bothered him. The trapper followed Caleb over to Pride and ran his fingers over the N.V. "Belongs to the man who fought for them during the war."

"Well, friend, I was First Nebraska! Joshua Bodine is the name!"

★ ★ ★

Caleb sat warming himself in front of the campfire, gnawing hungrily on a piece of buffalo jerky. Julie and Tilly tended to the camp, preparing the furs for a night's sleep. It was getting colder, and their breath fogged in the firelight. Joshua Bodine talked through the evening about his war adventures, fur trapping, and his life as a mountain man. Caleb checked his fur-laden mule for any weapons, but came up empty. As long as either he or Julie stayed on watch, he figured it was safe to offer the trapper a meal and a night's company.

"You say you fought under General Thayer?"

"The very same. Nebraska First, like I say," Joshua said, chewing on some jerky. "Never so glad we turned cavalry. Dern tired of walking all the time. We were beat to death. Covered a lot of ground all the way to Tennessee, I reckon. Ended up fighting the Sioux and running with the Pawnee on the Platte."

"I hear you had quite a battle with the Sioux at Whitestone Hill," said Caleb, remembering Blue Hawk's story. "First Nebraska under General Thayer, was it?"

"That's right. Took it to 'em pretty good." Joshua tossed Tumble a piece of the meat. Tumble gobbled it up and settled in between the trapper and Caleb. "All that's behind me now. Headin' to California. Try my hand at some prospecting. What do you say we play a little tune? Got a banjo in my bag."

"Yes!" cried Tilly as she wiggled out of her bed of fur.

"All right, but just a few," said Julie.

Caleb kept his eye on Joshua as the trapper dug into the pack on his mule and brought out the banjo. Then the man reached into a sack, took out something, and offered it to Tumble, then scratched the little dog's head.

"Good little dog. Kinda funny looking," chuckled Joshua as he tuned his banjo. "Here we go now!"

Joshua began a lively tune. Tilly danced and jigged, delighted at the fun. Julie even got into it and grabbed Tilly and picked her up, twirling her in the light of the campfire. Caleb took the Henry and leaned against a log and watched. It was good to see his sisters smiling and laughing. It was a rare sight since the tragedies of Great Bend. Tumble lay sound asleep, which puzzled Caleb, for it seemed when anyone in the family danced, Tumble was in on it, barking up a storm.

"Come on, Caleb!" shouted Tilly gleefully as she danced around the fire with Julie.

"Yes, come on, Caleb." Julie laughed and twirled Tilly. "Show us a jig!"

"No, you go ahead." Something didn't feel right to Caleb as he watched his sisters have their fun. He reached over to Tumble and scratched the dog's head. Tumble lay as still as a stone.

★ ★ ★

Something indeed was not right. Caleb sat still, pretending to sleep. In the early light of dawn, Caleb quietly brought the Henry to his shoulder and laid his finger on the trigger as he watched Joshua slip a rope around Tumble's neck and tie the other end to a tree. Then Joshua turned and gave a quiet whistle. Soundlessly, two more men emerged from the trees. Guns drawn, they entered the camp. One of them tossed Joshua a rifle. Thieves! Caleb's mind screamed out.

"Hold it!" shouted Caleb as he brought the Henry to bear. He would have to stand up to three of them!

BANG! The thieves turned to face Julie standing straight up with her pearl-handled Colt, gun smoke pouring from the barrel "Anyone takes a step, I will have no problem shooting you!"

"Now, ease up there, missy," said Joshua as he raised his rifle. "There's three men here, and I see just you children. We don't want to hurt you. We just want your wagon."

"Then you will have to shoot me for it, sir." Julie kept her Colt aimed at Joshua and stood her ground.

"We've come too far to give our wagon up to the likes of you." Caleb swung the big Henry at the other two thieves.

"Looks like we have ourselves a Mexican standoff," said Joshua. "Put your guns down and I promise we'll just take the wagon, nothing else."

"And we should just trust you?" scoffed Julie. "Not likely."

"What did you give Tumble last night to put him out like that?" asked Caleb, not moving an inch. "I saw you do it."

"Just a little valerian root. The dog'll be fine. That how you had me figured out?"

"That and the fact that some of your skins have bullet holes and can't be more than a day old and you say you lost your rifle a week ago. Plus, it was the Second Nebraska cavalry under General Sully at the Battle of Whitestone Hill, not the First under Thayer. I know the man who was there," said Caleb.

"Smart kid, you are. Too smart." Joshua gestured to one of the other men. "Jeremiah? You see that little girl over there under the bearskin?"

"Yeah, boss." Jeremiah slowly trained his pistol on Tilly, who was hiding under the grizzly fur.

"If either of these two fire, shoot the little girl," Joshua said with a victorious smirk. "That sort of changes things up, don't it? See, you and your big sister here trade shot with me and him, little sister gets killed. Now drop that Henry." Joshua pointed his rifle at Caleb's chest. Caleb stood firm, his mind racing. "Let me repeat that for you," said the trapper thief as he took a step toward Caleb. "I said drop it, or I'll…"

An arrow stopped Joshua in his tracks, piercing him

straight through the throat, sticking out the other side. *ZIP!* Another arrow hit Jeremiah in the leg. Several more arrows found their mark, and the third thief went down. Caleb ran to Tilly and grabbed her, taking her to the ground. Shielding Tilly with his body, he swung the Henry toward Jeremiah just as the wounded man raised his pistol to shoot. Julie beat him to it, firing her Colt, catching Jeremiah in the shoulder. Another arrow hit him dead-center in the chest, and he fell down, dead. Suddenly, all was quiet. The three thieves lay still. Six Indians emerged from the trees, their bows and arrows pointed at Caleb and Julie, who immediately gave up their guns and raised their hands in peace. Two of the Indians drew long knives and spoke in low tones as they carefully checked the bodies of the trappers for any sign of life. Satisfied there was none, they picked up the weapons of the dead. These were not the Sioux friends. These were the Nez Perce. The leader walked up to Caleb and Julie. He was a striking young warrior, broad-chested and powerfully built. He spoke to the other Indians and pointed down the river. Immediately, they began to drag the dead bodies away from camp.

"They will take these bad men down the river and leave them for the wolves," said the Indian as he looked over their belongings. He uncovered the stash of dried buffalo meat they had stored in the wagon. "I am called Yellow Wolf." He sniffed the meat. Satisfied, he smiled at them. "We will eat!"

★ ★ ★

"We had much talk of what to do with the white children. Some wanted to kill you; others said they did not want to kill." Yellow Wolf spoke clearly as he and the other Nez Perce sat with Caleb and Julie as they had their morning breakfast of bread and meat. One of the warriors walked over and gave them back their guns. "We decided we would kill those men for what the whites had done to our women and children at Big Hole."

"Why didn't you kill us too?" asked Caleb as he checked the Henry rifle. Julie spun the chamber of her Colt. Satisfied, she laid the pistol beside her.

"They know not why you wear Indian clothes and have the red Sioux buffalo mark on your wagon. There must be something about that. It is hard to know always what to do. Some say kill all the whites. Joseph does not want this. We have ridden many miles; we have fought many wars with the white man. We wished to settle in the valley of the Bitterroot, but there are whites who will not let us be. That is why they attacked us at Big Hole. That is why they come for us still." Yellow Wolf chewed thoughtfully as he gazed out on the field of purple flowers. "We must find a way out of this place. The soldiers are not far behind. Our scouts are all looking."

Caleb caught Julie's eye. "We know a way," he said.

"We were just with Touch the Clouds," said Julie. "It's his way into the park. He says only he knows of this pass. They go that way to stay away from the soldiers and the settlers."

"Will you show me this way?" Yellow Wolf's eyes shone bright with anticipation.

Caleb and Julie sat with Yellow Wolf and the other Nez Perce Indians and drew a map in the dirt as best they could remember of their travels the last few days. They described in detail the landmarks along the way, the geysers, the lake, and the rivers. Satisfied with the map's accuracy, they packed up their wagon and rode with Yellow Wolf and his fellow scouts, past the buffalo and the elk, the moose and the beaver. *It is hard to figure*, Caleb thought as Pride carried him through the Fireweed. The Nez Perce had killed the trappers, yet they had spared Caleb and his sisters and possibly saved their lives. He felt welcome in the presence of the same people who had just been needlessly attacked at Big Hole. *Perhaps the Indians will make their escape and settle in a new place, free to live as they desire*, Caleb thought. Then he remembered the words of Touch the Clouds. Change was happening and there was nothing they could do about it. Perhaps the old ways of the Nez Perce were gone.

Caleb and his sisters pulled to the side of the trail near a crashing waterfall that cut through a gorge. Yellow Wolf and his men disappeared briefly into the forest. Soon, Chief Joseph and hundreds of Nez Perce emerged from the trees. Like the Sioux, they were fast and efficient. These Indians traveled with almost military precision using forward and rear guards. Yellow Wolf raised his hand to Caleb in farewell as he trotted toward them with the Chief. Caleb and his sisters returned the gesture as Chief Joseph nodded to them and rode quickly past. In his heart, Caleb hoped they rode to freedom.

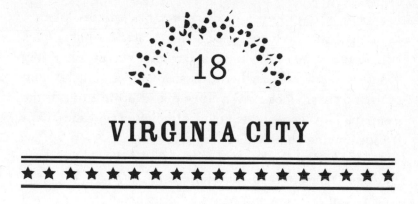

18

VIRGINIA CITY

★ ★

Caleb swallowed hard as they rode past the gallows that stood in front of the large brick courthouse. A man in a black hood was working on the hangman's rope, testing its strength. He pulled a lever, and a weighted sack tied to the noose crashed through a trap door. It jerked to a stop and then made an ominous creaking sound as it swung side to side. The gallows stood as a warning to all the murderers, con artists, and robbers entering the streets of Virginia City. Run afoul of the law and you will be hanged. The undertaker was often the busiest man in this rugged land. Resting in the hills of the Northern Rockies, the town was built on gold and blood.

Fashionable women mixed oddly with cowboys and miners among the wooden shops and stores that lined Main Street. Dressed in fancy clothes, the women crisscrossed the busy streets, chatting arm in arm as filthy men filed in and out of the saloons and assay offices. Prospectors, their horses laden with tools, mingled with fur-trading Indians and trappers. With its hotels, supply stores, blacksmiths, saloons, a bakery, school, Sheriff's office, and theaters, Virginia City, the former capital of Montana Territory, was in full swing. As they rode a little farther through the town, Caleb found what they were looking for. They pulled up in front of the Virginia City Bank. Julie grabbed the letter and they went inside, leaving Tumble tied aboard the wagon.

"Sarah O'Toole's kin?" The busy bank teller looked over the letter that Julie had given him.

"Yes, sir. We have a thousand dollars here that was wired by our mother in Great Bend."

"Don't have it," sniffed the bank teller as he handed the letter back to Julie.

"What do you mean, you don't have it? It's our money. The letter plainly says we are to withdraw the money and find Aunt Sarah." Julie tried to thrust the letter back into the man's hands.

"Well, we did have it. About a month ago, your aunt came in here and demanded the money. Says you children died of cholera in Great Bend. She's next of kin, so she took it. You want the money, you see her."

"But why would she say we all died of cholera?" protested Caleb. "We're supposed to live with her on her ranch."

"None of my business, but word is she fell on hard times. And I know that ranch. It's clear over in the Bitterroot and it ain't fit to be lived in. She tried to sell the bank that broken-down wreck of a place. She don't even live there anymore," said the teller. "Now, go about your business. I gotta lock up."

"What are we going to do?" asked Caleb.

"Find her." Julie folded the letter, eyeing the banker. "Where is she?"

"Like I said, it's none of my business. A woman's got to do what she can," said the officious little man. "You'll most likely find her working Skinner's Saloon in Bannack. Last I heard, she took up with a gambler. Now beat it." The teller ushered them out the door. "The show's about to start."

"What kind of a show," asked Tilly.

"The vigilantes are hanging a thief," said the teller. "Now git!"

"Come on, Tilly." Julie grabbed for Tilly's hand and hurried her to the wagon.

"Should we look for a place in town to stay for the night?" asked Caleb.

"No. I think we should find Aunt Sarah. The sooner we leave the better." Julie and Tilly climbed aboard the wagon.

Caleb mounted Pride, took out his map from the saddlebags, and studied it. "Looks like seventy or eighty miles to Bannack. I figure four or five days, depending on the road."

"Caleb, I'll not spend another minute in this town," Julie urged. "Our money and our lives depend on us getting to Bannack, and I will travel under the light of the moon if I have to. Let's go." Julie flipped the reins and brought Dusty into a quick trot. As they rode out on Main Street, the townsfolk began to spill out of the shops and saloons and rush back toward the courthouse to see the hanging. Several men in black hoods galloped past and headed toward the gallows.

"Must be the vigilantes," said Caleb with a shiver.

A commotion and shouts turned their heads. Other black-hooded men were dragging the thief up the gallows steps to meet his fate.

"Let's get out of here, Caleb!" shouted Julie as she gave the reins a snap. "Dusty, yah!"

★ ★ ★

They rode hard and fast for three days along the road to Bannack, passing mounds of dirt that had been dug up by massive steam-powered machines. Giant metal gears pulverized rocks, the earsplitting, grinding noise shattering the natural silence of the land. A hydraulic water-spewing cannon tore at cliffs and mountains, destroying all before it in the mad search for gold. They kept a watchful eye as they passed hollow-eyed miners and trappers housed along the river, avoiding the filthy desperate souls who lived in primitive caves under rocky overhangs. Murderers and thieves flourished along the road to Bannack. Caleb kept a firm hand on the Henry. Julie gripped the reins with one hand and rested the other on her pistol. They had traveled a thousand miles into the thick of it, and it paid to have your gun-hand filled.

★ ★ ★

"It looks like a stagecoach," said Caleb as he peered through his telescope. Several gunshots echoed through the hills.

"Riders are running up behind and shooting at it. We had better get off the road!"

They pulled into the trees and rocks by the river, hiding the horses and wagon from view as best they could. Caleb tied Pride off, grabbed his Henry, and took cover behind a boulder. Julie tucked Tilly and Tumble safely behind some rocks.

"Tilly, you stay here with Tumble," said Julie. Then she drew her Colt revolver and settled in beside Caleb. They watched as a Wells Fargo stagecoach raced toward them along the road, black-hooded riders tearing after it. The man who rode shotgun on the stagecoach turned and fired on the riders.

"Looks like the vigilantes from the hanging in Virginia City. They're robbing the stagecoach," Caleb whispered.

Caleb and Julie watched helplessly as four hooded vigilantes stopped the stagecoach less than a hundred yards away. The driver raised his hands, and the man riding next to him dropped his shotgun. Three men, passengers, were dragged out of the coach. The black-hooded men, guns drawn, stripped them of their coats, robbing the innocent travelers of their belongings. Suddenly, the man riding shotgun went for his weapon. In a flash, the vigilantes fired on him, and he fell from the coach to the ground. Then they turned on the three passengers and shot them point-blank. The vigilantes grabbed the driver of the stagecoach and dragged him over to a nearby tree. One of the thieves threw a rope over the biggest branch while the other murderers hoisted the driver onto a horse. They yanked the rope over the man's head and tied it off to the trunk.

"They're going to hang him, Caleb," whispered Julie as she clutched her brother's arm. "We've got to do something." Suddenly, the vigilantes pulled the horse away, and the poor stagecoach driver was left hanging by his neck, his feet dancing in the air.

"We've got to drive them off." Caleb, thinking fast, drew a bead on the murderers. Quickly, he fired several shots at a large granite rock next to the thieves. The ricochets echoed through the hills. Julie raised her Colt and blasted as fast as she could alongside her brother.

The vigilantes dove for cover, not knowing where the gunfire was coming from. They then quickly mounted their horses, shooting all around at their hidden assailants. Caleb and Julie kept up a deliberate fire as the thieves galloped away. "Let's go! We've got to cut him down!" Caleb raced over to Pride, leaped onto the saddle, and headed fast to the swinging, hanging man. Julie grabbed Tilly and Tumble and ran to the wagon.

Caleb drew his knife, slashed the rope, and the driver fell to the ground. He was alive! The choking driver clasped his neck, desperately trying to draw a breath. Caleb grabbed his Henry and began to reload in case the thieves returned. Julie pulled the wagon to a halt and ran to the fallen man to try to help him.

"Name's Mathew." After a few minutes, the driver of the stagecoach let Julie rub some ointment on the raw and nasty rope burn on his neck. "Got to thank you for what you did. I owe you my life. Real brave of you," he gasped, his voice straining from the injury. "It never ends in these parts. Highwaymen have been robbin' and killin' folks for years. Vigilantes are mostly crooks too. You're taking a big chance out here alone. I'll tell you, this is my last ride. If you'll help me with these poor dead folks, I'll make my way into Bannack and turn them over. Then I figure to take this rig south Utah way. It's just too murderous up here." Mathew rose and looked sadly at one of the dead. "Ol' Jim here was my best shotgun. Gonna miss him."

"Are things this bad in Bannack?" asked Julie.

"Vigilantes hanged Sheriff Plummer there some years back. Word was even he was a crook. Not much going on now. Used to be a gold town, but things have slowed some. Logan Porter is a good man. He's the new law there. He'll want to hear your story when he comes back from dealing with that Nez Perce mess in Big Hole," sighed Mathew.

"How far is Bannack?" asked Caleb as he helped Mathew carry Ol' Jim and lay him in the stagecoach.

"Just another day or so down the road."

"We'll ride with you, if that's all right." Caleb turned to another body and helped lift the poor man into the stagecoach.

"Son, the way you handle that Henry of yours, I welcome it!" said Mathew. "Let's go."

19

THE GAMBLER

★ ★ ★ ★ ★ ★ ★ ★ ★ ★ ★ ★ ★ ★ ★ ★ ★ ★ ★

They made it to Bannack without farther trouble, their hopes riding on finding their Aunt Sarah and the money that was owed them. As they rode down the sad, dusty street, Caleb wondered if his father's sister would even remember them. He dismounted and tied Pride off to the railing outside the rickety old Skinner's Saloon next to the Hotel Meade. Julie pulled up in the wagon next to him as Mathew brought the stagecoach to a halt on the other side of the street. Several men walked over on Mathew's signal and began to remove the bodies of the dead. The run-down wooden shacks and shops of the town spoke of decline and decay. Unlike the bustle of Virginia City, Bannack, the first territorial capital, felt empty of promise and riches. It had gone bust.

"You want to wait out here with Tilly, and I'll go find Aunt Sarah?" asked Caleb as he grabbed his Henry rifle.

"When you do, bring her out here," said Julie, her jaw set

with determination. "We've got a lot to straighten out about our money."

"Maybe she has a good explanation."

"For her sake, I hope she still has it." Julie reached for Tilly and hugged her close.

Caleb pushed open the weather-beaten swinging doors of Skinner's Saloon to the lively music that normally accompanies a drinking hole. As his eyes adjusted to the smoky, dim light, he could see cowboys, miners, and trappers lined up along the bar, draping their drunken selves on the three worn-out saloon girls. As he looked at the women, it was impossible to recognize anything of his aunt in them.

"Well, I'm feeling lucky!" said a sharp-looking gambler with slicked black hair at a poker table in the corner of the saloon. "I'm a little short on cash, but this watch is worth fifty dollars. All the way from Switzerland! Take a look at it, Gabe."

"I'll give you twenty, Roy," said Gabe as he examined the watch.

"Or I can sell you that glass eye of Taylor's if you'd rather have that!" Roy slapped another poker player on the back. As the man turned, guffawing at the joke, Caleb could see he had a glass left eye.

Caleb looked hard at the gambler, wondering if he was the one his Aunt Sarah was with.

"Boy, state your business and get on out," snapped the saloon owner. "Not right for you to be in here."

"Where can I find Sarah O'Toole?"

"She's in the back. She'll be a while. She's working the bath and the feller's caked in coal dust. You go wait outside. Go on!"

There was a time when Caleb would have politely done what the man said, but that seemed a long time ago. Instead, he walked straight through the door to the back of the saloon.

Caleb heard laughter from behind the door leading to the baths in the private rooms as he walked down the hall of Skinner's Saloon. He knocked on one of the doors.

"Sarah O'Toole!" called Caleb.

"Next one down!" cried out a woman's voice.

Caleb went to the next door. A man's voice could be heard on the other side. Caleb took his Henry and banged on the door with the rifle butt.

"Wait yer turn!" yelled a man from inside.

Caleb smashed the butt of the rifle even harder against the door. A woman jerked the door opened. Some gray graced her once pretty brown hair, and a thick coat of makeup and a frilly dress could not hide the years of struggle and the company of hard-living men. Still, Caleb could tell that this was their Aunt Sarah. Behind her was a man caked with dirt in filthy long johns, sitting in a tub.

"Get out of here!" said the man. "I ain't done yet!"

"Who in tarnation are you and what do you want?" Aunt Sarah demanded, looking Caleb up and down.

"I'm your nephew, Caleb O'Toole. Julie and Tilly are outside."

The woman's face went slack for a moment as she absorbed the news. "No! It can't be!" Sarah then exclaimed, "Go on, get out! I want nothin' to do with you!"

"Mother said you'd take us in the day she died. She said she sent a thousand dollars and the man in Virginia City said you have it." A cold wave passed through Caleb as he stood in the doorway. She was nothing like the laughing, smiling person his parents had described through the years. Instead, her eyes shone with suspicion and the corners of her mouth dipped in bitterness.

"Daggone it, Sarah," whined the filthy man. "I got soap in my eyes!"

"Shut up, Hank," snapped Aunt Sarah to the man. "I don't have it, Caleb. I loaned it to Roy. He lost it."

"You gave that gambler, the one in the saloon, our money?"

"He's gonna win it all back, he says. Then we'll go ahead with the plans," shot back Aunt Sarah.

"What plans?"

"We're heading to Chicago, where he's from. Going to live the life of luxury, he says. He's got a big house there," Sarah explained desperately, the guilt written on her weary face.

"What the spit is going on, Sarah?" growled the saloon owner as he burst through the door. "Kid, I said for you to get out of here."

"Not until we're done with our business," said Caleb, not giving an inch.

"It's just some family trouble, Cyrus. It's not anything," protested Sarah.

"Then take it outside. Boy has no business being in here," ordered Cyrus.

★ ★ ★

"Oh, Lord," gasped Aunt Sarah as she stepped outside into the bright sunlight and looked at Julie and Tilly. "You look just like your mother. It's been a long…"

"Years," snapped Julie. "I'm Julie. Tilly, this is your Aunt Sarah." Julie eyed her aunt pointedly. "You remember her from the pictures."

"My, you children came all the way here. I never thought you'd make it," Sarah said, smiling nervously.

"Apparently not," said Julie, keeping her temper in check. "The teller at the Virginia City Bank said that, according to you, we all died from cholera. Why don't we just settle up on our money now?"

"Why, I was telling Caleb here, I just don't have it. I gave it to Roy and he…" Aunt Sarah took a step back from Julie, fumbling her words.

"Well, maybe we should ride to your ranch and work this out," said Julie, her eyes boring in on Sarah. She pulled Tilly to her. "Tilly, we're going to stay with Aunt Sarah."

"No!" Aunt Sarah backed toward the saloon. "I don't want you. None of you. I never did. That was your mother's idea."

"You agreed to it!" exclaimed Julie as Sarah ran into the saloon. Julie hoisted Tilly aboard the wagon next to Tumble. "Tilly, stay out here in the wagon." Then she turned and followed her aunt inside, banging the saloon doors open. Caleb followed her with his Henry.

"Me and Roy, we have plans!" Sarah backed against the bar as Julie went after her. "We're going to travel the world together, get married. The last thing I want is you children hanging around my neck like a noose. What's more, there is no ranch. We lost it!" Sarah ran over to Roy. "Tell them, Roy!"

"You got a problem?" The slick gambler peered over his cards and eyed Caleb and Julie as they marched over to the poker table and stood in front of him. A pile of money was growing on the table. Along with the money was the watch from Switzerland, a few pouches of gold dust, and a yellow envelope.

"Tell them, Roy. Tell them how we lost the money and the deed to the ranch. Tell them how you're going to make it all back and it was just a little bad luck," said Sarah breathlessly.

"That's right," Roy offered slyly. "Just a bad streak. Couple of days, we'll be right as rain and out of here."

"You took our money?" asked Caleb as he tightened his grip on the Henry.

"Well, more like she loaned it to me. For our future. Like an investment, you might say," Roy replied calmly as he eyed Caleb and leaned back in his chair.

"And you lost it and gambled away the ranch," said Julie.

"It happens, Pocahontas," said Roy as he looked at Julie in her Indian dress. "Besides, that ranch is a worthless piece of junk. What's your stake in this anyway, Sarah darlin'?"

"They're my dead brother's kids. He sent them to live with me," said Sarah.

"Well, that's not likely to happen. Unless you want them. Do you? I sure as spit don't," said Roy.

"No, Roy. I want you," said Sarah desperately.

"You choose a man like this over your own family?" Julie questioned her aunt with disdain.

"Yes! I got one last chance at happiness and the three of you aren't going to take that away."

"Well, now, there you go," said Roy with a sinister grin. "Honey, get over here. You're bringing me luck. Working on a nice pot. You brats beat it, now. You can see she don't want you." He grabbed Sarah and pulled her toward him. Then he raked the money toward himself, sticking the yellow envelope in his vest pocket. With a practiced flair, he grabbed the cards and began to shuffle.

"How much is in that pot?" Caleb asked as he raised the Henry an inch and took a step closer to Roy.

"No you don't, boy!" As slick as grease, Roy whipped a pistol from under the table and aimed it at Caleb. "You lower your rifle right now. I got no problem killing anyone who draws down on me."

Instantly, the other poker players bolted from their seats and over to the bar. Julie quickly took a step around the table to the other side, drew her Colt, and aimed it directly at Roy's head.

"And I have no problem putting a bullet right through that cheating head of yours." Roy's smug expression changed in a heartbeat. "It looks like he's got nearly three hundred dollars. That right, Roy? Three hundred?" Julie cocked her Colt. Roy gently lowered his pistol to the table and folded his hands, grinning as he tried to salvage some of the dignity he lost, having been bested by Julie. Caleb picked up the gun and slid it across the room.

"And that envelope in your pocket. I'd like to see that." Julie stood firm as Roy, quietly seething, produced the envelope. Caleb aimed his Henry straight at Roy's head as Julie looked over the paper. "Well, now. Seems like this is the deed to the ranch, Roy."

"You said you lost it!" exclaimed Sarah, snatching the deed from Julie's hand.

"I won it back. I was going to tell you. It was a surprise," said Roy with a big grin, trying to laugh off his predicament.

"What should we do with him, Caleb?" asked Julie.

Caleb thought for a moment. "The stagecoach is leaving pretty soon. I'm thinking he should get on it and head south. I figure the three hundred dollars in this pot might cover it."

"Good idea." Julie pressed the Colt against Roy's head. "Roy, we're going to give Mathew your three hundred dollars, and when you get to Utah, you'll have it. Sound like a good deal?"

"Sounds like a good deal to me. I'd take it if I were you, Roy." Sheriff Logan Porter shouldered his way through the miners and cowboys and stood next to Caleb. His square jaw was set like a block of granite. Sandy blond hair peeked from underneath his hat and his piercing blue eyes danced in amusement at the predicament Roy was in.

"I've been lookin' for an excuse to ride you out of town. Let's go." Sheriff Porter snatched Roy up by his fancy vest. Caleb gathered up the money, figuring he should leave the watch and the gold dust on the table for the other poker players to divide up. Then Caleb, Julie, and Sheriff Porter marched the gambler out the swinging doors of Skinner's Saloon.

"Got a passenger for you, Mathew!" called Sheriff Porter as he dragged Roy over to the stagecoach. He opened the door and hoisted the gambler into the cabin. "You keep heading south, you hear me, Roy? There's a lot of folks will be happy you're gone. And you are real gone, you got that?"

Roy nodded in humiliation and sat back in the stagecoach, out of sight of the cowboys and miners who jeered from Skinner's Saloon.

"Mathew," said Caleb as he handed him the money. "I figure your fee is fifty. Give him the rest in Utah, OK?"

"Caleb, my pleasure," said Mathew as he took the money. "I owe you big."

"Roy!" cried Sarah as she ran to the stagecoach.

"Make your choice, Aunt Sarah," said Julie. "It's either us or him."

"Oh God! No. I just can't. I need him!" exclaimed Sarah as she opened the stagecoach door and climbed aboard. "Here, take that broken-down ranch. I don't want it!" Then she tossed the deed to her ranch in the street and slammed the door shut. "Roy, Roy…it's just you and me," she wailed as the stagecoach pulled away.

Caleb and Julie watched in the middle of Bannack's dusty

Main Street as Mathew drove Aunt Sarah and Roy the gambler out of their lives forever.

★ ★ ★

Caleb handed the letter he had just written to Sheriff Porter in the lawman's office. It felt good to get things off his chest. Julie and Tilly ate sandwiches from Skinner's Saloon.

"So this William Henderson is not the killer of Great Bend and you and Tilly witnessed it?" Sheriff Porter looked at the letter.

"Yes, sir."

"You say you saw the Blackstone brothers actually murder the Thatchers along with Jim Jackson and that Irishman in Dobytown? And Henderson killed one of the brothers trying to defend you. That the way it went?"

"That's right," said Caleb.

Porter rubbed his square jaw while he looked over the letter. "My gut says you're telling the truth. I know Sheriff Winstead of Great Bend. I'll telegraph him the information in a couple of days when we get the wires back up and working. Now, this Sheriff Blackstone and his brothers. My guess is you may not have seen the last of these boys. Sure you want to head out to the Bitterroot? Not much law out there, son."

"That ranch is all we have, sir. There's nowhere else to go."

"We'll be fine, Sheriff," said Julie. "We can handle things."

"No doubt you can," chuckled Sheriff Porter. "Caleb, Mathew told me about those vigilantes and what you did for him, cutting him down like you did. You're a good man. That means a lot in these parts."

"Thank you, Sheriff." Caleb shook the big Sheriff's hand and grabbed his Henry, which rested against the wall behind him. Julie and Tilly had finished their sandwiches, and they all headed toward the door.

"I get out that way from time to time. I'll check on you," said Sheriff Porter. "Good luck with the ranch. You'll need it."

20

THE BITTERROOT

★ ★

*W*e are going to need a lot more than luck, Caleb thought as they stared at the tiny broken-down ranch, sagging behind a rail fence that had fallen in disrepair. A rusty sign that swayed in the early autumn breeze creaked a sad and lonely melody and simply stated O'TOOLE. Caleb and his sisters had hoped against hope as they traveled over the past six days that their lives would begin anew, that they could plant their roots underneath the sharp painted mountains called the Bitterroot. They rode past the hills and river of the famous Battle of Big Hole and felt the sadness of the death that came to the Nez Perce Indians that day. They drove on through the pass between the mountains that led to the Bitterroot Valley and followed the river north, exhausted but nevertheless excited that their perilous journey was soon coming to an end. Smitty's Trading Post rested at the West Fork River some miles up the Bitterroot River, the last marker of civilization on their way up to the ranch. It had taken more than three months and over thirteen hundred miles to get from Great Bend to where they now stood alone to face their future. Golden colors mixed with red splashed from the granite rock cliff that towered above them. Deer, elk, and moose appeared in the dry grass and purple fields of fireweed that rested under the thick pine mountains. Their wooden shack of a house stood at the base of a pine-dotted hill next to a sagging barn. An old washtub and a privy rested on the other side. The only sound was the wind through the pines.

"Well," said Julie. "We may as well go inside."

"This going to be our home?" Tilly gazed at the run-down ranch, crestfallen.

"Yes, Tilly." Julie let out a deep sigh. "It is."

The door creaked on loose hinges as they stepped inside the little house. Spiderwebs and dust covered the kitchen. Filthy drapes fell across the broken windows over the old sink. There was a wood-burning stove in the corner, a fireplace, and a small table with four chairs. Some pots and pans lay stacked on the kitchen counter as if their Aunt Sarah simply abandoned her life one day. They entered through a door to the only other room. A half-made bed rested sadly against the wall. Rats, startled out of their home, scattered past them, fleeing for their lives.

"Well, let's get started," said Julie with resolve. "Caleb, why don't you check out the barn? Tilly and I will get to work on the house. There's no sense in crying. We're here now, and we'll make the best of it. Tilly, there's a broom in the kitchen.

You go get it and start sweeping. We'll get things in shape before you can say once upon a time!"

"Once upon a time!" exclaimed Tilly as she ran into the kitchen.

Caleb brought Pride and Dusty to the pasture by the barn and let them graze on the dry grass. He grabbed the handle of the pump nearby and worked the lever. After some time, fresh water came out and he took a long drink. Just the other side of the barn, a fair-sized creek gurgled along the side of the house and down the length of the valley. *Good*, he thought, *Dusty and Pride could have their fill there*. He unloaded the wagon of its furs and supplies and did an inventory. The barn was a disaster, but in it were some tools they could use. They would need lumber and paint, as well as some new glass for the windows of the house. He could see light through the roof of the small barn, and he made a mental note that it needed to be patched. He figured the main house probably leaked as well. He gathered some wood that lay chopped by the barn and hauled it to the house for Julie. *We need a fire*, Caleb thought, but before that, there was something he needed to do.

★ ★ ★

Caleb and his sisters sat on the granite rocks of the mountain ledge that rose above the ranch. Pine trees and wildflowers surrounded them as if the mountain offered up a sanctuary, a gateway that led farther into the mysteries of the painted hills. Two small wooden crosses that Caleb had made rested upright in the earth nearby. For the first time, Caleb quietly let the tears flow. Julie gently wiped his eyes and kissed him on the forehead, just like his mother used to do. His heart ached for both his parents, and the pain of their deaths filled his soul. Tilly nestled onto his lap, and the three of them held each other and watched the clouds roll in over their desolate little home a few hundred yards below. They looked at the photo of their parents in the locket.

"It's like they're here and looking down on us," said Julie softly.

"We can come up here to this place and talk to them?" asked Tilly.

"That's right, you can." Caleb choked back his tears and gathered himself. "But not alone. You might stumble on a bear or a wolf."

Tilly pulled the locket back over her head and began to pick some flowers. "Mommy liked flowers," she said as she laid them against the crosses.

"Yes, Tilly, let's pick lots of flowers!" said Julie, springing into action.

"Tomorrow I'll head over to that trading post with the wagon and see if I can pick up anything we might need around here." Caleb took a deep breath as he looked across their valley.

"Good idea, Caleb." Julie placed some flowers near their father's cross. "I'll go get supper ready."

★ ★ ★

"Folks just call me Smitty," said the older, wiry black man with a wooden leg as he carried some sacks of grain and stacked them on the porch of Smitty's Trading Post. "I been here near since the war. That's where I lost this daggone leg."

"Can I lend you a hand?" Caleb jumped off the wagon to help.

"Why not? Have to say, those are some nice skins you got. You been trappin'?"

"Some are from the game I shot near Yellowstone." Caleb grabbed a sack of grain and threw it on the pile. "The others I got from Touch the Clouds's people. That red mark of a buffalo on my wagon is from Sitting Bull."

"Well, I'll be. From Sitting Bull? Ain't that somethin'. That figures to be quite a story. What are you doin' up in these parts?"

"You know the O'Toole ranch up the West Fork?" asked Caleb as he stacked another sack of grain. "My sisters and I are taking it over from our Aunt Sarah. I'm Caleb O'Toole. It's a long story."

"I know the place. Pretty run-down," said Smitty as he stretched his aching back.

"There are things we need for winter. You wouldn't care to trade for some of these furs, would you?"

"Well, no. I got plenty of skins. But I tell you what. That Henry rifle there in the wagon. Now that is one fine thing. You let me have that and I'll go a long way in setting you folks up."

Caleb took the rifle from the wagon. It would be hard to give up Ben Johnson's gift. It had saved Caleb and his sisters many times. Even more, it was a piece of a man who was good to him and had respected him. But he needed what Smitty could offer. It was time to let it go.

"All right," said Caleb as he handed it to Smitty.

"I thank you for it." Smitty took the Henry and placed it against the wall next to his chair. Then he sat and took out a corncob pipe. "Now, Caleb. Pull up a chair. I want to hear that story."

"It's a long one." Caleb grabbed a stool and sat next to Smitty.

"Like I said," he said as he lit his pipe. "I got nothin' but time."

Caleb and Smitty traded stories that afternoon until nearly sundown. He helped him load supplies for other men who had stopped by the trading post. He liked the Civil War veteran, a man who had escaped slavery in Alabama to fight for the North against the South. A man who had laid down his life to be free and had lost his leg to a Confederate cannonball in Gettysburg. He had come years ago to find his fortune in gold like so many others. It was a life too hard for a one-legged man, but he found a way to survive with his little trading post. And he found a place to be free. And Caleb had found a new friend.

Smitty set up Caleb well, sending him back to the ranch with the wagon stocked with the food and supplies they would need for the winter. Come spring, they could do some planting. They had seeds for vegetables and fruit, and some day Caleb figured to add some cattle. All through October, Julie and Tilly scrubbed and cleaned and worked hard to get the house into shape. The two girls slept together in the little bedroom under the furs of the Sioux. Julie refused to be knocked off course and seemed to have a passion for fixing up their new home. She took to drying meat for the winter, just like their Sioux friends did. She studied the medical book Dr. Sullivan gave her nightly under candlelight, absorbing every word. Caleb made repairs on the ranch. He slept peacefully in the barn while it was still warm enough under furry animal skins on top of a pile of hay. From time to time, he would make his way to Smitty's to help him out, then up the road to the town of Darby if Smitty needed something. It was a fair deal. Smitty would pay him with more supplies for the ranch. Then they would spend an hour or so swapping stories, Smitty about the War and Caleb about the Oregon Trail, the Hole in the Wall outlaws, and the Indian friends he had met along the way.

★ ★ ★

Caleb led Pride to the edge of the Bitterroot River, letting him drink his fill. He had just spent the day poking around Darby, a few miles up the road. It was a nice mountain village, peaceful and quiet. Just the other side of the river, an elk stood grazing in the yellow grass on the forest edge. He took his Sharps rifle and sighted in on the elk, when the sound of a gunshot echoed softly in the distance. "Sounds like ol' Smitty got himself a buck, Pride. Let's see what's up," he mused as he spared the elk and put the Sharps back in the scabbard. It was almost routine now. If either Smitty or Caleb got a deer, they would both often clean it, skin it together, and divide up their food. It was more of an excuse to share stories. He laughed in anticipation at what his friend would come up with today. Sometimes it was hard to tell if it was a true story, for the man loved to spin a yarn or two.

Caleb pulled Pride up to the railing in front of Smitty's Trading Post. There seemed to be no one around. No horses were in sight, no sign of anyone or anything. He called out for Smitty, but did not get his friend's usual good-natured hello in return. He grabbed his Sharps and jumped off Pride and headed through the open doorway. It was dark inside. He heard a faint groan coming from the back of the store. He raised his Sharps and stepped around the counter. He found Smitty leaning up against the wall, blood pouring from a gunshot wound in his left shoulder.

"Smitty! What happened?"

"Get home, Caleb," groaned Smitty as he reached out with his right hand and pulled Caleb to him.

"Who shot you?" Caleb held on to his friend.

"There's four of 'em. Looking for you," gasped Smitty. "They're headin' up the Fork."

The blood suddenly ran cold in Caleb's veins. "What did they look like?"

"Black dusters. One of 'em had a sheriff badge. Another

one was missing part of his ear." Smitty struggled to get the words out. "I wouldn't tell them where you lived, so one with black teeth just shot me like I was nothin'."

"The Blackstones!" Caleb's worst nightmare had come to the Bitterroot. Quickly, he ripped up a cloth and pressed it against Smitty's bleeding shoulder and placed his friend's hand over it.

"Go on, Caleb! I been shot worse than this. Get home!"

"I'll be back for you, Smitty!" Caleb said as he rushed to the door.

"Caleb!" called Smitty as he pointed to the rifle in the corner. "Take the Henry!"

★ ★ ★

"Come on, Pride!" cried Caleb as they thundered along the West Fork River. His heart was in his throat. He pushed the fear of what was to come out of his mind; his only thought was to get to his sisters. He had hoped against hope the murderous brothers had lost the trail or had given up over the weeks and gone off to do some other mayhem. Or maybe even met their fates at the hands of Henderson. Sheriff Porter had been right. Caleb had not seen the last of them. Pride ripped over the ground as if he knew himself that this would be his biggest battle, the race of his life. Every ounce of the warhorse's soul and every fiber of his muscle surged and pounded beneath Caleb as they crashed through branches of pine trees and leaped over rocks and fallen logs. In no time, the Blackstones would find the ranch. Caleb shuddered to think what they might do to his sisters. If he could just get to them first, maybe together they would stand a chance. Caleb crouched low and gripped hard with his knees as Pride ate up the ground beneath them. Two gunshots rang out! It was Julie's signal. The Blackstones had found the ranch!

"Pride, it's up to you, boy! Give me everything you've got!" Pride bounded ahead with a burst of awesome power that came from deep within his big heart. Caleb, the reins in one hand and the Henry in the other, rode still and light as the mighty warhorse carried him into battle. More gunshots! As they crested the hill that led to the ranch, Caleb could see the Blackstones on horseback circling the little house. Tumble raced around in front, barking and snapping at the horses' hooves. Tilly broke from the door and tried to get to Tumble, but Julie grabbed her and yanked her back inside. He could imagine the Blackstones laughing as the brave little dog tried to defend his house, snapping at the legs of the horses. One of the brothers drew a bead on Tumble. With a yelp, Tumble rolled over in the dirt, shot. He tried to get up, but collapsed and lay still.

Caleb gripped the Henry rifle hard as Pride carried him over the purple fireweed. There was a time months ago when Caleb would not have dared what he did next. But he was not the same boy anymore. He could see the Blackstones turn to face him. The smoke from their guns puffed against the blue sky and the bullets whizzed past him. It didn't matter. Caleb let go of the reins and sighted the Henry at the closest

Blackstone. Rat Face! His heart pounded wildly as Pride charged over the purple field, hooves crashing and his great chest heaving. Barely fifty yards away, Caleb took one final calming breath and squeezed the trigger.

21

GOOD AGAINST EVIL

★ ★

Rat Face flew off the saddle and landed in a heap, his arm shattered by the single blast of the big Henry. He dragged himself to the horse trough and reached for his pistol. Caleb rode down on the Blackstones, firing the Henry and scattering the brothers. Blacktooth took his horse around to the side of the house as he fired at Caleb with his pistol. The bullet tore a patch from the side of Caleb's skin coat. Julie answered the call with her pearl-handled Colt from the window of the house. Caught between fire, Snake jumped off his horse and dove into the barn, drawing his pistol. Caleb fired the Henry as fast as he could, keeping the Blackstones pinned down as he rode to the back of the barn. Sheriff Blackstone ran to the side of the barn with his pistol. Caleb's shot tore off a chunk of wood, and the Sheriff clutched his face and hit the ground, cursing up a storm. Caleb had him right where he wanted him and sighted in on the Sheriff. *CLICK*. Empty!

With no more bullets that fit the Henry, Caleb grabbed the

Sharps from the scabbard and his pouch of fifty-caliber bullets, leaped off Pride, and dove toward the cover of the bushes along the creek as the Sheriff rose to fire. The shots went over Caleb's head as he crawled on his belly and hid behind a rock. He dug into the pouch and brought out a handful of shells. Quickly, he crammed one into the chamber and fired. The Sheriff retreated behind the barn. Caleb sprinted low through the creek toward the rear of the house. Like lightning, he shoved another bullet into the Sharps as Blacktooth appeared on the other side of the house. Blacktooth fired as Caleb took cover in the tall wet weeds of the stream. In a second, Caleb returned fire, driving Blacktooth to the front of the house, where he ducked behind a pile of wood by the fence. Caleb took a deep breath and ran fifty feet toward the back window. A bullet from the Sheriff nicked him, but he hardly felt it as he dove headfirst through the window of the little bedroom. Caleb rolled across the floor over the shards of broken glass. From the floor, he could see Tilly hiding under the bed, her hands over her ears, terrified and sobbing.

"Julie! Are you all right?" Caleb ran to the window and closed the wooden shutters and latched them.

"Yes!" Julie fired her Colt out the kitchen window. "Caleb, cover me, I have to reload!"

In a flash, he stuck more bullets into the webbing of his fingers and loaded the Sharps as he ran to Julie's side. Suddenly, a barrage of Blackstone bullets smashed out the remainder of the window glass and Caleb and Julie ducked for their lives. Quickly, Caleb rose and fired from the side as

Snake ran from the barn to the side of the house. Julie fired her Colt at the Sheriff as he ran from the other side of the house and shot through the window. Rat Face, his arm useless, ran toward the barn, firing his pistol with his good hand. Then everything stopped. The smell of gunpowder hung in the air.

"Pretty good shooting, kid!" shouted Blacktooth.

"Caleb O'Toole!" yelled Sheriff Blackstone. "You and your sister come on out now! I'm here to take you back to Dobytown. Give up and we'll go easy on you."

"We'll not likely give ourselves up to a family of murdering thieves!" shouted Julie. She turned to her brother, her face set in determination. "Caleb. There is no way we believe a word they say. They'll just shoot us down."

"I know. I say we stand and fight. How are you fixed for ammo?"

"Twenty or so, I think." Julie checked her pockets. "You?"

"Maybe thirty. If we make them count, we might get through this."

"What do you say, boy?" shouted Sheriff Blackstone.

"You don't come out, we will shoot you down or burn the house!" threatened Blacktooth. "Either way, it don't matter to me!"

"If you come for us, we will shoot!" shouted Caleb.

Caleb and Julie stood on either side of the window just out of sight. Caleb's ears strained to hear any sign of movement. As Julie reloaded her Colt, he saw a flicker of motion over her shoulder. A tiny ray of light peeked through a slight gap in the wood on the side of the house. For a split second, the light was blocked from outside, then the light appeared again. Someone was sneaking toward the door. The Blackstones laid down another barrage of fire as Julie swung the Colt toward the window. Caleb fired the Sharps at the gap in the wall. Then he grabbed the supper table and slid it hard against the door just as it crashed open, smashing it closed on the arm and head of the intruder. It was Snake! The killer threw all his weight against the door, trying to force his way inside, but Caleb held fast. Snake's lizard face peeled back in a ghoulish grin as he twisted his gun around and fired a shot at Julie. Julie dove to the floor just in time. In a flash, Caleb grabbed his knife and leaped toward the earless man, slashing down hard and slicing Snake's arm.

Snake shrieked as he yanked his bloody arm back and fell outside. Caleb slammed the door with the table. Then he reloaded and fired out the window as Snake scurried to the side of the barn.

"Burn them out!" shouted Blacktooth from the side of the house.

The Blackstones fired with everything they had as Rat Face ran from the barn, swinging a lit lantern. Bullets flew through the kitchen and chewed chunks from the window and the door. Caleb dove for the floor next to Julie who was reloading. Rat Face threw the lantern through the kitchen window and suddenly the wall burst into flames. Caleb rolled to his right and fired at Rat Face, but the rodent man ducked below the window. Julie quickly crawled into the bedroom and stripped the fur blanket from the bed. In a flash, she returned and began to beat back the flames as the Blackstones unleashed all their firepower. There was no way they could stand and return fire. In moments, the four mur- derers would rush the house. *In seconds our lives could be over*, Caleb thought as he slammed another shell into his rifle. He was determined to take at least one Blackstone with him. Suddenly, there was silence.

"They stopped!" said Caleb as he crawled toward the window.

Three gunshots echoed in the distance. Another shot, this time a little closer. Caleb rose carefully to his feet and looked out the window.

"Who is it!" cried Julie as she beat back the flames. "Who's firing?"

"I can't tell," said Caleb. "Wait. I see them. There're two men."

A tall lean rider, his long black coat swirling behind him, tore through the purple valley like he was sent on a mission from Hades. He thundered across the field on a mustang that was so red in color, it looked like he was riding on a flame. The reins in his teeth and a Spencer rifle booming in his hands, he swallowed up the ground, raking the Blackstones with his fire. Right behind him was a big man with a Winchester rifle, riding straight up and fearless on a snorting Palomino.

"It's Henderson! And Sheriff Porter is with him!" shouted Caleb as he reloaded.

Blacktooth turned and ran to the side of the house, firing both of his Colt pistols at the charging Henderson and Porter. Rat Face ran to the side of the barn, clutching his wounded arm as bullets dug the ground beside him. Snake, his arm covered in blood, dove for cover into the barn and snapped off two shots from his pistol. Suddenly, Henderson and Porter split off. Sheriff Blackstone ran away from the house into the field, trying to outflank them. Porter sheathed his Winchester and drew his Colt as he rode down on the Sheriff. Blacktooth fired from the side and Sheriff Porter jumped off his horse and dove for cover. Henderson rode hard toward the barn. In one motion, he sheathed his rifle and drew his Colt, leaping off the mustang. In a second, he was after Rat Face. Snake emerged from the barn, then crept around the side, trying to sneak up on Henderson from behind.

Caleb yanked the table away from the door. With the Blackstones now fighting Henderson and Porter, he took a chance and ran from the house to the barn and ducked behind the barn door. From there, he could see Sheriff Logan Porter and Sheriff Blackstone exchanging fire in the field on the other side of the house. Two lawmen, one good and one evil. Blacktooth appeared from around the corner of the house and drew on Porter from behind. Caleb fired from the barn at Blacktooth and hit him in his leg. Blacktooth grabbed his leg, turned, and fired at Caleb, but Caleb was already moving, diving across the barn and rolling to a stop on the other side. Through the gaps in the wood in the side of the barn, Caleb could see Henderson advancing on Rat Face. Henderson's shot knocked the man clear through the wall. Rat Face landed in a heap. He tried to raise his pistol to fire as Henderson stepped through the hole in the wall. Henderson finished off the murderer and Rat Face lay still. Snake suddenly appeared from behind Henderson and swung his pistol. In a flash, Henderson dove to his right and came up firing. Caleb beat him to it. The heavy slug from the Sharps blew Snake clean out of the barn and into the creek!

"Nice going, kid," growled Henderson as he ran to the barn door. "Let's take care of those other two."

Caleb crammed another shell into his rifle and ran to the other side of the door. Together they looked out as Sheriff Porter stalked slowly after Sheriff Blackstone as the man tried to flee for his life. Wounded in the leg, the man limped pitifully toward a grove of pines. The fleeing Sheriff tried to shoot Porter, but by this time he was near panic and his shots were wild and desperate. Sheriff Porter took his time as he advanced on the Blackstone lawman. He seemed an invincible force of good against the whimpering defeat of evil. Granite against fool's gold. Sheriff Blackstone lay down for good under the roar of Porter's Colt. Suddenly, all was quiet. But there was one more. Blacktooth. And then Julie screamed.

"He's got Tilly!" Julie ran from the house, blood in her beautiful blond hair, her chest heaving in fear.

"Are you shot?" Caleb ran to his sister and checked her head.

"No." Julie's breath came out in gasps. "I heard something in the back. He smashed through the shutters and then hit me in the head. He took Tilly!"

"Where did he go?" Henderson asked as he loaded his Colt.

"In back. Up the hill."

"He wants a hostage. Must be hit." Henderson reloaded his Colt and checked the Remington in his boot.

"I got him in the leg," said Caleb.

"Man's a coward," grunted Sheriff Porter. "We'll get him."

Caleb, Henderson, and Porter fanned out as they climbed the hill in back of the ranch. The blood trail was easy to follow, and it led straight to the sanctuary. Caleb swore that if Blacktooth harmed Tilly in any way, he would put a bullet into the murderer himself. With Henderson on Caleb's right and Sheriff Porter on his left, one thing was for sure. Blacktooth's days were numbered.

"Help!" Tilly yelled from the gravesite just fifty yards up the hill.

"Give it up, Blackstone!" shouted Porter.

A bullet went whizzing overhead. "You come any closer and I'll kill her!" yelled Blacktooth.

"You got nobody left, Blackstone!" shouted Henderson. "All your brothers are dead!"

Blacktooth fired off two more rounds and Caleb hit the ground hard.

Porter charged up the left side. "Back off, Sheriff!" Blacktooth, holding Tilly against him, fired toward Porter, and the Sheriff dove low into the grass. When the outlaw backed away from the rocky ledge and into the trees, Henderson bolted up the hill. Caleb, his legs churning, crested the hill after him and took cover behind a tree. Henderson, kneeling behind a fallen log, had his gun trained on Blacktooth. The outlaw cowered in the shadows of the trees, crouching against the granite boulders near the two crosses. Tilly kicked and screamed, struggling in the grip of the murderer's arms as he tried to reload his gun. They dared not fire and chance hitting Tilly. Before they could make a move, Blacktooth snapped the chamber shut and pointed the gun at Tilly.

"I didn't take you for a coward, Blackstone, hiding behind a little girl," taunted Henderson. "Let's just make this about you and me. It's what you really want, right?"

"You and me?" snarled Blacktooth, weakening from the loss of blood.

"Let the girl go. Maybe you can make it through the trees. Kill me and you have a chance. Wait much longer and you'll bleed out for sure. I see the boy here messed you up pretty good." Henderson, from the cover of the log, held his Colt rock-steady on the wounded outlaw. Sheriff Porter then eased himself closer from the hill below and took cover in the rocks on the other side of Blacktooth. "There's no way you'll stand up to three of us."

Blacktooth held Tilly against him as he swung his pistol toward Henderson, Porter, then at Caleb. Caleb didn't budge. Pressed against the tree, he was ready to fire if he had the chance. Still, there was no way he could risk a shot.

"You and me, face-to-face?" sneered Blacktooth as he swung his pistol back to Henderson.

"Face-to-face," answered Henderson with deadly calm. "We'll settle it. Let her go." Henderson knew the power of the temptation was too great for Blacktooth.

"The Sheriff and the boy head down the hill. When they

get far enough away, I'll let the girl go and we do this," snarled Blacktooth, his ugly black grin widening. Blood from Caleb's gunshot poured down his leg and he was running out of time. "I beat you in Dobytown, and I'll beat you here."

"You sure about this, Henderson?" Sheriff Porter was itching to get a shot at Blacktooth.

"You heard him, Sheriff." Henderson held his pistol steady on the outlaw.

It took everything Caleb had to leave his little sister in the clutches of the killer. But he knew Henderson was right. They had to get Tilly away from Blacktooth. Caleb, his Sharps held in front of him, backed toward the ledge and eased down the hill. Porter climbed down from the other side, ready to make a move with his pistol if he had to.

When Caleb and Sheriff Porter got halfway to the bottom, they waited for Tilly as she ran down the hill. Caleb opened his arms, and his terrified little sister flew into them. He felt her heart beating like a hummingbird. He wrapped his arms around her as she buried her face in his chest. Sheriff Porter gripped his Colt, ready to advance on Blacktooth should the murdering thief get the best of Henderson. Caleb checked his Sharps rifle. Carefully, he sighted on the ledge above.

It seemed an eternity. Finally Henderson appeared, standing tall and still in the sunlight. He slowly eased his Colt over to the left side and stuck it in his belt. His gun-hand! Then the murdering Blacktooth stepped forward from the shadows of the pines. They faced each other, waiting to see who would make the first move. It was their fate, their destiny. They drew out the time as if each knew it might be the last thing he ever did on this earth. It was deadly calm against blinding rage. The Civil War hero, his life torn apart by the evil done to him and his family, stared down the lightning-fast outlaw who burned with greed and destruction. Caleb held his breath. Quick as a snake, Blacktooth made a move for his gun. In a blur, Henderson's Colt appeared, smoking in his hand. Henderson fired two shots into Blacktooth before he could get off one. Blacktooth staggered, then stood still for several seconds as the life poured out of his black heart. The outlaw fired helplessly into the ground, and then he dropped his Colt. He took one step toward Henderson and tried to raise his arms before he slumped to his knees. Finally, Blacktooth collapsed to the ground, dead.

EPILOGUE

Caleb tore across the field on Pride, his Henry rifle in his
hand. Henderson had made sure he got it back. For two
weeks, Julie had nursed Smitty to health. She even tried to
use the last of the chloroform on him so she could dig the
bullet out of his shoulder. Smitty refused. So she used it on
Tumble and took the forty-five slug from the hind end of the
most stubborn dog in the West. Only a cat could have more
lives than mighty Tumble. Smitty and Henderson got good
and drunk while Julie dug around for Blacktooth's bullet, trading war stories into the night. They traded other things too,
including Henderson's Medal of Honor, which Henderson
said Smitty deserved more than he did. Smitty's eyes glistened
with tears of wonder and gratitude as he clutched the medal
to his heart. They gave a toast to Abraham Lincoln, and then
Smitty gestured toward the Henry rifle. And lo and behold, by
the time Sheriff Porter and Caleb had returned from taking the
Blackstones to be buried in Darby, Caleb had his Henry back.

Caleb gave Pride a squeeze with his knees, and the great warhorse thundered ahead through the gentle snow that began to cover the valley beneath the rugged mountains of the Bitterroot. Another squeeze and Pride flattened out his head and his tail and they raced, smooth as glass, toward the house. Caleb let go of the reins, sighting in on his target. He took a deep breath as Pride pounded beneath him. Time seemed to stand still. He gently squeezed the trigger and fired. Dead center! The can of beans sitting on a log in the field exploded and the beans went everywhere.

"I told you!" squealed Tilly, a bandaged Tumble barking at her feet.

"Well, I'll be," mused Smitty, his arm trussed up in a sling. "That's some shootin'!"

"Daggone straight," said Henderson, walking over to the fence as Caleb rode up with Pride. His reddish-brown mustang was loaded up and ready to ride. "That's great riding, boy. It's like you're a part of him. I know you two have been through a lot." Henderson stuck out his hand and Pride walked over to him. Gently, Henderson stroked the big horse's head and ran his hand down its flank. Pride's coat shivered and shook. His panting eased as Henderson whispered to him. The love of the man for his horse and the devotion of the horse for his master could not be denied.

"You sure were right about Pride." Caleb slid easily from the saddle. "He got me out of a lot of scrapes."

"Yeah, I heard about a couple of those," chuckled Henderson. "Took a while for my leg to heal. I started tracking those Blackstones all the way to Bannack. I figured they'd go after you. Stories about you and Captain Bellows's wagon train and Scotts Bluff were all over Fort Fetterman. Then some old Sioux friends I met up with had a few things to say. They talked about this kid on a fast black horse who could shoot the eye out of a hawk like you were a legend or something. After what happened here, I believe it. Logan Porter thinks pretty highly of you. We shared a drink at Skinner's Saloon. You learn good, kid."

"I had some good teachers. This is a real nice horse you have now." Caleb stroked Henderson's mustang.

"She's beautiful," admired Julie as she and Smitty walked over and stood beside Caleb. "What's her name?"

"I call her Glory. Darn near as fast as Pride. Blue Hawk's best. In a couple of years, she's going to make a great horse. She's only two now." Henderson checked the saddlebags and his packs.

"I'm almost seven!" exclaimed Tilly.

"That a fact?" smiled Henderson as he picked up Tilly and gave her a kiss on the cheek.

"Trade you for her," said Caleb.

"What?" Henderson put Tilly down, and then turned to Caleb and Julie.

"I'll trade you Pride for Glory." Caleb gave Julie a quick glance. "I've got Dusty and…"

"And I could use a good horse," said Julie with a twinkle in her eye as she stroked Glory. "She's a pretty one. I like her."

"Besides, you're going to need Pride where you're going."

Caleb knew the gunfighter would not rest until the Redlegs who killed his wife and child paid the ultimate price. As much as Caleb would miss him, Pride belonged with Henderson.

"And tell Dr. Kathleen Sullivan when you see her I thank her for her father's medical bag. It's come in real handy," said Julie matter-of-factly.

"What makes you think I'll be seeing her?" Henderson flushed as Caleb began to transfer his saddlebags from Glory and onto Pride.

"Men," teased Julie with a wink. "A woman knows these things."

"There's no way I'm gonna...that woman..." Henderson growled sheepishly as he crammed his Spencer rifle into the scabbard on Pride's saddle.

"Mr. Henderson, you are welcome here anytime. When you come back up this way, please pay us a visit." Julie offered her hand to Henderson. Then she suddenly embraced the big man.

"That I will, Miss O'Toole," said Henderson as he held Julie. Then he let her go and offered his hand to Caleb. His piercing eyes revealed the slightest hint of warmth. But the pain in his soul also held him away. He was already pushing south to the trail.

Caleb shook Henderson's hand and fought the lump that was building in his throat. There was too much to say. "Thank you."

"Caleb O'Toole. You're about as good as a man gets, and I am the better for knowing you." Henderson mounted Pride and stroked his big horse. "I would ride alongside you any-where." Henderson touched his hat, turned Pride toward the field, and urged the big warhorse into a gentle run. White puffs kicked up from Pride's hooves as the gunfighter parted the swirling snowflakes. He reached back and pulled up the collar of his duster as he rode across the valley and into the cold fading light.

"Let's eat." Julie laid a gentle hand on Caleb's shoulder.

"Be right there. I'll put Glory in the barn first."

"Smitty, you'll stay, of course," said Julie, turning toward the house. "Tilly, how about a story? Once upon a time!"

"Once upon a time!" cried Tilly.

"A story!" said Smitty. "I do love a good story."

"Once upon a time there was a very sad knight." Tilly took Smitty's hand. "They cast a spell on him and he had to wander off into the Petrified Forest to slay the dragons with his magic fire wand!"

"What's a magic fire wand?" asked a confused Smitty.

"This one turns dragons into stars!" cried Tilly as she walked Smitty to the porch.

"Stars? What for?"

"Once the knight turns the dragons into stars, he can leave the Petrified Forest and ride to the castle where the beautiful and lonely princess is waiting for him…" explained Tilly as she led a mystified Smitty into the house.

Caleb watched as Henderson and Pride reached the end of the valley and disappeared into the pine trees. Then he grabbed his Henry and led Glory into the barn. He leaned the rifle beside the plow against the wall and lit a lantern against the dimming light of day. He took the saddle off Glory and brushed her down, noting the ripple of muscle. She had a bright, smart look to her. Henderson said she was fast. He would find out in the morning. Just then, he heard the soft whinny of his best friend. Dusty pawed the dirt, signaling his attentions. Caleb walked over and gave him a handful of oats.

"Hello, friend," said Caleb as he stroked Dusty's nose. "You were the best of us all. Without you, we never would have made it." Dusty tossed his head up and down as if he could understand. Then he let out a loud whinny. Caleb brushed his loyal horse gently as he looked through the barn door at the house. Smoke from the fire inside rose from the chimney. The smell of supper wafted through the mid-November cold. He heard the cackle of Smitty's laughter and the squeal of Tilly's glee. The door opened and Julie stuck her head out. Firelight danced off her golden hair. "Caleb! Supper's on!" she called.

"Coming!" As the comforting smell of Julie's cooking lingered in the cool air, Caleb's heart ached for the time when he looked across the supper table into the loving faces of his parents. There would be so much to say to them. He wondered how his father would react from behind his newspaper to the tales Caleb could tell. He would be proud, he thought. "Dusty, this spring, we've got work to do," said Caleb to his horse as he glanced at the old rusty plow that leaned against the wall. He grabbed a bale of hay and tossed it easily down for Dusty and Glory. His arms and back were much stronger now. He had even grown two inches since that fateful June night in Great Bend. He felt he was nothing like the small boy who escaped from his burning home with his sisters those months ago, and yet, he was. He had stood strong for his mother, like a big oak tree. He kept his promise to her and never wavered. He discovered the things that lived deep inside him, the strength and the courage to keep going, no matter how hard the trail. And he had something else inside. It was something Touch the Clouds had once said. He had the roots of a warrior. It was here he would set these roots, in their little ranch under the painted mountains of the Bitterroot. He gave Dusty a final pat. Then he checked his knife, grabbed his Henry, and headed toward the house.

THE HISTORY
BEHIND THE STORY

In the summer of 2009, I packed up my car and my dog, Joey, and headed for the Oregon Trail. I have always had a great love for Westerns. My own family has a pioneer history. They came across the Oregon Trail, the California Trail, and the Mormon Trail. Many settled in Utah near Salt Lake City. The pioneer part of my heritage produced very rugged individuals, women who became prairie doctors whose sons became doctors. But as I sat down to pull this story from my mind, I found that many of my "facts" about the Wild West came from Hollywood. Not good enough, I thought. There was only one thing I could do. Trace the route the O'Toole children of this book took in the summer of 1877, from the flat prairies of Great Bend, Kansas, along the Oregon and Bozeman Trails, to the Bitterroot Mountains. This is what Joey and I learned:

The Railroad Strike of 1877

By 1869, train travel had grown in popularity after the transcontinental railroad routes were established. Instead of spending months of rough travel on the Oregon, California, and Mormon Trails, a person could be whisked across the country in a matter of days. However, the Great Railroad Strike during the summer of 1877 forced many travelers heading west to face the many dangers of the Oregon Trail.

The Oregon Trail

By the 1830s, routes of rocky dirt roads had been established by fur traders and explorers traveling to the western United States. In the 1840s, these routes opened up to thousands of immigrants, pioneers, prospectors, and settlers during what was known as the Western Migration. The Oregon Trail was a two-thousand-mile route that began in Missouri and went west through parts of Kansas, Nebraska, and along the Platte River. It continued through Wyoming, Idaho, and Oregon. Thousands of wagons would gather near the Missouri River and cross in steady streams over the land. It provoked the many Indian nations. Forts were established to protect the settlers from these dangers.

The Bozeman Trail

Referred to often as "The Bloody Bozeman," this trail split off the Oregon Trail near Fort Fetterman in southeastern Wyoming. Fort Fetterman was considered the last remaining outpost of civilization along the Platte River, as many of the forts of that time had been dismantled. Prospectors, miners, and fur traders caused great conflict with the Plains Indians as they made their way over the Bozeman Trail to and from Virginia City, Bannack, and the gold fields of Montana. Soldiers were sent to try to control the Sioux, Arapaho, and Cheyenne nations and attempt to force them into reservations. Indian attacks were frequent, because the Indians felt their way of life and rich hunting lands were being taken away from them by the expansion of whites during the Western Migration. For a while, the army shut down the trail due to treaty agreements and violence. It was reopened in 1876 after the Battle of Little Big Horn.

Dangers of the Oregon and Bozeman Trails

Cholera, disease, contamination, flash floods, tornados, snake bites, gunshot wounds, theft, murder, and attacks from hostile Indians were among the many dangers facing pioneers as they pursued their dreams of land, gold, and a new life.

The Indians

The Pawnee, who lived in mud huts and turned to farming, were prevalent along the Platte River. They had a peaceful existence with whites and traded with them. Many fought for the U.S. Army against other warring Indians and were used as scouts. One such scout was named Blue Hawk. **The Sioux** (Lakota) had a fearsome reputation. Washington bowed to pressure to drive the Sioux out of their lands for the sake of the settlers and put them on reservations, only to drive them from those too. Thus, the great Sioux Wars continued. The year 1876 saw the Battle of Little Big Horn, which resulted in the massacre of General George Armstrong Custer and his troops by chiefs Sitting Bull, Crazy Horse, and others. Greatly respected chiefs Touch the Clouds and Red Cloud stopped fighting and lobbied for peace in Washington. **The Nez Perce** were surprise-attacked in Montana by soldiers and settlers at the famous 1877 Battle of Big Hole, their women and children gunned down in their sleep. After the battle, the greatly revered Chief Joseph led his people through Yellowstone Park toward Canada. Later, in Washington, Chief Joseph told his story and gained much sympathy. People finally began to understand the plight of the Native American People. Yellow Hawk was a scout for Chief Joseph who described a Nez Perce encounter with several young white settlers and some trappers in Yellowstone. The Indians killed the trappers, but for some reason let the children go free.

Wagon Trains

The Great Migration began in 1843, and over a half million pioneers over the next twenty-five years joined the push west. They traveled in or walked alongside ox- or horse-drawn wagons of different sizes, ranging from large Prairie Schooners that could haul a ton to hand carts and even wheelbarrows. Some wagon trains were quite large and were led by experienced wagon masters, sometimes escorted by the military to protect them from Indian attack during the Sioux Wars. The settlers mainly circled their wagons to provide a temporary corral for their livestock rather than to protect themselves from Indians. Often they could only make from two to ten miles a day. Children played games and were schooled along the way. So many traveled the land from 1843 to 1869 that the main trails were a graveyard of discarded objects and broken-down wagons. The bones of pioneers and livestock dead from violence or disease were scattered along the trail. Much of the Oregon Trail lacked any wood, so the pioneers would collect buffalo chips to burn in their campfires. Typical meals may have been a combination of coffee, beans, bacon, dried bread, buffalo, deer, and antelope.

Weapons

The Colt was the revolver of choice. It was single-action and held six .45-caliber bullets. **The Enfield** was a single-shot musket and mainly a leftover from the early Civil War. **The Sharps** was a heavy and very accurate single-shot breech-loading rifle. A skilled shooter could cock back the hammer, load a bullet, and fire at about ten rounds per minute. Lawmen preferred the lever-action and more modern and efficient **Winchester** rifle, which became known as "The Gun that Won the West." The powerful lever-action **Henry** rifle came out of the 1860s and held up to twelve rounds. **The Spencer** rifle was a bolt-action gun that held seven cartridges. It was a preferred choice for cavalry soldiers in the Civil War and the Indian Wars.

Women as Doctors

Prairie doctors were women who were not educated in medicine in any formal way, but were quite competent in caring for the sick or injured along the Oregon, California, and

Mormon Trails. However, there was an emergence of women who got their certified training and medical degrees at the University of Cincinnati beginning in 1870. Treatment of a bad gunshot wound was primitive. If the injury was deemed to be too severe, it was common practice to cut off the limb with a saw and the help of either chloroform or whiskey to anesthetize the patient. However, some doctors were on the leading edge in their knowledge of surgery and infection, and amputation was not always necessary.

Cholera

The primary cause of this horrible disease that struck the pioneers and Native American Indians along the Oregon Trail and many towns along the Missouri River was contaminated water from refuse and human waste. There was no real cure for cholera. Some tried opium. Another primitive solution was something called bleeding. A vein was sliced and the patient was "bled," the theory being that the cause was infected blood. Louis Pasteur of France theorized that water should be heated to expel germs. He experimented in the late 1860s and felt that hydration was the only helpful action taken, since so much fluid of the body was lost due to vomiting or diarrhea. Victims were often dead in hours. Through advanced trial and error over the years, ingestion of herbs, water, and rice in varying combinations was known to work once someone came down with the disease. Among the ingredients proven to be effective were onion, ginger, and bitter gourd. In Tilly's case, Dr. Sullivan gave her a mixture of water with herbs, rice, citrus, pepper, and bitter gourd to help cure her.

The Telegraph

This Morse code method of communication was lightning fast compared to the railroad or the Pony Express. By the 1860s, messages and letters could zip across the telegraph wires, and money could be transferred between banks. The military could send word of troop movements or Indian activity. Lawmen could give a town advance warning of outlaws on the loose. The Indians would also burn the poles and destroy the wires during the Indian Wars.

The Route

The story of twelve-year-old Caleb O'Toole and his two sisters begins in June of 1877 in the town of **Great Bend, Kansas**. Run with an iron fist by Sheriff W. W. Winstead, Great Bend was a booming cattle town and cattle shipping center that had been founded formally in 1871. Many shops and businesses emerged, along with nine saloons. Buffalo roamed the area in great numbers. Colorful characters passed through this town, including the gunfighter Wild Bill Hickok and the famous scout and buffalo hunter, Buffalo Bill Cody.

In the story, cholera and violence leave the O'Toole children orphaned, and they flee in their wagon north to the Northern Railroad in Kearney Junction, Nebraska, to catch the train west and eventually to Montana. They travel to the **Smokey Hill River** and seek shelter for three days before riding north one hundred miles and seven days in the stifling heat to **Red Cloud, Nebraska**, a booming pioneer town named after the great Sioux Chief, Red Cloud. Though trains were not running there until 1878, it was a bustling, lawful town, though smaller than Great Bend. Culture, businesses, and commerce were on the rise in anticipation of the coming railroad. The children head north seventy-five miles over four days to the **Platte River** and **Kearney Junction** to catch the train. There they learn that the trains were not running because of the Great Railroad Strike of 1877 and that the Montana line had not yet been completed. This forces them to journey west on the **Oregon Trail** in their little one-horse wagon. They ride to **Dobytown, Nebraska**, on July 4th to wait for a wagon train to build up in order to travel under its protection. This western town was as lawless as it could get. Even the U.S. Army avoided it. Gamblers, thieves, cowboys, and the women who catered to them whooped it up in towns like this all over the West. Caleb and his sisters flee west for several days on the Oregon Trail and eventually to **Cottonwood Springs, Nebraska**, one of the numerous supply towns that had emerged to serve and supply the wagon trains along the Oregon Trail. Many became ghost towns after the railroads took over. The children are forced to push farther west for another twenty miles to a Pawnee Indian camp, and then back on the Oregon Trail a hundred miles to **Ash Hollow** in western Nebraska. Ash Hollow was a place known for its ash trees and fine water, where the Platte River split off north and south. It was shallow enough to cross. The waters there were safe to drink. Often, the pioneers would lower their wagons by rope since the steep trail made it almost impossible for the horses or oxen to pull the wagons safely.

By the end of July, Caleb and his sisters catch up with a wagon train on the North Platte River and make their way past **Chimney Rock**, **Courthouse Rock**, and **Scotts Bluff**. These giant rock landmarks were famous in their pioneer history, signaling the end of their plains travel and into grander territory ahead. Another week and a hundred miles from Scotts Bluff put them into **Fort Fetterman, Wyoming**. This was considered the last fort left along the Platte River and the Oregon Trail. It was an outpost not well-liked by any soldier, because it was so remote and devoid of human interaction. Here, the Oregon and California Trails split off west and the **Bozeman Trail** went north toward Montana Territory. Mormons mainly took their wagons across the Oregon Trail on the northern Platte road to avoid conflict with others who did not approve of Mormons or their religious practices. They crossed over near Fort Fetterman and continued west until they picked up the Mormon Trail to Utah. The O'Toole children continue north on the Bozeman Trail. After a week of rough travel over a hundred miles, they come to the secret hideout, **Hole in the Wall**. This famous hideout near the Big Horn Mountains in Wyoming was home to outlaws from the late 1860s, built up in the 1880s, featured pastureland for stolen cattle and several cabins, and was easily defended against the law or Indians. It later became the refuge of train robber Butch Cassidy and many other notorious figures of the Wild West. Farther north on the Bozeman Trail, the children meet Chief Touch the Clouds and are escorted for several weeks and over three hundred miles along the **Big Horn Mountains** into **Yellowstone Park**, which was established in 1872. They come face-to-face with the notorious Sioux Chief, Sitting Bull. So far, they have come a thousand miles in nearly three months.

They continue nearly one hundred miles alone through Yellowstone to **Virginia City, Montana Territory**. Virginia City was a town built on gold, mining, and fur trading. Even though there was considerable social activity, dances, and entertainment, there also existed one of the most dangerous roads in the land. Highwaymen, murderers, thieves, and con artists controlled the eighty-mile stretch between Virginia City and **Bannack,** another gold-strike town. It was nearly impossible to pass unharmed. One notorious man, Sheriff Henry Plummer of Bannack, vowed to clean up the lawlessness and erected a gallows. His power stretched to Virginia City and he and his henchmen hanged anyone suspected of thieving. He himself was accused of the very deeds he claimed to prevent and was hanged on his own gallows by hooded vigilantes, who also had vowed to clean up the towns. They in turn were accused of running a crooked ring and were threatened with hanging by miners, traders, and town folk if they continued their evil ways.

Caleb and his sisters travel the final hundred miles to the ranch in the **Bitterroot Mountains**, passing the site of the Battle of Big Hole where the Nez Perce Indians were dealt a fatal blow by the U.S. Army in a surprise attack just one month before. The story comes to a rousing conclusion with an epic gun battle in the shadows of the **Painted Mountains** of the Bitterroot. It is a journey of three and a half months and over thirteen hundred treacherous miles.

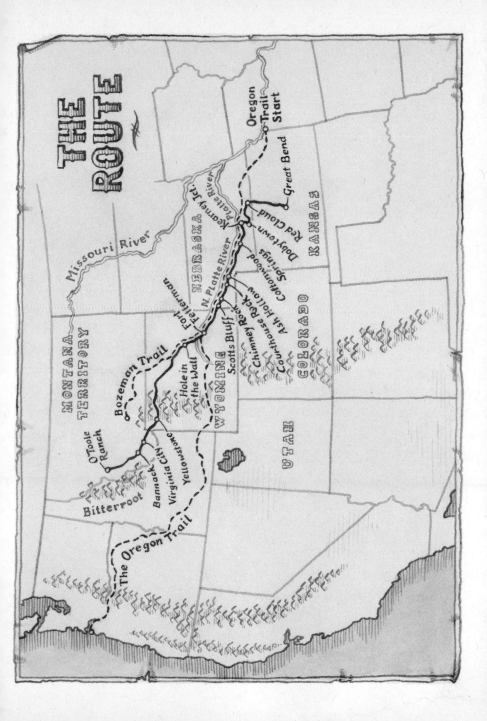

ACKNOWLEDGMENTS

★ ★ ★ ★ ★ ★ ★ ★ ★ ★ ★ ★ ★ ★ ★ ★ ★ ★ ★ ★

I would like to thank the following people who helped make this book possible.

Tom Dixon, my English teacher at Landon School, for trying so hard to make me pay attention in class.

Deijon Erkins, my companion and Little Brother from the Big Brothers of Greater Los Angeles, for his inspiring friendship along our many adventures.

My family, for their constant support and encouragement.

My manager, Marilyn R. Atlas, who has been after me to write for many years.

My agent, Adriana Dominguez, for all her hard work and wonderful insights.

My publisher, Steve Geck, for giving my book wings.

All the wonderfully helpful people I met along the way, from Kansas to Montana.